This GLITTERING WORLD

**Center Point
Large Print**

Also by T. Greenwood
and available from Center Point Large Print:

Two Rivers

**This Large Print Book carries the
Seal of Approval of N.A.V.H.**

This
GLITTERING
WORLD

T. Greenwood

CENTER POINT PUBLISHING
THORNDIKE, MAINE

This Center Point Large Print edition
is published in the year 2011 by arrangement with
Kensington Publishing Corp.

The text of this Large Print edition is unabridged.
In other aspects, this book may vary
from the original edition.
Printed in the United States of America
on permanent paper.
Set in 16-point Times New Roman type.

ISBN: 978-1-61173-004-3

Library of Congress Cataloging-in-Publication Data

Greenwood, T. (Tammy)
This glittering world / T. Greenwood. — Large print ed.
p. cm.
ISBN 978-1-61173-004-3 (library binding : alk. paper)
1. Friendship—Fiction. 2. Domestic fiction. 3. Large type books. I. Title.
PS3557.R3978T48 2011
813'.54—dc22

2010049205

For my sisters—
Ceilidh Greenwood
and in memory of
Jillian and Miranda Greenwood

ACKNOWLEDGMENTS

With thanks to my parents, Paul and Cyndy Greenwood, for their tremendous help in researching this novel. To Derek M. Begay, Milford L. Belin, and Eric M. James, who, besides keeping my dad humble at the poker table, generously offered their insight into Navajo culture. To Duncan Thayer for giving me the spark that lit this story on fire. To my lovely student, Nada Shawish, whose early morning writing sessions got me from start to finish. To Henry Dunow, the best, best agent. To Peter Senftleben, my incomparable editor, who always knows exactly how to make my work better—and to the rest of my Kensington family for their tireless support. To my brilliant girls, Mikaela and Esmee, for making every day better than the one before it. And to the city of Flagstaff, Arizona, where long ago I found both a home and my amazing husband, Patrick.

Give sorrow words:
the grief that does not speak
whispers the o'er-fraught heart,
and bids it break.

—Malcolm, Act IV, scene iii
Shakespeare's *Macbeth*

RED WORLD

Winter came early to Flagstaff that year. Ben hadn't split the firewood that lay in a cluttered heap in the driveway. He hadn't cleaned out the chimney or bought salt to melt the snow from the sidewalk in front of the house. Sara hadn't gotten the winter coats out of storage, hadn't taken down the artificial spiderwebs and plastic decals she'd hung in the windows for Halloween. The harvest dummy sat ill-prepared and coatless on the porch. The jack-o'-lanterns hadn't even started to bruise and rot when the first storm brought twelve inches of snow.

They weren't prepared.

It came while they were sleeping, as Sara dreamed of something that made her scowl and Ben dreamed of something that softened his features into a face he might not recognize in the mirror. This dreaming face was the face of his boyhood. Only in sleep did the hardness of the last twenty years subside. At thirty, his face already bore the quiet evidence of things gone wrong. It was etched in the fine lines in the corners of his eyes, in his clenched jaw, and in his worried brow. But in sleep, when he did sleep, the road map tracking the journey from possibility and promise to anger and ennui and disappointment almost disappeared.

The house was cold, though neither of them knew it. Sara insisted on sleeping with a heavy down comforter year-round. Usually, Ben slept on top of it while she lay nestled like a small bird underneath its feathers. But tonight, maybe sensing the coming storm, he too had hunkered down, his dog, Maude, at his feet. The one window in their room, the one that would have revealed the falling snow, was veiled in the heavy curtains Sara had bought to keep out the morning sun and prying eyes. She was worried about the neighbor, Mr. Lionel, who she claimed looked to her like he might be dangerous, a pedophile or worse. The one who spent hours rubbing Turtle Wax into his old blue Ford Falcon. The one Ben made sure to wave and nod to each time they both happened to be outside in their yards at the same time, as if this would make up for Sara's paranoia.

The furnace was set to OFF. The woodstove was bone cold.

Sometime during the night, as they slept, it began to snow. And when it snows in Flagstaff, it doesn't stop until the entire world is sheathed in white. Ben had lived here long enough to have experienced this, to have gone to sleep at night and awoken to a world obscured.

Ben moved to Flagstaff eight years ago *because* of the snow. He'd just graduated from Georgetown and was done with the city, done with its grit and grime and heat. He planned to get his Master's, and maybe even his PhD, in history, and he wanted to go somewhere clean and quiet for grad school. Somewhere without steaming streets and honking horns and subways always rumbling under his feet. Then he cracked a tooth on a chicken bone on a Friday afternoon and wound up in the dentist's office, where an issue of *Arizona Highways* lay buried beneath a pile of other magazines. If the dentist hadn't been running so late, Ben might have simply finished the article in *Newsweek* about the missing girl in Utah and not even seen the picture of the San Francisco Peaks. He might never have seen the turquoise sky with the ocean of clean white snow beneath. He might never have felt that strange tug in his chest, amplified by the ache in his jaw, and decided then and there that this is exactly where he belonged.

Here, snow was no different from air or breath. It was simply part of the landscape, part of how one lived. And he loved everything about it: the cold pristine white of it, the soft sharpness of it. The crunch and glisten. He was never as happy as he was when it snowed, each storm like a small baptism. He knew, even after he had finished his dissertation, he wouldn't leave, couldn't leave. And so here he was eight years later, an underpaid adjunct and part-time bartender. Though all of it (the financial worries, the late hours, the work overload) was softened by the presence of snow. But still, he wasn't expecting this. Winter, while a welcome guest, had shown up early to the party.

There had been no sign of a storm when they went to bed, Sara angry and Ben too drunk to care. They'd gone to a Halloween party at Sara's best friend Melanie's A-frame in Kachina Village the night before. He'd had too much to drink. Spent most of the party listening to a girl playing Jane's Addiction songs on an acoustic guitar. Sara was furious, but she didn't say so; she'd simply grabbed her coat and stood there waiting for him. They'd driven home in silence, gone to bed without saying good night.

And while they slept, Sara fitful and Ben oblivious, icy fingers curled around their ankles and hips. Winter crept in.

It wasn't the cold that woke him. The shiver through the old window. The icy breath that skipped across his exposed cheek. It was Maude, his seventy-pound golden retriever, nudging, prodding. He ignored her for a moment, feeling shaky and too hungover to open his eyes. But she persisted, whimpering in his ear.

"Hush," he said, and quietly got out of bed so as not to wake Sara, whose face had softened by now, the dream apparently having passed. He hoped that her anger also might fade by the time she woke.

The floors were icy. He grabbed the pair of socks he'd worn the night before, some long underwear, and a sweater that was crumpled up on the floor. But it wasn't until he went into the dark living room and pulled back the curtains that he saw the obliterated sky. His head pounded, but his heart trilled. Maude knew too and raced to the door, anxious to go out and piss and play in the snow.

"Hold on, girl," he said, his voice crackling like a fire. "Let me get the coffee on first."

While the coffee bubbled and hissed and Maude romped in the backyard, sinking into the wadding of snow, Ben backtracked through his fuzzy recollections of the party, tripping and stumbling over the conversations until he remembered the girl, the guitar, and Sara standing over him, pissed. He remembered that the girl was very pretty, dressed up like Dorothy with sparkly red shoes, and that she had one slightly lazy eye which, for some reason, captivated him. He also remembered wanting only to curl up inside the hollow mahogany body of the instrument and listen to the music from the inside out, and he recalled whispering this to the girl. This is what Sara must have seen. *Shit.* It was Sunday, a day that should be easy, and already he knew he'd have to spend the day tiptoeing, making amends for this transgression and all the others she was sure to bring up.

He knew the Sunday paper wouldn't be there yet. Theirs was the last house on the delivery route, he was convinced, because the paper almost never arrived before seven. He looked at the clock on the stove: 6:52. Maybe just this once it would be early, maybe today would be his day.

The thermometer hanging on a tree outside the kitchen window read twenty-five degrees. He found his winter coat in the back of the coat closet and his Sorels buried deep inside as well. He yanked them on and opened up the front door to the blizzard.

From the doorway, he contemplated the journey to the sidewalk for a newspaper that was likely not even there, and almost turned around to go back inside. But then the blue sliver of something in the distance caught his eye, and he imagined his newspaper lying swaddled in plastic. So he pulled his hat down over his ears, shoved his hands in his pockets, and trudged through the snow, squinting against the icy shards that seemed to be falling sideways.

But it was not his paper.

It took a minute before what he saw registered, before his brain, thick with the hangover and disbelief, could make sense of the image before his eyes. The absurdity of it was what hit him first, and he almost laughed; this would later make him wonder if it was evidence that he was, as Sara would suggest time and time again, incapable of empathy and capable of the most frightening cruelties.

At first he just thought the man was sleeping. He was curled on his side, facing the street, hands tucked quietly between his knees. But he wasn't dressed for the cold: just a flannel shirt tucked into a pair of jeans held up by a concho belt. No coat, no hat, no gloves. Only a pair of Nike basketball sneakers on his feet. His black hair in a braid, curling like a snake into the snow.

There was a half inch of fresh powder covering his entire body.

Ben squatted down next to him and touched his shoulder, as if he could simply wake him up. "Hey," he said.

The wind admonished Ben, and then hit him hard in the chest, like an angry fist. It was *twenty-five* degrees outside.

The man didn't move, not even with a second nudge, so Ben started to roll him over, pulling his shoulder until his body yielded. He was big, maybe six foot two, a couple hundred pounds. And then the man was on his back and Ben stood up, stumbling backward.

"Jesus Christ," Ben said. "Shit."

Both eyes were sealed shut, crusty with blood and circled in blue-black. His nose was crooked, bent at an impossible angle, with dried blood in two lines running from each nostril to his lip. His bottom lip was blue and swollen, split in the center. And slowly, a fresh stream of blood began to pour from his ear, the crimson blooming like some horrific flower blossoming in the snow.

He should have run back into the house then, gotten Sara. She was a *nurse,* for Christ's sake. But he was suddenly paralyzed, quite literally frozen in place as he realized: He *knew* this guy.

Of course, he couldn't remember his name. . . . Jesus, why couldn't he ever remember a goddamned name? But he *knew* him. He was the kid who came into the bar almost every single night to shoot pool. Ben knew he couldn't be old enough to drink, but he never carded him, because all he ever ordered were Cokes. And because Jack's served food, minors were allowed in as long as they didn't sit at the bar. The kid always sat alone in a booth, eating cheese fries, waiting for someone to show up at the tables. He was a good pool player. Didn't talk shit like some of the idiots that came into the bar. A gracious winner and loser. Jesus fucking Christ.

Ben dropped back down to the ground, feeling the cold wet seeping through the knees of his jeans. He pressed his hand hard against the kid's chest, waiting. When he felt nothing but the resistance of bone, he leaned over and pressed his ear against his chest, listening. He didn't know what he expected, but it wasn't this. It wasn't the silence that was suddenly as loud as drums. And the harder he pressed his ear against him, the louder the blood in his own ears got.

When it snows like this, the sun never rises. The air simply turns lighter and lighter until things come into focus. Until there is clarity.

Ben stood up again and shoved his hands into the pockets of his coat, looking for his cell phone. Shit, where the hell did he put his phone last night? He was afraid to leave the kid there in the snow, as if something worse than what had already happened could happen to him now if Ben left him alone.

He thought of Sara, sleeping angrily in the bedroom, and knew that he had to wake her. She would know what to do. He needed to call 9-1-1. And so as the sky filled with hazy white light, he backed away from the kid whose head was surrounded now by a bloody halo, back through the blizzard, back to the house.

Even before the ambulance arrived, he knew what the newspapers would say about this. *Young Native American man found dead in Cheshire neighborhood. Alcohol-related death suspected.* He knew because this was how too many Indians die here. They come from the reservation to Flagstaff, looking for jobs, for a way to change their lives. And when they get here and find nothing but disappointment, they find places like Jack's or the Mad I or Granny's Closet. Ben had worked at Jack's long enough to know that this was one of many, many sad truths. He'd seen men drink until they couldn't see, and then watched as they stumbled out into the snow. And at least once a winter, one of them would wind up on the train tracks, where he would fall asleep and not wake up. Ben wasn't sure how many people had died since he got here, but it seemed as if there was always some story—buried deep in the paper, mentioned in passing on the news, whispered about at the bars. This, like the snow, was a fact of life here.

Still, you don't expect to walk out of your front door on a Sunday morning looking to retrieve your newspaper from a snowbank and find someone dead on the sidewalk.

After he woke Sara and called 9-1-1, watching as Sara made her way through the snow to the man, he started to think that maybe he wasn't dead after all. Maybe Ben had been mistaken. He'd had a roommate in college who'd drunk almost an entire bottle of vodka by himself one night. They'd found him passed out in the bathroom at a party and called 9-1-1. The EMTs had revived him, and at the hospital they pumped his stomach and sent him back to the dorms with a crisp plastic bracelet to remind him how close he'd come. But this kid didn't drink. At least not at Jack's. He *knew* this. And besides, you don't bleed from your ears when you're drunk, and your face certainly doesn't look like you ran into a brick wall head-first from drinking either. Somebody did this to him, and when Ben had listened for his heart, all he'd heard was his own.

After the ambulance pulled away, he and Sara stood on the sidewalk, watching the twirling red lights disappear down the road.

"You okay?" Ben asked.

Sara nodded without looking at him.

"Do you think he'll make it?" he asked.

She shook her head. "It doesn't look good. He had no pulse. No blood pressure. He was bleeding out."

Ben stared at the place where the kid's head had been, at the violent bloom slowly turning pink as the snow kept falling.

Their neighbors were watching from the windows, their faces pressed to the glass. A few had come out onto their porches, clutching their robes around their waists. Sheila, from next door, had ushered her two sons back inside when she realized what was happening. Mr. Lionel stood on his porch, nodding grimly. Now the ambulance was gone, and Ben could hear the plow coming. In a few minutes it would barrel down this street too, pushing away any evidence that a man had just begun to die there.

The police were quick. They sent only one car, and they took Ben and Sara's statements without even coming inside the house. Ben was surprised by how soon he and Sara were alone again. By the time the paper boy finally threw the newspaper into the yard, it felt almost as though they had just woken from the same terrible dream.

They sat at the small oak table that used to belong to Sara's grandmother, sipping coffee, staring at the pages of the paper. Sara said, "I wonder if he has family here."

Ben looked up, grateful for her breaking the silence, for her willingness to set aside whatever it was that had transpired between them the night before. "I don't know," he said. "He had ID on him, so they should be able to find out pretty quickly."

"What was his name?" she asked. Her eyes were soft with tears.

He thought about the kid sitting at the booth at Jack's. Always alone. Ben had a problem with names. He blamed his job. Both of his jobs. So many people in and out of his life. At the bar, he had a talent for remembering the names of every single patron for exactly the amount of time they spent bellied up, drinking, tipping. But the moment they were gone, the second they'd slapped down a five or a ten and walked out the door, any recollection of what they called themselves was gone. It was like this at school too. He had anywhere between forty and eighty students a semester. He knew the first and last names of each and every one of them until the final exam. Then he'd run into one of them on campus (*Hey, Professor Bailey!*) and there was nothing but that white-hot shame of forgetting. Though maybe Ben hadn't ever known the kid's name. It was possible that he hadn't forgotten at all, but rather that the guy had always been anonymous.

He should tell Sara that he recognized him, he thought. That he was a regular at work. But for some reason, he didn't. Sometimes it was easier to keep things from her. To lie. And so he said, "I think they said it was Begay? His last name. I don't remember his first name."

"He was just a kid. Who could have done that to him?"

This was the Sara he loved. *Old Sara,* he thought of her. She emerged sometimes from New Sara's body and face, like a slippery ghost. This was the true Sara, the sweet Sara, the Sara who wasn't sarcastic and always rolling her eyes as if she were always, always disappointed. Sara without her guard up. Vulnerable Sara. Her hair was messy, in a pale puff of a ponytail. Her makeup from her witch costume last night was smudged under her wide green eyes. She was wearing the robe he'd bought her five years ago for Christmas. He'd filled the pockets with green- and red-foil-covered Hershey's Kisses. It was pilly now, frayed at the cuffs.

"God, Ben. What the hell?"

He reached across the table for her hand. Her hands were small, like a child's, with short fingers and tiny palms. He studied the ring on her finger, the one that had been resting there, waiting there, for almost two years. He could barely remember most of the time now what it was that had gripped him, what emotion it was that had assailed him two summers ago. He remembered buying the ring; he'd found it at an antique shop on Route 66. He remembered her happy *yes*. But ever since that initial moment of elation, sitting in the alley courtyard at Pasto, dizzy with too much wine, he remembered feeling almost nothing but regret.

He'd somehow managed to convince Sara that they should wait to set a wedding date. His reasons, at first, were good ones: They needed to save money if they were going to have the kind of wedding she wanted. Then his mother passed away, and he just needed time. Later, he suggested that he really wanted them to own their own house first, wanted them to be more stable. When her father put the down payment on the place in Cheshire, he couldn't help but feel he was being bribed. Angry now, he became even more reluctant. Let's wait until summer. Fall. No, winter. A winter wedding. Wouldn't that be beautiful? And finally, they stopped talking about it altogether. By now, the ring had become a constant reminder of his biggest broken promise.

He hadn't realized that he was playing with the ring, until she yanked her hand away and grabbed her coffee mug. "What time do you have to go in to work?" she asked.

"I might check at the hospital first, to see what happened," he said.

"Why?" she asked.

"Maybe he didn't die," he said.

She shook her head. "I really don't think he made it. Couldn't you just call? That way you won't miss your shift tonight."

"So *that's* what this is about?" Ben said. "The fifty bucks I'll make at work tonight?"

New Sara raised her chin, hard and sharp, and stood up, disappearing into the kitchen. "Do what you need to do, Ben."

But he *wasn't* dead. At least not right away.

If he'd died right away, if not for the body's stubborn insistence upon living, then it might have ended here: the snow plow carrying away the crimson snow, Ben and Sara sipping coffee at the kitchen table. They would have gone on with their lives, and this man-boy, body frozen, breath stolen by winter, would just be a sad memory shared between them. They might talk about it sometimes, about the tragedy of this life cut short. Another casualty of winter. Just another sad disaster.

But when Ben closed his eyes, he could almost see time slipping backward, events unraveling . . . a woven Navajo blanket made by the boy's ancestors, the pattern slowly coming undone, each thread revealed, the intricate design disassembled. He saw him riding a rusty tricycle in the dirt, a hungry rez dog nipping at his ankles as he pedaled furiously away, his face flushed with heat and joyful. Ben imagined him at his grandmother's feet as she braided his hair. His soft moccasins. His small feet. He could hear the sound of her voice as she sang the boy to sleep. He watched his eyes close and then watched as he packed a duffel bag, as he hitched a ride to Flagstaff. Ben wanted to tell him not to come. To stay home. He wanted him to see the finished picture, this picture of himself, lifeless in the snow.

Sara might be able to let this go, to will herself to forget, but Ben couldn't let it end like this, with the uncertainty of whether or not the boy had survived. He couldn't just pretend it hadn't happened. He couldn't let everything just disappear into the new snow.

Sunday night was a shit shift. Hippo could handle the kitchen and the bar by himself until Ben got there later. He grabbed his coat and said good-bye to Sara through the bathroom door. Melanie was on her way up from Kachina with a bottle of wine and a movie. He knew that by the time he got home, Sara would be asleep; she had to work tomorrow. There were children with strep throat, kids with chicken pox, babies waiting to be immunized. And so he walked out the door and drove to the hospital.

Ben hated hospitals. He could count on one hand the number of times he'd been inside a hospital, and each recollection was still sharp and nauseating. The first time was when he fell out of a tree, snapping his elbow like a twig. The second time was when he was five and his sister, Dusty, was born, one month early, her head as small as a tiny peach. He'd been terrified of the wires and tubes and the blue veins running and pulsing under the transparent skin of her chest. The third time was when Dusty died. He was eleven years old then, and he remembered the hallways smelled like chlorine, cold chicken soup, and bleach. He could still recall something bitter in his throat and the swell of something awful in his chest. And so years later, when he was away at grad school and his mother was diagnosed with ovarian cancer, he'd only gone back east to see her in the hospital a couple of times. Each time he'd felt his pulse racing, felt his knees and spine melting into liquid bone. He'd been almost relieved when she was sent home, when she stopped the chemo treatments and opted to acquiesce rather than fight anymore. Hospitals made him sick, made his skin prickle. He didn't know if it was ironic or masochistic or simply sad that he'd wound up engaged to a nurse.

Until now, he'd managed to avoid the hospital in Flagstaff as well. Even the time Hippo had nearly sliced off his thumb at work, he'd just dropped him off at the emergency room entrance. But now, here he was again.

He went to the visitors' information desk and told the receptionist the story about the kid, asked if he had been admitted. He told her he only wanted to find out if the guy had survived, that he thought his last name was Begay.

She clicked and tapped at the computer without looking at Ben and said, "ICU. But you'll need special permission to go in to see him. Down that hallway, then take a right."

He hadn't planned to actually go see him, but he found himself muttering, "Thank you," and following her directions anyway. He tried to concentrate on his own breaths rather than the smell, the silence, the loamy green walls. By the time he got to the ICU waiting room, he wondered what he was doing there. He knew the kid was alive. Wasn't that enough? He could go to work now. He could leave. But what then? Did he just go on as though nothing had happened? When you find someone beaten nearly to death in your front yard, what is expected of you? Are you tied to them, inextricably bound in some intimate way forever?

There was one old man in the waiting room. He was reading the *Daily Sun* but had fallen asleep.

His chin rested on his chest, and he was snoring. Ben approached the nurses' station and spoke softly so as not to wake the man, repeating the story he'd told the lady at the information desk.

"I'm sorry, sir. Mr. Begay is in grave condition, and only immediate family is being allowed in at this point."

"Does he *have* family in town?" Ben asked.

"His sister," she said. "She just went to get a cup of coffee."

Ben felt his chest heave with relief. The kid wasn't alone. Perhaps this was all Ben really needed. To know that if the guy were to die tonight, he wouldn't be here, in this hospital, by himself.

"You can wait for her if you'd like. I'm sure she'd appreciate your being here."

"Okay," he said.

He sat down next to the old man and picked up a magazine to busy his hands. It was quiet here, just the ticking of the clock and the distant beeping and humming and buzzing of the machines.

He looked up when he sensed someone coming into the room.

The girl was blowing into the top of a Styrofoam cup. She was tall, thin, and her thick black hair ran down her back to her waist. She was wearing overalls splattered with paint and red high-top sneakers. She spoke to the nurse, who gestured toward Ben, and the girl turned to look at him. She scowled and then came over.

Ben stood up. He felt shaky, unsteady on his feet.

"Hi. I'm Ben Bailey. I'm the one who . . ." he stumbled. "I found him. This morning."

She looked at him, skeptical, and sat down in one of the chairs and took a sip of her coffee. She gestured for him to sit as well.

"How is he?" he asked.

She shook her head. "He won't live through the night."

It felt like someone had punched Ben in the chest. "Are you sure?"

She nodded. "We could keep him here, hooked up to these machines, and he would keep breathing. But his brain is dead. It's too late."

Ben took a deep breath.

"Do you know what happened to him?" she asked. Her voice was crackly, like timber just catching fire.

He shook his head. "No, I just . . . he was just out there. In the snow."

She rubbed her temples. Her long fingers were stacked with thick silver rings. Her nails were clipped short, clean.

"*Somebody* knows something," she said, looking up at him. *Questioning* him. "Somebody must have seen something."

"I don't," he said, shaking his head, "know anything."

31

His eyes were stinging, and his throat was thick. He hadn't felt this sensation in so long, he barely recognized it anymore. A relic of childhood. This sorrow so big it fills your entire chest—he hadn't felt that way since he was eleven years old. Not since Dusty died. It was déjà vu of the worst kind, like re-dreaming a terrible dream. *Somebody knows something. Somebody must have seen something.*

This was not what he had expected. He just came here to make sure the kid had lived. That was all. He would check in and then make his way back to work. That had been his plan.

"Hey, are you okay?" she asked, her furrowed brow softening.

He nodded and looked at her. Her face was striking, with high cheekbones, amber skin, and eyes a confusion of brown and gold. She wore a thin leather choker around her long neck, a rough nugget of turquoise dipping into the deep hollow below her throat. There was a streak of white paint across her collarbone.

"You want me to get you some water or something?" she asked.

"No, I'm fine," he said, laughing awkwardly. He stood up. His mind was reeling. "I should be going. Will *you* be okay?"

She nodded and stood as well.

As he turned to leave, she said, "If he does die tonight, the funeral will be in the next couple of days. If you give me your e-mail address or phone number I can get you the details."

He turned to look at her. She was smiling sadly.

"Sure," he said, reaching into his pocket for a slip of paper to write on. He found a grocery receipt and asked the nurse for a pen. "And I'm sorry," he said. "I didn't get your name?"

"Shadi," she said. "Shadi Begay."

He nodded and scratched his e-mail address on the slip. "That's an unusual name," he said, looking back up at her. "I mean, it's a beautiful name. . . . Is it . . . ?"

"It's my nickname. It's Navajo for *older sister*."

Ben looked back down at the receipt, felt his throat swell.

"You'd really come?" she asked, taking the paper from him. Her eyes were warm and still. Something about her face made him feel calm.

"Of course," he said, nodding.

A long time ago, everything was whole. Ben remembers those times as if they belonged to some other Ben. A distant smiling happy Ben. A flickering black-and-white Super 8 life projected on a sheet suspended in a basement rec room. This was when he had a father and a mother and a sister. When he and Dusty made forts underneath the dining room table and chased fireflies while their parents drank wine out of fragile glasses in the backyard. It was a time of poison ivy and climbing trees. Everything smelled of cut grass and barbeque. Even the bee stings were good then. Even the cuts and bruises and humpbacked crickets and screeching cicadas.

Then he was eleven and Dusty was six, and in one moment, one sliver of a moment, everything changed. It was October, cold and sunny. The trees were alight in the bright autumn sun. They'd gotten off the bus after school and were walking home, and Ben wasn't paying attention. He was cracking gum and cracking jokes with Charlie, the only other kid who got off at their stop, and Dusty lagged behind, dragging her ladybug backpack behind her, humming a song she'd learned that day at school. He and Charlie gave each other high fives before Charlie disappeared into his little brick house, and then Ben kept walking with Dusty following behind. Ben was thinking about basketball tryouts. About how to ask for new sneakers. About his math test. About what there might be to eat in the cupboard at home.

He imagines now that something beautiful caught her eye: a silvery dragonfly, a monarch with painted wings. Maybe just a falling acorn from one of the giant oak trees that lined the street. But that day, he wasn't paying attention. And so when she darted out into the road and the car sped past them, into her, picking her up and then setting her down like just another autumn leaf on the pavement, he didn't see anything except a blur disappearing in the distance. It happened so quickly, it was as though it hadn't happened at all.

Later, when his father demanded, "You had to have seen something, Ben. Try to remember!" he hadn't been able to remember anything. Not the color of the car, not the face of the driver, not even the song that Dusty had been singing.

For a while they tried to believe that someone would be caught. That there would be some sort of explanation, even if it was one they didn't want to hear. They waited for the driver to come forward, for his conscience to kick in, for the guilt to overwhelm him. They waited for Ben to remember. But Ben hadn't been paying attention. And Ben couldn't remember anything. And so hope slowly turned into desperation and desperation into sad resignation.

That winter, when the trees were stripped of their leaves and their branches looked like blanched and arthritic bones against the sky, they cleaned out her room, and soon it was as if she'd never existed at all. It was also when his mother stopped making them go to church and stopped making pancakes on Saturday mornings and stopped playing her old records on the stereo. Eventually, she stopped speaking to his father. And so his dad left, moved into the city when Ben was fourteen. And then Ben graduated, left home, and his mother got sick. Since then, instead of feeling whole, Ben had felt slivered. His life fractured into *before* and *after*. And the chasm between was Dusty.

He never talked about her. Not even with Sara. There was no way to share that sort of grief with someone who had never known sadness. It would be like trying to explain the color red to a blind man. Trying to describe snow to someone who has never felt cold.

And so he held on to this secret, kept it folded into tiny squares inside his pocket. Sometimes he could forget it was there, on good days. But when he spoke to Shadi that night at the hospital, it was as though she had found it, unfolded it and smoothed the worn, soft creases. As though she were asking him to share this ragged grief.

He didn't know how to tell Sara, how to explain this sudden urgent need to console a stranger. He could never have articulated the feeling that this was somehow serendipitous, that there might be a *reason* he was the one who found the kid. He knew Sara would never understand, was incapable of comprehending the new sense of purpose that swelled in his chest like a storm.

And so when Shadi Begay sent an e-mail with the details about the services, Ben lied. He said he was going down to Phoenix with Hippo to look at camper shells for Hippo's truck, and instead drove two hundred desolate miles to Chinle for the funeral.

Ben bought his truck as a gift for himself the day he graduated from Georgetown. Little did he know then that the PhD he planned to get would likely never make him enough money to pay the truck off. It was a 1952 Chevy pickup, completely restored, the color of a candy apple. The guy who sold it to him had tears in his eyes as Ben drove away. He and Maude had driven all the way from DC to Flagstaff in this truck, windows rolled down, both of their noses to the wind. Since then, it had seen eight Flagstaff winters, and thousands of miles. He figured he might drive this truck to his grave. If he could, he'd take it with him.

Now, Ben watched in the rearview mirror as the San Francisco Peaks disappeared behind him. The sun had come out on Tuesday morning and quickly melted the snow from the roads, as it always does in Flagstaff. The snow would remain on the Peaks, though, dappling the ashen gray in white. He yanked his sunglasses from the glove box and put them on, glancing at his reflection in the rearview mirror. He'd been thinking about growing a beard for a couple of weeks now, despite Sara's obvious lack of enthusiasm. Or, perhaps, because of it. This morning he'd shaved the few prickly whiskers that had sprouted up like spines on a cactus.

He thought about his kids showing up to his 8:00 A.M. class, finding the note he'd written in Sharpie on a piece of notebook paper. It had been too early to have anybody in the History Department do it, so he'd double-parked and run into the building like a bandit, sticking notes on the two classrooms where he taught, *Prof Bailey's US History to 1865 Class Canceled Today: Family Emergency.*

He'd told Sara he was going into his office early to grade papers and that he and Hippo were leaving for Phoenix right after his second class. He promised he'd be home sometime later tonight. He left her still sleeping, getting dressed in the dark. His suit, which he hadn't worn since he'd had his interview at school, was already in the truck.

Ben still wasn't sure why he didn't just tell Sara he was going to the funeral. He found himself doing this a lot lately, lying about where he was and what he was doing even if he had nothing to hide: telling her he was getting a burrito at Ralberto's when he was really sitting next door at Crystal Creek with a turkey sub. Saying he was going to meet Hippo for a drink and instead ducking into the movie theater and watching an entire movie alone. Since the engagement, he'd found his actual life and the one he fabricated becoming two entirely different things.

He glanced down at his cell phone and saw that

the reception had already disappeared. He hoped Sara would be too busy today to call him. He hoped she wouldn't need him for anything.

According to the map, Chinle was close to the Canyon de Chelly. For someone who'd made Arizona his home, Ben had done surprisingly little sightseeing. In the eight years he'd been here, he'd been to the Grand Canyon only once. He hadn't been to Four Corners or Window Rock either. Growing up just outside DC in Maryland, the only reason he'd ever seen the monuments was because of class field trips. He'd spent four years at Georgetown and not once made his way to the National Mall. He hated tourists. He hated the sense that people were ticking off the items on their lists of *Things to See*, as if their lives suddenly gained meaning when they had their photo snapped in front of some stone memorial. The connection between the monument and what it was meant to memorialize was too often lost. And the bickering families in oversize T-shirts, sweating and frowning and gathering together and smiling for the brief moment it took for a bystander to take their picture before returning to their misery, always made him feel sad.

It was seven thirty now, and he'd been on the road for over an hour. His ears popped as he descended out of the clouds. Already, he could feel it getting a little warmer outside. He pressed his hand against the window, and the glass no longer held the cold. He rolled down the window and stuck his hand out. Fifty, maybe sixty degrees.

The funeral was at ten A.M. at Our Lady of Fatima Catholic Church. Shadi had told him in the e-mail that her brother's name was Ricky.

At nine thirty, Ben pulled into town, stopped at a gas station, and changed into his suit in the restroom. He checked his reflection again and barely recognized himself. Normally, he wore T-shirts and jeans year-round, changing only his shoes in response to the weather. He needed a haircut; his dark hair stuck up in several directions. He ran his hand through it, trying to tame it into some sort of submission. He peered in closely at his reflection in the mirror and noted that his eyes looked tired. Flat blue-gray irises under heavy eyelids. He tightened his tie and stepped back.

As per Shadi's instructions, he took a right onto Route 7 off the 191. He parked in the church parking lot and began to wonder what on earth he was doing here.

The parking lot was virtually empty. There was a rusty Lincoln and a couple of trucks. The church looked like an octagonal log cabin. He peered down at the e-mail he had printed out: *Our Lady of Fatima Catholic Church.* This was it.

He got out of the truck and walked up to the front doors, and just as he was about to open them, the girl emerged.

"Hi," she said, grabbed his hand, and pulled him to the side of the building, leaning against the wall and sighing. She was wearing a black dress, her hair pulled away from her face. She smelled like freshly mowed grass. "God, I need a cigarette," she said, and then as she located the pack, she sighed and smiled. "I didn't think you'd come."

On Monday night, Ben had asked Hippo if he remembered seeing the kid when he was working that weekend. Hippo was usually in the kitchen, but sometimes he helped out behind the bar if it was busy.

Hippo was sitting at the bar after his shift, eating a basket of fries and a cheesesteak. "It was Halloween, dude," he said. "Everybody was dressed up. He could've been here, but with everybody in costumes, I don't know." Melted cheese dripped down his chin.

"You got a little . . ." Ben said, pointing to Hippo's face.

Hippo wiped at his mouth with the back of his hand and kept eating.

"There weren't any fights, then? You didn't need to kick anybody out?" Ben asked.

"Nah. Nobody except for Leroy. But we always have to kick Leroy out."

Leroy was the old guy who lived upstairs in the apartment above the bar. He was in every night, most nights until closing. When he got too rowdy, they sent him back upstairs. Sometimes, Ben or Hippo would walk up with him, make sure he got into his place okay.

"So it looked like he got beat up?" Hippo asked.

"Or run over. He was a mess. Shit," Ben said, opening up a Bud Light and putting it in front of Hippo. "I can't get it out of my head."

Ben had taken the job at Jack's to supplement his income at school. But he quickly realized that he could make as much in a month at the bar as he did teaching a class for a whole semester. And he'd made some good friends at Jack's—both coworkers and patrons.

Hippo had been working at Jack's since he dropped out of NAU as an undergrad. He was here for the snow too. In the winter, when he wasn't working, he was skiing. He operated the chairlift to get a free pass. Contrary to what his name might suggest, Hippo was tall and rail thin with a skinny goatee that he banded together with colored rubber bands. He was tattooed from the neck down. His girlfriend, Emily, owned the tattoo shop south of the tracks on San Francisco.

"Have the police been in here?" Ben asked, thinking the cops, assuming the kid had been drunk, would probably have interviewed the local barkeeps. He was only nineteen after all.

"Nah. And I haven't seen anything about it on the news, either," Hippo said, dipping a fry into a glob of ketchup.

Ben had scoured the paper that morning, looking for something, anything. Nothing. He'd watched the local news as well as the Fox station in Phoenix, but there was no mention.

"I'm going to the services tomorrow," Ben said. "Up in Chinle."

"Jesus," Hippo said. "You want me to come with?"

"Nah. But I told Sara you and I were going to Phoenix. So that's the story, okay?"

Hippo, his perpetual alibi, shook his head. "You gotta get out of that situation, dude."

"Easier said than done," Ben said, grimacing a little. He wasn't an asshole, didn't want to be an asshole, but here he was.

"What are we doing in Phoenix?" Hippo asked.

"Looking for a camper shell for your truck."

"Cool," Hippo said, popping the last bite of cheesesteak into his mouth and taking a long pull on his beer. "Gotta go wax my skis. They got twelve inches of fresh powder at Snowbowl. And I've got tomorrow off."

Outside the church, Shadi pulled a pack of American Spirits out of a small leather purse and shook one loose from the pack. She offered it to Ben, and at first he shook his head. He'd pretty much quit smoking when he and Sara started dating except for every now and then if he was out with Hippo. He'd steal a drag or two, but never around Sara. She was allergic to cigarette smoke and could smell it even a mile away. The few times she'd smelled it on him after a night out, she'd made him leave his clothes outside in a heap on the porch. But Sara was *two hundred* miles away, and he could use a smoke. His stomach was in knots for some reason. He was still a little worried that Shadi might think he was withholding information about what he saw, about what he knew.

"Actually, sure . . . do you mind?" he asked, gesturing to the pack before she crammed it back into her bag.

"Help yourself," she said. "Thanks again for coming all the way up here." She lit her cigarette with a Zippo, which she passed to him. It hissed and lit, the flame leaping into the air before his face.

"That your truck?" she asked.

He nodded, took a heavy drag on the cigarette. The rush of nicotine made him feel swimmy.

" '51?"

" '52."

"Our grandpa had a '51. Course it wasn't restored like yours. Piece of shit, actually. All rusted out, missing the rear bumper. Ricky and I used to like to ride in the back, feel the wind. Taste the air." She pulled a piece of loose tobacco from between her lips and flicked it onto the dirt. She looked up at Ben, and looked him hard in the eyes. "They're saying he was drunk. That he passed out, hit his face, and died of exposure. Just another drunk Indian. It's total bullshit. Goddamn *Belaganas.*"

Ben stared at the ground.

"I knew him," he said. He should have said something sooner. "Not well. But he came into the bar where I work, to play pool. I never saw him drink anything."

Her eyes narrowed then. "Jesus Christ. I told him to stay away from the bars. It's asking for trouble." She tossed her half-smoked cigarette onto the ground and snubbed it out with the toe of her shoe.

He did the same.

"Do you know who did this to him?" she asked.

He shook his head. "I wasn't there that night. My friend who was working said he didn't know whether or not he was there either. Everyone was dressed up for Halloween."

The girl took a deep breath and lifted her hair off her neck, closing her eyes. When she opened them again, she looked at Ben, as if gauging whether or not she should trust him.

"He left the rez, came to Flagstaff, to play music. Guitar. He was in this band. They played the prom at Chinle High. He was really, really good. He thought that he would have more opportunities in Flag."

They stood there for another minute or so. Shadi slipped off her shoe and shook out a pebble. "We should go inside," she said.

After the funeral, Ben followed behind Shadi and her grandmother in the Lincoln as they left Chinle. The roads became rougher, the dirt thicker. Through the rear window of the Lincoln, he could see the back of Shadi's head, but her grandmother was small, hidden in the passenger's seat. The woman had not said a single word to him when Shadi introduced them after the service. She was dressed head to toe in thick purple velvet, weighted down in silver and turquoise necklaces. She had shuffled past him to the car, waving her hand dismissively.

"Are you sure it's okay for me to be here?" he had asked Shadi quietly as she helped her grandmother into the car.

"She didn't want this," she said, gesturing to the church. "She wants him to have a traditional burial. Come," she said. And so he did.

They turned down so many roads that didn't

even look like roads that he suspected he'd have to ask to follow her back into Chinle afterward. The sky was warm and pink as the Lincoln stopped in front of a single solitary structure that looked as though it had sprung from the ground: her grandmother's hogan, he suspected.

The other people from the funeral were already there, milling about in front. The coffin had been loaded into Shadi's uncle's F-150, which pulled up next to his truck, dwarfing it, making it look like a child's toy. Ben felt uncomfortable and stiff in his suit. He was sweating, and the tie was tight around his neck. He got out of the truck and went to Shadi, who was helping her grandmother out of the car.

"Can I get a ride back to Flagstaff with you?" Shadi asked, looking over her shoulder at him.

"What?"

"Can you give me a ride back to Flag?"

"What about the burial? I thought that's where we were going."

"No. My grandmother wants things done the traditional way. My uncles dug the grave last night. They'll take him, with the shaman. My grandmother insists it's the only way he can make it safely to the underworld."

"And you don't want to be there?" he asked.

"I'm not *allowed* to be there. It's no good to be around the dead. And I need a ride home. This is my uncle's car."

"Okay," Ben said, shrugging.

"Thanks," she said and grabbed a bag from the cavernous trunk of the Lincoln, tossing it into the bed of his pickup.

By then, Shadi's uncles had all piled into the cab of the F-150 and were heading north, the wooden coffin bouncing around in the back. They watched the truck disappear in a cloud of dust.

"You been to Canyon de Chelly before?" she asked as he opened the passenger door for her and she hopped up into his truck.

"No," he said, shaking his head. He looked at his watch. It was almost one o'clock.

"Then I'll take you. It's a sacred place. A good place to be today."

The house Ben grew up in backed up to a creek with thick woods on either side. At night, with his window cracked open, he could hear the water bubbling and stumbling over rocks. When spring came, the trees of the forest made a fortress around their house, the new green leaves pressing against all of the windows. At night they made moving shadows on his walls. The woods were his private playground. He knew how to climb every tree, he was familiar with every rock, he could always find his way home. But after Dusty died, his mother forbade him to go to the woods. She was afraid of everything then. Everything good became a possible disaster. He could drown in the creek, fall from the tender limb of a tree, get bitten by a rabid raccoon. And so he was exiled from the one place where he felt at home.

In high school, he and his friends found their way back to the woods, but it wasn't the same anymore. Now they smoked weed and made out with girls, emerging from the woods with twigs and pitch and burdocks in their hair. They drank beers and crushed cans and left their candy wrappers at the water's edge. They pissed in the creek and carved obscenities into the aging elms. Sometimes he felt as though he owed the woods an apology. But how do you say you're sorry when you can't undo the damage you've done?

This is the way he felt about Sara sometimes. He knew what he was doing was hurting her, harming her. Destroying what was left of what had been beautiful. But he couldn't seem to resist. There was something strangely thrilling in wondering how far he could go before she snapped. There can be a terrible joy in knowing that someone won't fight back no matter what you do. It's the kind of joy that makes you sick to your stomach. The kind of joy that makes you ashamed of what you have become.

This is what Ben was thinking as he pulled the truck up to the overlook. If Sara knew where he was, how far this lie had gone already, she would be hurt.

He and Shadi got out of the truck, and he looked over the edge.

"That's Spider Rock," she said, gesturing below at two looming red rock towers jutting up into the sky from the bottom of the canyon. The cliff must have dropped down five hundred feet. He felt dizzy and exhilarated.

"The Diné believe this is where Spider Woman lives. She is the one who taught us how to weave. She also punishes disobedient children. See how the rock is white at the top? Those are supposed to be the bones of bad children."

"Jeez," Ben said.

52

When they got to the next overlook, she pulled her backpack out of the bed of the truck and put it on her back. "Let's go," she said. And she gestured to the path marked WHITE HOUSE NATURE TRAIL.

"You want to go on a *hike?*" he asked. He had taken his tie off but was still wearing his suit. She was also still wearing her funeral dress but had changed into the high-tops she'd had on at the hospital. "It'll just take a couple of hours. I have plenty of water," she said.

This was ridiculous.

He looked at his watch. It was a few minutes past one o'clock. If they were on the road to Flagstaff by three, he'd be home by six or six thirty. Jesus, what was he thinking? But before he had time to argue, Shadi had pulled her long hair off her neck into a ponytail and was headed down the sandstone path.

He thought about the time he and Jason had gone into the woods behind his house with a bunch of firecrackers they bought at a Fourth of July firecracker stand set up at the Sunoco on New Hampshire Avenue. Jason had thought it would be fun to put a brick of firecrackers in the crook of a tree. Ben thought about the hiss of the flame, the crack, and the explosion. And he thought about the robin's nest, the shards of blue shells, and the small featherless embryo motionless on the ground when it was over.

D id you grow up in Chinle?" he asked as they descended deeper into the canyon.

"Yeh. We lived in town until my mother took off, and then Ricky and I lived with our grandmother until I graduated."

Ben nodded. He tried to imagine all of them living inside that small hogan. He didn't ask where her mother went.

"My mother's father was a missionary," she said. "She went to high school on the rez, got pregnant with me, and married my dad. When her family went back to Kingman, she stayed with us. But by the time she had Ricky, she'd realized she made a big mistake." Shadi shrugged. "She was only twenty. She went back home. And my dad sent me and Ricky to live with my grandmother."

Ben could feel the sun on his back; the back of his neck was hot. "When did you move to Flagstaff?" he asked.

"I got a scholarship through the Navajo Nation. For college. And then I went straight to grad school for my MFA. This is my last year."

"Are you a painter?" Ben asked, thinking about her paint-splattered clothes at the hospital. "You'd been painting, right? At the hospital?"

"Oh no," she said, laughing. "I was just painting my kitchen."

They were at the bottom of the canyon now. Looking back up at Spider Rock, which loomed above them, framed in clouds. Ben felt small, at the feet of a giant.

"I'm in textiles," she said. "I'm a weaver."

It was only five o'clock when they pulled back into town. Shadi had suggested they go back through Leupp, on a shortcut through the endless barren expanse that is northern Arizona, which thankfully cut more than an hour off the trip. They'd stopped in Winona to get gas, and Ben had called Sara at work, told her he and Hippo were on their way up from Phoenix. That they were grabbing some dinner at Camp Verde. He said he'd be home by six thirty.

Shadi rolled down the truck window. They were climbing back up into the clouds, into the cold. Ben stared out the window at the ribbon of asphalt unfurling in front of them.

"Did Ricky live with you in Flagstaff?" he asked.

"Up until a month ago. It was too crowded, though. So he got a studio at the Downtowner. He was washing dishes at Beaver Street Brewery. Trying to put together a new band."

Ben knew those apartments; they weren't far from Jack's. Lots of short-term residents, very transient. Lots of people coming and going.

"Do you think it could have been someone at

the Downtowner?" he asked. "Was there anyone there he had problems with? Anybody giving him a hard time?"

Shadi turned to look at him, shaking her head. Her eyes were filling with tears.

"Ben?" she said. "Do you have anything you regret? Anything you wish you could take back?"

Ben nodded. He considered all of his regrets, like barbs on a wire fence circling around him.

"I shouldn't have kicked him out," she said. "He was my brother."

As they pulled into town, the sun was setting, the air becoming cold.

"Where should I take you?" he asked as they drove past the motels and strip malls along Route 66.

"You can take me home," she said. "It's been a long day."

They drove past his neighborhood off of Fort Valley Road, past the road up to the Snowbowl, and into an RV park. She directed him through the woods to her space, where a vintage silver Airstream was parked. "This is it," she said, and he parked the truck. "You want to come in for coffee or something?" she asked, opening the door.

It was five thirty now, and getting dark. It was cold outside, the sky cloudy and starless. He grabbed his jacket from the seat and pulled it on.

"No," he said, thinking of Sara getting home from the doctor's office soon. "I should get home. I've got papers to grade."

She turned to look at him. "You'll come back, though," she said. This was not a question.

He cocked his head at her quizzically, wondering what she meant. What it was that she wanted from him.

Her cheeks were pink in the cold, and she shivered inside the thin fabric of her black dress. She grabbed his hand and squeezed it, and it sent a trill through his entire body.

"I need you," she said. "To help me find out who did this to my brother."

At home, Sara was in the kitchen making a salad, patting dry the lettuce with a paper towel. "Hey," she said without looking up at him. She was still wearing her scrubs but had pulled a thick wool cardigan over them. "How was Phoenix?"

He felt a knot in his stomach twist tight. "Okay."

"Any luck?" she asked.

"Huh?"

"Hippo find a camper shell?"

"Nah."

She started to tear the lettuce into pieces. "You ate already?" she asked.

"Just a couple of tacos. I'm still hungry." He went to the fridge and pulled out a bag of carrots, a pint of cherry tomatoes, and a bottle of blue cheese dressing. Another lie; he hadn't eaten since this morning. He was starving. "Can I help?" he asked.

She looked at him and smiled a little suspiciously. "Sure."

Silently they worked together, assembling the salad.

"I can't stop thinking about that boy," she said. "I dreamed about him last night. I dreamed he didn't die."

Ben stiffened. "He *did*. I told you I stopped by the hospital." He grated the carrot on top of the two bowls.

"Have you seen anything in the paper about it?" she asked. "I mean, it's so weird, don't you think? There was nothing in the police log. It's like it didn't even happen. You'd think there'd be something. An obituary at least."

"He was probably from the rez," Ben said. He thought about the pink light enclosing him and Shadi as they descended into the canyon. He thought about the way the light caught in her hair, how he'd wanted to reach out and feel if it also held the sun's warmth. The lie was so big it seemed to fill the room, all of the empty spaces.

"It's such a shame," Sara said.

"What's that?"

"The drinking. The *alcoholism*. You wouldn't believe how many Indian kids we see with fetal alcohol syndrome. It's not just the men who drink."

"Who says he was drunk?" Ben asked, feeling heat rising up his neck as he tossed the brown carrot stubs into the garbage.

"Well, how else would you explain it?"

"It looked to me like somebody beat the shit out of him," Ben said angrily. "You don't have to be a drunk to get the crap beaten out of you."

Sara's lips tightened and she sliced a cucumber into perfect transparent disks. "I'm not being a racist, if that's what you think," she said. "There have been studies done, *genetic* studies about Native Americans' predisposition to alcoholism."

"Jesus Christ, Sara. I didn't call you a racist. Let's just stop."

Sara grabbed the two bowls from the counter and brought them to the table. She sat down hard in her chair and shook the bottle of dressing.

"Is this it? Just salad?" Ben asked. "I'm starving. Do we have any of that leftover chicken?"

"I'm on a *diet,* Ben."

Ben sighed.

They ate silently. Ben took a long drink of ice water; it made his whole body go cold.

"I was thinking we could have the reception up at the Snowbowl," she said quietly, staring into her salad.

"What?"

"I called up there yesterday, and they still have two weekends open next summer. But they fill up fast, so we need to decide."

"Right now?" Ben asked, pushing a cherry tomato around his bowl. His appetite was suddenly gone.

"No, Ben, let's wait another year. Hell, let's wait two more. What's the fucking hurry anyway?" she said, grabbing her bowl and going to the kitchen, where she dumped it in the trash. He heard her slam it onto the tile countertop.

She came back into the dining room and stood in front of him, hands on her hips. There was something unidentifiable (*Blood? Chocolate?*) smeared across her pale pink scrubs shirt. "I'm going to take a shower," she said. "I feel disgusting."

Later that night as Sara slept curled tightly away from him, Ben thought about all the ways to tell her this was over. He imagined the conversation that would free him. He thought about all the ways to say, *I don't love you anymore.* He tossed and turned.

When he finally fell asleep, he dreamed of the Spider Woman perched at the top of her red stone spire, spinning a web that stretched all the way across the canyon in shimmering filaments. And as he descended into the abyss, he could feel her silken trap slowly entangling him, enclosing him.

At Jack's on Wednesday night, Ben asked all of the regulars if they'd seen Ricky Begay on Halloween. He got in at six o'clock, just as the day crew was stumbling out, replaced by the nine-to-fivers.

None of the day crew would know Ricky. These were the folks who came in after the bar opened at eleven and stayed all day, shooting pool or watching CNN on the one TV over the bar. Hippo called them the Retirees, but the truth was, most of them were just out of work, disabled, or career drunks. And there's no retiring from that.

The nine-to-fivers, the people who worked at Gore or at any of the businesses downtown, were the folks who came in straight from work before heading home. Single guys mostly, though there was the occasional gaggle of women enjoying a ladies' night away from their husbands and children.

Jack's was one of those bars that appealed to everyone by appealing to no one in particular. There was no theme: no sombreros on the wall, no Irish or Italian paraphernalia. No sports motif, no mounted marlins, no fancy microbrews or cocktails with silly names. It was just a small, dark bar with three beers on tap, two good pool tables, and one rarity: really good food.

On any given night, you could expect to see a wide assortment of people crammed into the booths or bellied up to the rough-hewn bar. Sorority girls flirting with bikers, bikers hanging out with lawyers, lawyers offering free legal advice to the recently paroled. Ben considered Jack's the great equalizer. A place where all those walls we build around ourselves, all those labels we cling to, disappear into the frothy foam of beer.

Tonight he asked all of them if they remembered seeing Ricky on Halloween.

"I wasn't here. Out with my kids trick-or-treating," said Nancy, who worked at an oral surgeon's office up on Cedar but found her way to Jack's at least a couple of nights a week.

"I was up at Havasu last weekend," said Huck, who ran one of the many outdoor sporting goods stores in town.

At a Halloween party, stomach flu, mother-in-law in town. Not a single person was even at the bar, never mind watching to see if anybody was giving some quiet Indian kid a hard time.

The weekenders were a less predictable crowd, primarily because of the college kids. In Flagstaff, bars fall in and out of popularity with the college population. For a while, everybody's hanging out at the Monte Vista, and then all of a sudden that love affair is over and they're back at Jack's. By the time the season changes, or the semester ends or the summer begins, some other bar is calling their name: Beaver Street, the Mad I, or Collins'. There's a restlessness about small towns, and with restlessness comes infidelity. But the good news was, they almost always came back. And there was never a weekend night when the bar wasn't full.

"Who was tending bar Saturday night?" Ben asked Hippo.

"Ned," he said. "I came out to help when it got crazy, but he was out front most of the night by himself."

Ned had been working at the bar off and on for ages. He was a river rat, disappearing into the canyon for weeks at a time on rafting trips. But when he wasn't river running, he was here at Jack's, pulling beers and dealing with drunks and making sure people had fun and also making sure they got home safe. Ben had seen Ned walk girls to their cabs and even drive a few folks home who might be stranded otherwise.

Tonight, Ned was in as a patron rather than an employee and sat at the end of the bar near the condiments tray, drinking whiskey and stealing olives.

"Hey, Ned," Ben said, giving Ned a fist bump across the bar.

"Dude," Ned said, throwing back his third shot of Jameson since he'd gotten there. Ned had the skin of a fifty-year-old man who'd spent too much time in the sun, but he was probably only in his twenties.

"Listen," Ben said. "I'm trying to find out if there was something going on Saturday night with one of the regulars."

"Who was it?" Ned asked, swiping another olive. The pimento slipped out and fell on the bar.

"You know the kid who comes in and shoots pool? He usually sits over in the booth by the bathrooms?"

"Ricky?" Ned asked.

"Yeah," Ben said, surprised that Ned knew his name. "You know him?"

"Sure," he said. "Cheese fries and a Coke. Good pool player."

Ben nodded.

"Lot of folks in on Saturday," Ned said, jutting his chin out and rubbing the bristly whiskers there. "I had to throw out some frat boys. Stupid motherfucker broke one of the pool cues."

"They giving Ricky a hard time?"

"Shit. I don't remember if he was here then. I think he might have been here early on, before all the idiots started showing up in costumes. Place went fucking crazy after that. But I don't remember seeing him at the tables after ten or so. That's about when I got rid of the kids. One of them fell down on the sidewalk afterward, split his lip and started threatening to sue." He laughed and slammed the fourth shot of whiskey Ben had set down in front of him.

"You know if there's anywhere else he hangs out?"

"Uptown sometimes, Brews and Cues. The V . . . any place that's got pool tables. He's got a bad fake ID, says he's thirty. Doesn't drink, though, so nobody gives him a hard time about it."

Ben sighed. This wasn't going to be as easy as he thought. Ricky could have been anywhere that night. The question was, where did he start out and how the hell did he wind up five miles from his room downtown in front of Ben's doorstep, left there like some god-awful gift?

"Wait!" Ned said, as Ben reached under the bar for the jar of olives to replenish the depleted supply. "He *was* here," he said, smacking his palm on the bar. "Early on. I remember because he was talking to some chick dressed up like a cowgirl. Some drunk bitch who kept trying to get her boyfriend to take a picture of the cowgirl and the Indian."

"What time?" Ben asked.

"Shit, maybe nine, nine thirty? It was early, because I remember thinking that she must have gotten a head start. Meathead boyfriend I recognized from the gym."

Ben dumped the olives in the tray.

"Guy's name is Higgins, I think. Weird thing was, after the stupid girl finally shut up, he and his buddy ended up playing pool with him."

"Ricky and this Higgins guy?"

"Yeah. I think they even took off around the same time."

"Did he have a coat on?" Ben asked.

"What?"

"Was he wearing a coat?"

"Yeah. He had on that big army coat he always wears."

Ben thought of Ricky lying in the snow, in only a flannel shirt and a pair of jeans. What the hell happened to him after he left Jack's? He looked at his watch. It was only ten o'clock. He still had three and a half hours until last call. It was pretty slow tonight, so he might get home by two thirty. But he had to teach at eight, and he hadn't even planned his lessons yet. Jesus, he was ready for the semester to end. He wasn't sure how much longer he could do this.

On Thursday, after his second class, he went upstairs into his office, which he shared with three other adjuncts, and was glad to see no one was there. That was the advantage of teaching early morning classes. He almost never had to deal with anybody lurking around in his office. He set down the new stack of essays and clicked on the monitor of the one antiquated computer.

Early on he'd tried to make his office feel like it belonged to him, putting books on the bookshelves, hanging up a couple of posters on the walls and the back of the door. But after three or four rotations of grad students and other adjuncts, any attempt to make it feel more permanent than it was seemed futile and pathetic. The truth was, he didn't know if he'd even have a job lined up from one semester to the next. There had been times when he'd been able to get only one section of US History to 1865; when he was lucky, they'd offer him two or three. Only one tenure-track position had come open the whole time he'd been there, and it had gone to a woman who had published four books already. He knew that if he wanted a real academic job, he'd have to go on the job list and be willing to move. He'd have to relocate to Mississippi or Kansas or Florida if he wanted tenure. Benefits. All those things you're supposed to have by the time you're thirty with a PhD. But what he'd realized in the last several semesters was that, while he loved history, he really didn't like teaching it.

Sara was constantly suggesting that he should be willing to look beyond Flagstaff. She could work anywhere, she said. And it was true, as a nurse her options were limitless. *California,* she said. *New England. I don't care where I am as long as I'm with you.* She'd gone as far as to print out real estate offerings in places like Maine and Oregon, places where she knew there were openings at universities. "We could sell the house and have a good down payment," she said. "It would be an adventure."

He knew that although Sara had grown up in Arizona, there were times when she was envious of her friends who had left. One of her girlfriends from high school went to Los Angeles after graduation and had made a pretty good career in commercials. They'd see her at least once a month on TV selling Jell-O or laundry detergent or tax software. And her friend Stacy from nursing school had married some guy she met on spring break and moved to Manhattan, where he got a job at a big financial firm. Sara talked about Los Angeles and New York as if they were the most exotic places in the world. "We could move to DC," she had said. "Wouldn't it be nice to go back home?"

The only thing that kept Sara from insisting they move was that her family still lived here, her parents just a couple of hours' drive to Phoenix, her brother in Tucson. And while she claimed to dream of leaving, Ben suspected that he could probably call her bluff at any moment. They had dinner with her parents at least once a month, her mom was always coming up to take her shopping, and her dad showed up every time something needed to be fixed whether or not Ben was able to fix it himself. What would have made her happier than anything was if Ben would agree to move to Phoenix.

Ben sat down at his computer, looked at the desktop photo of one of his office mate's daughters, and checked his e-mail. He clicked through the excuses and apologies from his students who hadn't made it to class, through the spam, and then stopped. He clicked on the first e-mail Shadi had sent and nervously clicked REPLY.

Can you meet me for lunch today at Café Espress? Around 1:00? he typed and looked around the office guiltily, as though someone might be peering over his shoulder.

Within moments, she responded. *I'll be there.*

Café Espress on San Francisco is one of the few places in town where you can actually get something healthy to eat. Organic produce, sandwiches on crunchy homemade bread piled high with sprouts. Sun tea. Punks and hippies. Sara called it Café Patchouli. He'd picked it because it was a place that Sara never went.

Shadi was already there, sitting at a table in the window; she waved and motioned for him to come join her. He thought about being on display like this, like a clothing store mannequin or a sports shop kayak. He thought about who might see him and what they might say.

The warm air enveloped him as the door closed behind him. It smelled good in here. Like homemade bread. He went to Shadi's table and took off his coat, unwrapped his scarf.

Today she was wearing jeans and boots and a turtleneck sweater. Her hair was up in a bun, held in place with a pencil. She smiled and stood up, leaning into him for a hug. She smelled good, that fresh-cut grass smell.

"Sit," she said.

Ben sat down and picked up a menu. He tried to focus on the lunch items, but the words blurred together, swimming across the page. He put the menu down and looked at her. Her eyes were warm pools; she was waiting for him.

"Ricky *was* at Jack's that night, but he left early," Ben offered.

She nodded.

"There was a girl, some stupid girl who kept bothering him," he said. He didn't want to repeat

71

what it was that she was doing. The cowgirl and Indian shit. It made him feel guilty, ashamed. But if he didn't say it, it was like he was protecting the girl instead of protecting Shadi.

She tilted her head and looked at him for an explanation.

"She was trying to get her boyfriend to take a picture of the two of them. She was dressed up like a cowgirl. For Halloween."

Shadi's eyes grew dark.

"Her boyfriend and Ricky left Jack's around the same time. They'd been playing pool together."

The waitress came over to take their order. Her arms were tattooed, and she had a large silver lip ring that looked a little infected. She seemed put out by their requests. Dressing on the side for Shadi. Jack instead of Swiss for Ben. She scratched their orders on her pad and huffed as she walked away with their menus.

Shadi shrugged and smiled.

Ben peered out the window. The lunch crowd and students and tourists filled the streets. It was a cold but gorgeous sunny day, with almost no evidence of the weekend's snowstorm remaining. A train rumbled and then screamed past them on the tracks a block away. Ben studied the faces of the people on the sidewalks, worried about seeing someone he knew. Sara usually ate lunch at work, part of the diet. He could picture her watching her Lean Cuisine spinning around inside the microwave in the break room. He used to meet her for lunch. He used to bring her rolled tacos or slices of pizza from Alpine Pizza. They'd eat in the break room together or, if it was nice, out at the picnic table on the office park's lawn. Even eating had turned into a sort of drudgery for her lately.

"Have you talked to the police anymore?" Ben asked.

She shook her head. "They say that he got drunk and passed out. Fell down, hit his head. He died of exposure."

"But he wasn't drunk. Didn't that show up in the autopsy?"

"There was no autopsy," she said, shaking her head. "It's against our beliefs. Well, my grandmother's beliefs anyway."

"They must have done a blood alcohol test at the hospital," Ben said.

Shadi looked out the window. A woman was tethering a collie to a bike rack. "They did. His blood alcohol was point-oh-eight."

"That doesn't make sense. You said he doesn't drink, and even if he did, point-oh-eight is hardly drunk enough to pass out. And what about his injuries? What about the trauma to his head? That was no fall." Ben felt anger spreading from his gut to his arms. He felt his hands clenching into fists.

"You don't understand," she said, shaking her head. "The rules aren't the same."

"What do you mean *rules?*"

"They found alcohol, they found their answer. That's enough for them. Case closed." Shadi shut her eyes and turned toward the window. The sun was so bright it almost hurt. "God, I'm starving. Where's our food?"

After lunch, Ben drove Shadi back to campus. She had an art history class at three o'clock, and Ben needed to pick up the essays he'd left in his office. He parked near campus and they walked together. Ben was already formulating his excuses in case anyone saw him. *She's a student of mine. A grad student TA. A friend.* A friend? What was she really? *Who* was she to him?

At the entrance to his building, Shadi said, "I know it's a lot to ask, but is there any way you could meet me tomorrow at the Downtowner? I need to move things out of Ricky's room. I don't know anyone else with a truck."

"You don't have a car?" he asked.

She shook her head. "This is my ride," she said, pointing to a rusty three-speed bicycle locked to the bike rack outside the building.

"What do you do in the winter?"

"Hang on tight," she said, laughing. Then she unlocked the bike and hopped on. "Can you meet me out in front of the building at ten o'clock? You don't teach tomorrow, right?"

"No," he said, and watched her pedal away. "I'm free."

The first time Ben saw Sara was on campus at school nearly six years ago. He was studying, sprawled out on the grass in front of the library, surrounded by a fortress of books. She was walking along down the sidewalk, a backpack slung over her shoulder, smiling like someone had just told her a joke. She even shook her head, as if she couldn't believe what she'd just heard. He watched her because she was so pretty and so *happy*. It's such a rare thing to see people so joyful. So absolutely content.

He asked her once later what she was smiling about, and she said that someone had just hollered, *Hey, beautiful!* at her as she walked across the grass. And Ben said that he'd almost done the same.

He was in the throes of finals after his second year. He was miserable, wondering what the hell he'd been thinking. Pursuing a PhD in history had seemed like a good idea two years before (when he was twenty-two, fresh out of Georgetown, and in love with the prospect of teaching someday).When he started graduate school, he romanticized the life he'd one day have: the handsome young professor in jeans and a tweed blazer, fawning coeds vying for the front-row seats, him brilliant and funny as he taught his students to love history as much as he did. But suddenly, as he crammed his brain full of facts and time lines, theories and speculations, he started to wonder if this had been a big fat waste of time. He was living in a dumpy studio south of the tracks. The train rattled his windows every single time it went by, and there was the faint scent of raw sewage every time he opened his back door. Getting his PhD, if he wasn't willing to leave Flagstaff, seemed like nothing other than a feather in his cap. A useless frilly feather that did nothing but blow about in the wind. And then he saw Sara walk across the quad, smiling to herself, almost laughing out loud, and any doubts he'd had flew out the window.

He'd leapt up and decided to follow her, leaving his books on the grass behind him. She'd gotten all the way to the student union before she turned around and said, "Have you been following me this whole time?"

When he said, "Maybe just a little," she laughed and said, "Well, you must be thirsty, then. Let me get you something to drink." And she'd taken him to a vending machine, popped a dollar in, pressing the button for a Mountain Dew without even asking what he wanted, and handed it to him. "There. Now tell me your name."

Within a month, she was spending the night in his room four nights a week, going home only to shower and do her laundry. She lived with three other girls in an apartment off of Lonetree Road. Melanie was one of them. They had grown up together in Phoenix, come to Flagstaff for college, and now they were both in their final year of nursing school. She and Melanie both got jobs at Dr. Newman's office as soon as they graduated. Sara moved out of her apartment and signed a lease on a place closer to downtown. She never asked Ben if he wanted to move in with her; she just brought him a bunch of boxes from the grocery store and started packing.

He used to love that she took charge with everything. He loved that she was so decisive. And he really loved that she liked to sleep with him. He was surprised by how easy the sex was with her. No game playing, no pleading. She seemed to know when he wanted her, and a lot of times she wanted him first. Either way, she let him know. He loved to follow her into the bedroom, loved the way her soft wide hips swayed.

He loved that she sang at the top of her lungs in the shower. He loved that the smallest things gave her pleasure: a pint of ice cream on a hot day, thunderstorms, a nice long hike in Oak Creek Canyon. She was so *happy* all of the time. She was optimistic, positive that everything would eventually go her way.

What he finally realized was, her optimism was grounded in the fact that nothing ever, ever went awry in Sara's world. She'd never been denied anything. She'd never been truly disappointed. She'd always had enough money. Good friends. Parents who were still married, a brother she adored. Not a single person she was close to had died. This might seem like a ridiculous reason to fall in love, but for Ben, something about the simple lack of sorrow in her life was almost magical. It was as if she were somehow blessed, golden. And maybe he thought that by virtue of being her boyfriend, some of this good fortune might rub off on him.

But instead, he'd let her down. He'd been the first and only disappointment in Sara's life. He was the curdled milk in the fridge. The weeds in the garden. The cloud shrugging off its silver lining.

In six short years, he had systematically turned her life from sublime to miserable. From simple and contented to ordinary and mundane. Nothing made her happy anymore. She deserved better than this.

Ben parked his truck near Jack's and walked down to the Downtowner Apartments, where Shadi was standing out front smoking a cigarette. She had her bike with her, and the basket was brimming with pears. Her face lit up when she saw him. "Where's your truck?" she asked.

"It's up the street." He didn't want to have to explain to Sara what he was doing if she, or anybody else, saw his truck down here. "Are those *pears?* Where did they come from?"

"That tree over there," she said, gesturing to a lone pear tree that, despite the weather, was replete with fruit.

They went inside the apartment building and down the hall. For some reason, he'd imagined the place cordoned off with yellow police tape. Instead, there was nothing. Just an empty hallway that smelled vaguely musty and a lot of closed doors. She put her key in the lock and opened the door to Ricky's room. Inside, there was an unmade mattress and box spring on the floor, a guitar stand with an electric guitar, and a laundry basket full of clothes. A fridge, a microwave, and a small TV. Next to the bed were a stack of books, all of them Stephen King paperbacks. Shadi sat down on the bed and put her face in her hands.

He hadn't seen her cry before. Not at the

hospital, not at the funeral. But now, in this quiet room, she was falling apart.

"Hey," he said tentatively. He sat down next to her on the bed and slowly put his arm across her shoulder. Her entire body was quaking.

"He was so lonely," she said, looking up at him. "What kind of life is this?" she asked, gesturing to the monastic room. "I told him not to come here. That at least in Chinle he had friends. He had family."

"He had you here," Ben offered. "Maybe he wanted to be closer to you."

"He drove me crazy!" she said, wiping her tears hard with the back of her hand. "I asked him to move out because I couldn't stand him living with me. His music, all day and all night. He's messy," she said, pointing to a crumb-covered dish and a glass with a hard disk of orange juice at the bottom. "He always told the dumbest jokes. His feet smelled. He was so big! There wasn't room for him."

Ben suddenly felt awkward holding on to Shadi, and he lifted his arm off her shoulders and coughed so he'd have something to do with his hands.

"Ben, what do *you* think happens when people die?"

Ben took a deep breath. After Dusty died and they went home from the hospital without her, he'd curled up in his bed alone. He'd waited for someone to come and explain to him what would happen next. What to expect. Not for him, for them, but for *her*. But neither his mother nor father offered anything. There was no heaven in his house, no God.

Ben shook his head. "I don't know."

Shadi wiped away her tears. "My people believe that you shouldn't cry when someone dies. That too much emotion can interrupt their journey to the underworld. That the dead person's spirit might attach itself to you, or to a place, or to an object if the journey is interrupted. Do you think that's possible?"

This time, he nodded. Without heaven, without angels, Dusty became a ghost. She lived in every particle of dust, in every shadow. She lived in all the empty places; maybe she still did.

"Well," she said, standing up from the bed. "At least it shouldn't take long to clear this shit out."

Shadi put everything into the laundry basket (the books, the clothes, the TV, a small amplifier, and a carton of cigarettes), which Ben carried, and she rode her bike next to him to the truck, the guitar slung over her back. "Thanks for helping me out," she said.

"No problem," he said, shrugging.

She took the pears out of the bike basket and threw her bike and Ricky's stuff into the bed of the truck. Ben drove up Humphreys so they wouldn't have to pass the doctor's office on San

Francisco and then pulled out onto Fort Valley Road.

When they drove into her spot at the RV park, she got out of the truck and he got out to help her. "It's okay, I've got it," she said, lowering the bike to the ground and grabbing the rest of the stuff. "Listen, thanks for helping me out and I'm sorry about that earlier. I didn't mean to fall apart like that. It's not usually my way."

He waited for her to invite him in. It was early; Sara wouldn't be home from work for another couple of hours, and he didn't have to work that night. He wanted to keep talking to her. He wanted to stay.

"Okay, I'll see you," she said.

His heart sank a little. He got in the truck, and she started to chain her bike to the trailer. He leaned over to the passenger side and rolled the window down.

"Hey, I'm going to see if I can find anything out about the other places Ricky might have gone that night. I've got friends who tend bar at some of the other places he might have been hanging out. Somebody had to have seen something."

She stood up and smiled. She came over to the window and handed him a pear. "Thanks," she said, and then she unlocked the trailer door and disappeared inside.

He sat in the driveway for a minute. He couldn't believe she and Ricky had lasted as long as they had, sharing such a tiny space. He wondered what it looked like inside. He wondered what she was doing in there. And then he shook his head, *no,* this was crazy, and he put the key in the ignition and backed out. On the way home, he ate the pear, just a couple of bites. It wasn't ripe yet, though, too hard and too green, almost bitter.

B en?" Sara's voice came from the kitchen as
Ben walked in the door.

He took off his coat and poked his head around
the corner. She was standing at the counter,
making lasagna, layering noodles and sauce and
cheese. Ben's favorite. She'd changed out of her
scrubs and was wearing a soft pair of Levi's and
one of his sweaters. Barefoot, her hair loose
around her shoulders.

She stopped what she was doing and looked at
him. Her chin trembled. "I'm sorry. I'm just a
mess. I didn't mean to be such a bitch the other
day. God, I don't know what's wrong with me,
Ben. I think everything with that kid, it just
finally got to me. I see broken bones and bloody
faces all day long, but this is different. At work I
feel like I have control over things. That's why I
couldn't work in the ER. It's just too much. I can
give shots and draw blood and hand out stickers
to scared little kids, but I can't *deal* with death
like this. I've been rattled all week. And then that
stupid stuff about the wedding . . . I'm just . . ."
She took a deep breath. "Sorry."

She must have been saving this up for days.

"It's okay," he said. He hated seeing her like
this.

She turned to him and shook her head. "It's *not*

okay. It's like things are changing between us, and I don't want to be so angry all the time. I want to be who we used to be. God, what happened?"

And then she was leaning into him, pressing her cheek against his chest, and his chest ached. He rested his chin on the top of her head and closed his eyes hard. The house smelled like her mother's homemade tomato sauce. There were candles burning on the dining room table.

"Did you do this for me?" he asked.

She pulled away from him and looked up, smiling. "I got the sweet sausage you like, and I made homemade garlic bread." She went to the pan, covered it with foil, and put it in the oven.

"What time is it?" he asked, glancing down at his watch. It was only five.

"I left work early. I just wanted to come home and be with you. Start the weekend right."

He raised his eyebrow at her. She was pressing her whole body into him now, and he could feel himself giving in to that old feeling, that wonderful feeling of Sara, Sara. God, what *had* happened to them?

And then she took his hand, leading him out of the kitchen, through the living room and down the hallway to their bedroom. She put her hand against his chest, pushing him down on the bed. She pulled the heavy curtains, and in the darkness he went through the motions, trying to remember what it meant to love Sara.

On Tuesday morning, he walked down the rows of seats, handing back the graded essays. He was met with all of the requisite groans and sighs. He hated teaching at eight A.M., but it came with the territory of being an adjunct. The full-time faculty got first picks with the schedule, and the rest of the available courses were doled out to him and the rest of his colleagues at the bottom of the academic totem pole.

There are two types of kids who take eight o'clock classes: the overachievers and the underachievers. The overachievers are the ones who wake up ready to go each day, the ones who go to bed early during the week, the ones who do their homework and visit during office hours. These are the students who manage to graduate in four years, which is no small feat in a town with so many opportunities for distraction. The underachievers are the ones who forget to register for their classes until all of the sections held at reasonable times are full. These are the second- or third- or fourth-year seniors who *have* to have this class to graduate. The ones who have spent more time snowboarding than studying. More time at the bars than at the library. And this makes for a terrible classroom dynamic. The overachievers sitting in the front row, raising their hands, eagerly jumping in anytime Ben poses a question while the underachievers hold court in the back rows, fighting off sleep or texting their grievances, clackety-clack, all through class.

This morning as Ben began his lecture on American colonialism, Hanna Blum, fresh out of the shower and Starbucks in hand, raised her hand to ask a question, and Joe Bello yawned in the back. It was a big yawn, an exaggerated yawn. The kind of yawn that is meant to send a message.

"Joe?" Ben said. "Am I boring you?"

There were some chuckles in the back. His buddy, Drew Miller, punched his arm. "Wake up, dude."

Joe had been a pain in the ass all semester. He was a rich kid from Scottsdale, probably on his third or fourth school. His parents had likely sent him here thinking there would be fewer temptations than back home. He was a frat kid, but he probably had an apartment off campus, a BMW, top-of-the-line skis. He probably woke up this morning with a bong next to his bed, smoking $500-an-ounce weed for breakfast. Ben was pretty sure Joe had a job all lined up working for his daddy or one of his daddy's friends back in the valley after graduation next spring. School simply did not matter.

Ben thought about Ricky, about him coming to Flagstaff to make a better life. About his not being able to afford to go to school. It was probably a prick like Joe who beat him up. Some entitled little shit.

Ben kept talking, talking, talking. Emphasizing his points with random scratches on the whiteboard. Behind him he heard the clackety-clack of a BlackBerry and his neck stiffened. He stopped talking and turned around.

Nestor Yazzie in the front was about to ask a question, but Ben held his finger up in a *wait a minute* gesture and looked down the rows to the back, where Joe was now sitting upright, hoodie pulled down over his head, hands in lap. Clackety-clack.

Ben set his Expo marker on his desk and walked down the aisle between the seats. He got to Joe before Joe even realized that he was coming. He held out his hand, palm up, and said, "Give it."

Joe looked up from whatever electronic missive he was tapping out and said, "I'm done."

"Mr. Bello, I said give it to me."

"You're not taking my phone," Joe said.

Ben planned on taking the phone, confiscating it until the end of class, and then giving it back when class was over. But as he stood there, he felt his skin prickling, anger swelling inside him. "Why are you here, Joe?" Ben finally asked.

"What?"

"I said, *Why. Are. You. Here?*"

Joe shrugged.

"You're a waste of time," Ben hissed. "A waste of all of our time. A waste of your folks' money. A waste of fucking space. Give me the goddamn phone."

"Dude, chill out," Joe said, setting it down, raising his hands in some sort of stupid surrender. "Forget it. It's off."

Ben watched his hand grab the phone. He—and Joe—watched as he hurled it across the room. He—and everyone else in the class—watched in disbelief when it hit the back wall and shattered, its electronic innards splattered all over the floor.

And then he went to the front of the room, picked up his briefcase, and said quietly, "There will be a test on Jamestown on Tuesday."

It took about ten minutes for word to spread across campus that Ben Bailey had lost it in his eight o'clock. His next class looked terrified. A few nervous whispers but not a single text message sent during class. Ben was feeling pretty good about himself as he made his way to the History Department to get his mail.

The second he poked his head in to say hi to Rob, the interim chair of the department, he realized he'd screwed up.

"Hey, Bailey, I just got a call," he said, motioning for Ben to come into his office.

"From?"

"Martin Bello. His son is in your eight A.M.

American history class? He said there was an *altercation* this morning."

Ben wondered how Joe had managed to get ahold of his father so quickly without his cell phone.

Rob's face was red, his already large eyes popping. "What the hell were you thinking, Ben?"

Ben knew exactly what he was thinking. He was thinking he was sick and goddamned tired of getting paid $15,000 a year to stand in front of a bunch of entitled brats, compressing the entire early history of this nation into thirteen weeks as they slept or texted. He was tired of not being able to answer Nestor Yazzie's questions because of the douche bag sitting in the back. He was tired of pretending that anything he had to say or think about America's history had any impact on America's future because obviously this was not the case. Because *nothing had changed*. Not here.

Someone beat the shit out of Ricky Begay and left him for dead in the snow. And no one seemed to care.

"Ben, I hate to do this to you, buddy, but this just can't happen. This has to be a safe place for these kids. They can't be worried that their profs are going to hurt them."

"What the hell are you talking about?"

"He's threatening to press assault charges," Rob said.

"For throwing his cell phone at the wall?"

"Never mind what the university might do."

"What are you saying, Rob?"

"I'm saying that Martin Bello, Joe Bello's father, is in the Arizona state house of reps. He's also an alumnus and a significant donor to the school. What I am *saying* is that you draft a formal apology to Joe and his family. We'll transfer him into a different section. Maybe with Rose? You just need to make it through the next month until the end of the semester without any more incidents, and then maybe you can take a little sabbatical after that. Joe Bello graduates in May. We can start a new contract for you next fall if there are some sections available."

"A sabbatical is a paid leave," Ben said, seething.

Rob shook his head sadly. "Not for adjuncts."

Ben was grateful for the mind-numbing routine of washing and sanitizing the glasses, dusting the bottles of liquor, sweeping the peanut shells off the floor. He relished the mundane tasks: wiping down the bar, slicing lemons, cleaning the mirror that reflected the patrons' faces. There was only one customer today, a regular who sipped slowly on his Jack and Coke. Ben refilled his glass about once an hour.

He hadn't told Sara about his conversation with Rob at school, about the great cell-phone fiasco. Since the weekend, she'd been so happy. He didn't want to wreck it.

On Saturday they had gone for a hike down in Oak Creek Canyon. It was at least twenty degrees warmer down there, sunny and so quiet. Sara had made a picnic lunch and brought a six-pack of Sierra Nevadas. They spent the whole day hiking and got home Saturday night sunburned and exhausted. On Sunday they'd curled up on the couch together all day watching football and eating bean dip.

For a little while, it was as though they had spun backward through time, as though none of this had happened. It was an amnesiac weekend, when Ben began to wonder how he could ever have thought about leaving Sara. Thoughts of

Shadi became whispers, like a hazily recollected dream. And this is what Sara had wanted, wasn't it? Perhaps this was proof that Ben's theory about her was true; things always worked out for Sara. She always got what she wanted. Her glass was not just half full but brimming.

They didn't talk about Ricky once.

But here he was two days later, and everything had gone to shit. And it was all his fault. He had no idea how to tell Sara that he'd lost his job, that he was now officially the only full-time bartender with a PhD in town. He imagined how angry she would be, how disappointed. He could already see the furrow of her brow, the lines in her forehead, the ones he'd certainly put there, deepening with another new worry. And then, as he was sweeping up the shards of a glass that had slipped through his soapy hands, Shadi came in through the heavy doors of the bar, breathless.

"Ben," she said.

"Hey," he said, startled but happy to see her.

She sat down on one of the bar stools and set her purse on the bar. She looked anxious. She leaned in close and said softly, "There's a kid bragging about being the one who beat up Ricky."

"What?"

"My girlfriend who works over at the Laundromat on Milton said that she overheard some guy talking about tipping Indians on Halloween."

"What the hell does that mean?" he asked.

"You know, find a drunk Indian and knock him over?"

"Jesus," Ben said, wiping his hands on his apron. "Did she tell you what he looked like?"

"*Belagana*, white guy, college age. Blond hair, baseball cap."

"That could be anybody." Half of the guys at the university fit that description.

"Wait," she said, her eyes lighting up. "She said he was driving a Mustang. A bright blue one."

"That should narrow things down," Ben said.

He swept the broken shards into a dustpan and dumped them in the trash.

"You want something to drink?" he asked.

"Coke," she said. "Please."

He scooped some ice into a pint glass and filled it with Coke from the fountain behind the bar. "Straw?"

She shook her head. "Did you get a chance to talk to anyone else about it this weekend?"

"I didn't have time this weekend," he said, feeling strangely guilty that he'd been at home with Sara. "But I will. I actually get off around ten tonight, and I can stop by a couple of places before I go home."

"Do you think we should talk to the cops too? If we can find this guy, maybe they can question him."

Ben thought about how quickly the cops had

dismissed Ricky. How determined they were to wash their hands of the whole thing.

Shadi took a drink of the Coke and then rifled through her purse. "Hey, have you got fifty cents I could borrow?"

He dug into his front pocket and pulled out two quarters. She snatched them out of his palm and went to the jukebox in the corner.

She studied the glowing menu of songs, flipping through until she found what she was looking for. Then she dropped the coins in, and the music started. She returned to the bar, smiling.

"Shake your hip, babe," sang Mick Jagger against a bluesy bass.

"Exile on Main Street was our daddy's favorite album," she said. "It's what made Ricky want to learn guitar. He listened to that record so many times, the grooves wore out."

She sat back down at the bar and ran her finger down the glass, drawing a line through the condensation. She peered into the cola as though she were peering into a crystal ball. When she looked up again, she sighed. "Our daddy was a drunk. A nasty, mean drunk. And we were scared to death of him."

Ben nodded. "Is that why Ricky didn't drink?"

"Not even at weddings."

The spell with Sara was broken the second Ben opened his mouth.

"I'm not going to be teaching next semester," he said. She was sitting on the couch in her pajamas, flipping through a wedding magazine, when he got home that night.

He probably wouldn't have said anything at all except that he'd had a couple of drinks on his way home. Alcohol was worse than truth serum for Ben. After his shift ended, he had searched up and down the streets for a blue Mustang. He had also asked the bartenders at the Mad I and Uptown Billiards if they remembered any fights on Halloween night, if they recognized Ricky. Shadi had given him Ricky's high school yearbook photo. In the picture he looked about fifteen years old, a wide, smiling baby face. Ben had had a beer at work, then a shot of Jameson at the Mad I and another at Uptown. No one had seen Ricky. And nobody remembered any fights on Halloween except for one between two girls who had both dressed up as slutty nuns.

"What did you *do?*" Sara asked, clearly livid.

"I chucked a kid's cell phone against the wall, and his dad threatened to charge me with assault." He laughed at this, waited for her to laugh too. It was ludicrous, really, if you thought about it.

"What?" Sara asked, her eyes growing wide.

"I'm taking a sabbatical," he said, smirking.

"There's no such thing for adjuncts," she said.

"No shit," he answered and plopped down on the couch next to her. He grabbed the magazine she had set down. Glossy models in slinky white dresses, zillion-dollar flower arrangements, diamonds as big as boulders. The smell of the pages was nauseating. He felt acid rising in his throat and burped quietly into his hand.

"Are you drunk?" Sara asked.

"No."

"Well, you reek."

"I'm not drunk. I just had a couple of drinks after work."

"Well, you better figure out what to do for a job come Christmas," she said. "Two shifts at Jack's is not going to pay the mortgage, and I'm already working fifty hours a week with overtime." She picked up the magazine and started flipping through it angrily.

All of the doubts and regrets rose to the surface again, corpses bobbing in still water.

He was actually drunker than he thought. He probably shouldn't have driven home. His tongue felt thick.

"My dad could maybe get you a job at one of his dealerships," she said, without looking up at him. She knew this was the one thing she should not suggest. "We could move to Phoenix."

His heart started to race. He tried to keep the words in, but he couldn't stop himself. He looked at her and felt nothing.

"I don't think I want to get married," he said. It felt awful and wonderful to finally say it out loud.

"*What?*" Sara asked, stunned.

Her obliviousness, her ignorance, pissed him off. "Really? You're surprised?" he said.

When she slapped him, any sort of buzz he'd had went flat. His face stung. Jesus, what had he done? His skin was hot from where she had hit him.

"You're one stupid asshole, Ben Bailey," she said, standing up and grabbing her coat. She lurched forward and yanked her car keys from the table. She stopped and pointed the keys at him. "Does this have something to do with that girl?"

That girl. His head was spinning. This was it. Was he this transparent? His thoughts like glass?

"What girl?" he asked.

"That bitch with the guitar?" she said, her voice shrill, and he thought of Shadi riding her bike, Ricky's guitar slung across her back. Someone must have seen him with her. Someone must have told.

"I don't know what you're talking about."

"*Rory?* That stupid hippie chick at Melanie's on Halloween? Jesus, I saw you that night."

Relief came over him in one hot liquid splash. "No. God, no. Sara, listen. . . ."

"I'm going down to Melanie's."

The front door slammed, then her car door slammed. Her headlights swept through the living room, and then she was gone. Blood was pounding hard in his temples, but beyond that thrumming was something quiet, something close to peace.

And suddenly the only thing he wanted was to see Shadi. He knew he shouldn't drive, but maybe he could walk. It couldn't be more than a mile to the RV park. Sara was gone. Sara was *gone*.

By the time he got to Shadi's Airstream, he had sobered up. It was cold out, bitter and windy. He pulled his hat down over his ears, cupped his hands together, and blew hot air into them. He thought about turning around and heading back home. He looked up at the clear bright sky, and the stars made him dizzy. There was a faint pink light coming through the curtains in the window. She was awake. Before he had time to change his mind, he stepped up to the door of the camper and knocked.

"Who is it?" Her voice was gruff.

"It's me," he said. "Ben."

She opened the door and peered out at him. Her voice softened. "Ben?"

"Hi," he said.

She leaned out of the trailer and looked around. "Where's your truck?"

"I walked."

"Jesus," she said, trembling. "Get in here. It's freezing out there."

Inside, it was warm. There was a butane heater right next to the door, and he could feel the heat coming off it in waves. Shadi was wearing gray long johns, thick wool socks, and a red plaid flannel shirt. It was unbuttoned, and underneath was a thin white cotton T-shirt. He tried not to look. As if sensing his discomfort, she wrapped the flannel tightly around her waist.

"Sit down," she said, gesturing to the kitchen table. "You want some coffee or something?"

"Sure," he said. A cold shiver ran through his body.

The outside of the Airstream was deceiving; the inside was much more spacious than he'd imagined. There was a small stove and fridge. A decent-size counter with a sink, and the table where he sat while she made coffee. At the front of the trailer was a built-in couch with cupboards underneath. On the opposite end of the trailer was a door, probably to the bathroom, and a curtain behind which he assumed was Shadi's bed. And next to the counter was a large weaving loom. He recognized it from the trips he'd made to the Museum of Northern Arizona during grad school.

She sat down next to him in a metal folding chair and smiled. "It's late."

"I know," he said. "I'm really sorry."

"It's okay. You must have a good reason for being here. Did you find anything more out?"

He tried to think what reason he might offer her. But the only thing he could think about was the stillness after Sara walked out of the house and that tug somewhere deep in his chest that had pulled him out his door, into the cold starry night, and through the forest to find her.

"I lost my job."

"At Jack's?" she asked.

"No, at school."

"Why?" she asked.

"I threw some kid's phone at the wall when he wouldn't stop texting."

She laughed. Her voice sounded like wind chimes.

"You know, there's going to be a position opening up at the museum. In their educational outreach program," she said.

"Really? That sounds interesting."

"I've shown my work there a few times; I know the director. I can put in a good word for you," she said and gently reached for his hand.

Her skin was so soft. He felt his entire body tremble.

"I have a girlfriend," he said. "A fiancée. And I told her tonight that I don't want to marry her anymore."

She took a deep breath, let go of his hand, and stood up, reaching into the cupboard over the sink.

"Do you love her?" she asked, her back to him.

"No," he said without hesitation. "I did. But I don't anymore."

"Milk?"

"No. Thanks," he said.

She turned and handed him the hot cup of coffee. The steam drifted toward his face, getting rid of the chill. He could still feel the place where Sara had hit him.

"People fall out of love," Shadi said matter-of-factly. "Everything is always changing. It's hard to stay in love."

He nodded.

"Is this some of your work?" he asked, gesturing to what appeared to be a work in progress on the loom, the colors of sunset unraveling into evening. There was a large basket full of wool on the floor.

She nodded.

"It's beautiful," he said, feeling stupid. Trite.

"My grandmother would hate it. I don't make the traditional designs like she does. I use the traditional techniques, the skills she taught me, but the pictures are mine. I tell her I am making my own traditions."

"Do you miss her since you left Chinle?" he asked.

"I'm learning not to grow too attached to things. To people. I am attached to my work. I am attached to my home, to Arizona. I am attached to my memories. These are the only things that really belong to me. Especially now."

He rubbed his beard with his hand; it prickled his palm. She poured more coffee into each of their cups. He tried to think of what belonged to him.

The warmth from the coffee spread through his body.

"I had a sister," he said. "Dusty." And as he said

her name, he conjured her: the memories of Dusty suddenly appearing, the threads of their lives, those separate moments wound together. He wanted desperately to offer Shadi one strand, one precious filament, that would say, *I know how it feels. I know.* But how could he pick just one? It's not the individual threads that make the pictures, but how they're woven together. That's the art. That's the dream. And so he closed his eyes and gave her the first one he saw, and when he pulled it from his memory, he felt how tightly it was bound to every other moment. Even this moment here in Shadi's trailer in the woods in November.

He could remember the bottoms of her feet, small and pink, dirty with early summer mud. The sprinkler ticking in the backyard, his mother in a beach chair, straw hat, sunglasses, metallic tumbler of lemonade. Dusty sitting cross-legged on the wet grass in her bathing suit, watching a caterpillar crawl up her arm. She was five and he was ten.

He could remember every single thing about that afternoon. The light filtering through the leaves of the oak tree, the hard bumps of last year's acorns under his feet. He could remember the smell of charcoal, and his father's pale legs as he stood at the barbeque, cooking hot dogs. He could remember the slivers of grass, newly mowed, sticking to his hands and feet as he ran through the sprinkler. The softness of his beach towel as his mother wrapped it around his shoulders. The freckles scattered across Dusty's cheeks.

He could remember the lazy tick, tick, tick of the sprinkler. The thrill of cold water against hot skin, a small cut on his lip and the sting of lemonade. Dusty, peering at the fuzzy brown caterpillar, luring him onto her finger and then running to Ben. *Here,* she said. *Take care of him while I play.* And he had sat shivering inside his towel at the edge of his mother's lawn chair. He'd held on to the caterpillar, kept him safe, until Dusty came back dripping wet and breathless with her own bliss.

He remembered the crisp skin of the hot dog resisting his bite, the sweet potato salad, the flimsy paper plates. He remembered the flicker of fireflies like the flick, flick, flick of streetlights and porch lights up and down their street. He remembered how Dusty cried when her father insisted they leave the caterpillar outside. The change from bathing suits into soft pajamas. The cold smell of Noxzema on burned shoulders. He remembered sleep.

And then the next summer she was gone. Just like that.

"You were just a boy," Shadi said.

He nodded.

She reached for his hand again and took it. She stroked his fingers; he could feel the cool silver rings on his hot skin.

"Remember I told you my grandpa had a truck like yours?" she said. "In the summertime, when Ricky and I were kids, we used to drive all the way to Winslow to the drive-in movies. My grandpa put an old mattress in the bed and we'd wear our pajamas and eat popcorn. Ricky was just a baby then. I went there last summer, and it's just an empty field now. The screen's still there, but it's torn up. The marquee is gone."

Ben kept holding her hand, stroking her fingers now.

"Things disappear," Shadi said.

And then their fingers laced together, interlocking.

He knew even as she clicked out the pale pink light in the kitchen and they were swallowed in darkness that he would remember every single thing about this night. The smell of hickory, the alignment of the stars outside the window. The crisp smell of her sheets and the musky scent of her hair. He would remember the impossible softness of her skin, and every bone he touched. He would remember the way his entire body trilled as her lips whispered on his neck, and he would remember the heat of her breath. Even if this all disappeared too. Even later when this was just a memory. Just one pristine and perfect filament woven so tightly into the pattern, you couldn't even see it anymore.

The next morning, Ben woke at dawn and slipped out of Shadi's bed, kissing her naked back from the base of her neck down to her tailbone. He pulled the sheets up and covered her, kissing her neck. It was torture tearing himself away from her, away from this quiet sanctuary.

"I have to teach," he said.

She rolled over and opened her eyes. She propped herself up on one elbow. Her hair covered one eye.

"Will you come back?" she asked sleepily.

"Yes."

"What will you tell her?"

"The truth," Ben said.

"Do you promise?"

He nodded and leaned over to kiss her again. He closed his eyes and felt the smooth skin of her cheek on his.

Outside, the world smelled of pine, of winter. Since last night, the sky had clouded over, and he knew it would probably snow again soon. Clouds shivered across the tops of the Peaks. He walked along the edge of the road, hands shoved into his pockets, his stride quick and long. For the first time in a long time, he was happy. Thrilled to simply breathe the cool air in and out, to feel the earth beneath his feet.

Sara was not at the house, had not been back to the house as far as he could tell. There were no messages on the machine. None on his cell phone, which he'd left on the coffee table, either. He quickly showered and changed and grabbed his things, got in the truck and drove to school.

Joe Bello was not in class, for which he was grateful. Rob must have managed to get him transferred out, or, maybe, he'd just opted out today. Ben handed out the tests and pretended to be absorbed in a book as his students hunched over their work. His heart was racing, his head thumping. He could barely keep from smiling as he thought about Shadi, as he recollected every inch of the night before. Every tremble, every shudder. He wanted to leap out of his skin, leave the shell of him there and race back to her, to disappear into her trailer, into her bed, into her body forever.

The wall clock ticked off each excruciating second. And he still had another class before he could go back to her. Finally, the students came up one by one and gave him their tests and left. At last, there was no one in the room but him. He stuffed the papers into his bag and made his way to his next class.

Again, he passed out the tests and pretended to read, and time slowed down, the minutes arthritic. By the time it was over, and he could leave, he was exhausted, as though he'd been trying to swim upstream for hours.

He couldn't get the key into the ignition of the truck fast enough. He had to concentrate not to press his foot to the floor as he drove through town. He cursed at the train that held him up at the railroad tracks. Car after car after car, the rumble and whistle of the longest train in history a moving wall between him and his future. That's how he saw her, as the beginning. He felt like he'd just woken up from a terrible dream.

When the train had finally passed, the wail fading into the distance, his heart was pounding. As much as he wanted to go straight to Shadi's, he knew he should stop by his house and let Maude out. She'd been alone all night and cooped up all morning. He figured maybe he could take her with him. There was nothing else in that house that he cared about or really needed. If he got Maude, he could just leave. He could be gone.

Sara would be at work. In the entire time he'd known her, she'd never missed a day. She'd had a perfect attendance record in school too. In thirteen years of school, she hadn't missed a single class. She'd never been sick. Never woke up with a sore throat or the flu. And so when he pulled up to the house and saw her Camry parked in the driveway, he hit his palms against the steering wheel. "Goddamnit."

He considered not stopping, just driving. Just

forgetting about Sara, even about Maude. But then something snagged in his chest like a rusty fishing lure. It bit and then held on. Christ, Sara hadn't done anything but love him. Didn't he at least owe her an apology? Six years; he couldn't just run away. He felt like an asshole. *Was* a stupid asshole. Just like she'd said.

And so he pulled into the driveway, turned off the ignition, and tried to figure out what to say to her to make this less painful. He figured she was home for lunch, probably making a sandwich, a salad, heating up a bowl of soup in the microwave. But when he opened the door and went inside, she wasn't there. Not in the living room, not in the kitchen.

"Sara?" he said, walking down the hallway to check in the bedroom.

Maude lumbered toward him. "Hey, girl," he said, rubbing her head. She whimpered and rubbed against him.

The bedroom was empty. The bathroom door was shut.

"Sara?" he said, knocking gently on the door.

Maude flopped down at his feet. He didn't hear the shower running. He leaned into the door, listening.

"Sara, are you in there?" he said and gently turned the doorknob. The door was unlocked. "Hey, you okay?"

He pushed the door open slowly, leaning into

the room. Sara was sitting cross-legged on the furry blue bath mat on the floor. She looked up at him, and her cheeks were streaked with tears, mascara in dark smudges under her eyes. She smiled weakly, and held up the stick.

"I'm pregnant," she said.

Everything went white hot.

Her smile widened and her eyes lit up. "We're going to have a baby."

BLUE WORLD

B en's beard was starting to fill in. It had been two weeks since he'd tossed his razor into the wastebasket, and it was starting to look like a real beard instead of just a patchy mess on his face. He liked the way a beard made him feel. It was the same way his truck made him feel. Unbound. Untamed even.

"Ow," Sara had said this morning when he'd kissed her. "You need to shave."

"I've stopped," he said.

"Stopped what?" she asked, pulling away and looking at him, at his sad beard.

"Shaving. I've stopped shaving."

"Oh," she said, and then, "How long do you plan to grow this beard?"

He hadn't thought much beyond tossing the razor and its associated irritants (the time it took, the money spent on shaving cream and aftershave, the sore bumps that made his neck feel like a column of fire).

"I guess I'll grow it until it stops," he said, suddenly hell-bent on a full, thick beard—like Grizzly Adams, like Santa Claus. In his mind, he aged forty years, grew a belly, sported a pair of suspenders and a bow tie. Years passed. His life neared an end.

"Well, I'm not going to kiss you like that," she said. "It hurts."

There she went again, ruining everything, holding him and his dreams hostage. And so he did what he always had to do with Sara: change the subject. "I've got to bring the truck into the shop for an oil change. Can you give me a ride to school?"

"Listen, Ben. I've been thinking we're going to probably have to sell the truck."

"What?" he asked.

"Daddy could get us a deal on a minivan, and you could have the Camry. You can't put a car seat in the truck; it's not safe."

The baby. God, when he thought about himself in his new beard and his truck, he never thought of the baby, the one that was, as they spoke, no bigger than a peapod in Sara's belly.

"I hate that you do this," Sara said.

"Do what?"

"Pretend that this isn't happening." She was sitting on the couch now, pulling off her winter boots, and she looked more sad and tired than pissed off.

"I'm not . . ." he started, but she beat him to the punch like she always did.

"Because it is," she said, her eyes angry and wet. "Happening."

He hadn't said the word, *abortion,* but she must have known what he was thinking, because after he'd found her in the bathroom that morning two weeks ago, he'd left her there, gone to the living room, and said to no one in particular but loud enough for her to hear, "We shouldn't do this."

She'd come out of the bathroom, raging. "Where were you last night? Where the fuck did you go?"

She'd thrown herself at him, pounding her fists into his chest.

He could still smell the musky scent of Shadi on his hands.

"How did this happen?" he asked her.

She looked at him as if he were an idiot. "This happened because you slept with me. Because you *made love* to me. This happened because you *fucked* me, Ben," she screamed.

"You're on the pill," he said. "You've been on the pill for years."

"We're *engaged,*" she said and backed away from him as though she were afraid of him. She laughed, the kind of laugh that is verging on hysteria. "We're in *love.*"

"We can't do this," he said.

"That is not an option," she had said, her hands on her hips.

"What?"

"I am not killing this baby."

"Sara," Ben had started, studying her face, which was bloated and red from crying.

"Where were you last night?" she cried, no longer angry, just broken.

And he thought about telling her the truth. He thought that if he told her the truth, she might actually let him go. Maybe if he told her about Shadi, then she might just set him free. He imagined himself getting in his truck and driving up the road to Shadi's. He imagined hitching that Airstream to his truck and driving away with her. He could almost feel the air rushing through the open window. Hear the radio. Feel Shadi's hand as she touched his leg.

And then he thought about cells dividing, about what was taking shape inside of Sara. About the fact that he had set into motion a *life*, and something fell in his chest. Something primitive and scary. He was going to be a father. This was his child. And so he did what he always did. He lied.

"I was at Hippo's."

Sara looked at him, waiting, giving him a chance to backtrack, to tell the truth. She waited, expectant.

He thought again of cells dividing; he felt himself dividing. He watched one self walk out the door, turn the key, roll the windows down to the frigid air, and drive. He watched this self disappear into the woods, into the dark canyons of Shadi's hair and skin. And he watched the other self stay. He felt the baby in his arms, the weight and heft of it. He heard the cries.

"With Hippo?" Sara asked.

And he saw himself, fourteen years old, standing alone at the front door, knowing his father had left. Dusty was gone. His mother had retreated into her own world. And now his father was gone too, our of their lives, out of his life. *Stay.* How would his life have been different if his father had just stayed?

And so he said what he needed to say.

Yes. I was at Hippo's.

But now, two weeks later, he thought about that other self, the one driving away, the bearded man in the truck, wondered where he had gone. Wondered if he'd made a terrible mistake. Thanksgiving was tomorrow. Sara's parents were coming for dinner. They would tell them about the baby then. They had set a date for the wedding after the baby came. They had reserved Hart Prairie Lodge up on the mountain for the reception.

Sara handed him the grocery list. "And get some razors. It looks ridiculous."

Ben would forget Shadi. He would unremember her. He would lose his memory, drop it like a coin into the snow. He would become an amnesiac. He would work backward, unraveling the moments woven together to make that other picture.

Because there could be only one end.

The day after Sara told him she was pregnant, he went to the trailer when he knew Shadi wouldn't be there. He'd written his apologies on a fragile piece of paper. *I'm sorry,* the note said in careful cursive. *I have to stay. I have no choice. There's going to be a baby.* He folded the paper in half and slipped it under the metal door.

Then he drove away from her house, back through the forest, imagining the days in reverse: warm coffee and the scent of her hair, a basket of unripe pears, Ricky's lonely apartment. Spider Rock, her grandmother's velvet dress. A turquoise sky. The truck with Ricky's casket, barreling down a dusty road toward a waiting grave. *The first lie.* The smell of the hospital, the beeping and ticking, and Shadi's paint-splattered overalls. The snow plow backing up, the snowbank restored. Ricky, still nameless. Bloodied and dying in the snow. Asleep, dreaming next to Sara, as snow falls upward from the ground into that starless sky. November becoming October. Halloween. A keg of beer, a Nixon costume, a silly argument. A girl with a guitar.

He could undo this. He could untangle these threads, the ones the color of sunset unraveling into evening. And then he would begin again.

Now he walked through the aisles at Bashas', checking off everything on Sara's list, pretending that he was just a man out shopping for dinner with his future in-laws. That all of this was good and right.

Sweet potatoes, russet potatoes, cranberries, green beans. Sour cream, whipped cream, heavy cream. Pumpkin pie filling. Evaporated milk. Stuffing and tangerines. At the giant freezer, he picked up the largest turkey he could find. Twenty-two pounds, as heavy as a small child in his arms.

He waited in line behind a Navajo woman with her three children. One of them stared at him, clinging to his mother's legs, his nose crusty with a cold. His cheeks pink and chafed. Ben smiled, the child scowled, and Ben felt scolded.

In the parking lot, he loaded the bags into the bed of his truck. Looking toward the Peaks, he could see clouds thickening, descending. He could smell snow in the air, feel the promise of it when he took a deep breath.

As he got in the cab of the truck, he realized he'd forgotten to get wine. The Shiraz Sara's mother loved. He ran back into the store, went straight to the beer and wine section, and searched for the bottle with the kangaroo label. When he found it, he grabbed two bottles, went through the express lane, and trotted back to his truck.

He would go back to the house and start to get ready for her parents. He'd promised to clean the bathroom, the kitchen, scrub the floors. The smell of bleach made Sara sick. The smell of everything made her sick. He would do their laundry. He would make everything clean.

As the first flakes of snow tapped at his windshield, he turned the key, revved the engine, and started to back out. He looked in the rearview mirror to make sure there was no one walking behind him and his throat began to ache. Because there, parked in the row behind him, was a bright blue Mustang.

He looked at his watch. Sara would be home from work in twenty minutes. He imagined her finishing up with the last patient of the day, trying to keep her nausea at bay as she administered a measles shot or took a throat culture.

Ben waited for the guy to come out of the store. He couldn't just drive away. Not when he was this close. He thought about getting out of the car and approaching him. Making up some story about needing a jump. About his battery being dead. He thought about asking him if he knew a kid named Ricky.

He sat in the truck with the engine running for five minutes, then ten, glancing into his rearview mirror every few seconds to make sure the Mustang hadn't gone anywhere.

He scratched the tag number onto the grocery list with a stub of a pencil he found in the crack of his seat. There had to be a way to track down the owner of the car if he had the plate number. He was getting ready to pull out when he glanced into the mirror one more time and saw the trunk of the Mustang was lifted up. He watched in the rearview mirror. He was sweating, despite the chill. There was an empty shopping cart next to the car. When the trunk lid closed, he gripped the steering wheel tightly and craned his neck to see.

It was a girl, a brown-haired girl in a light blue parka and pink Ugg boots. She got into the Mustang and closed the door. And then the Mustang was pulling out of the lot and zooming down the steep drive onto Humphreys.

Sara would be home in ten minutes, so he called her from his cell phone and left a message on their answering machine. "Hey, it's me. The turkeys at Bashas' were too small. I'm going over to Fry's to find a bigger one."

And then he was behind the Mustang, following the girl close behind, the frozen turkey rolling out of its bag and across the bed of the truck as he turned the corner.

The Mustang pulled into the parking lot of the video store. Ben followed. While the girl parked, Ben kept driving slowly, circling, keeping the Mustang in sight. When the girl got out, he pulled into a spot and let the truck idle for a minute. When she disappeared through the electronic doors, he turned the truck off and followed her.

He pretended to peruse the glossy rows of movies. New releases had just been stocked, and he pretended to be absorbed in the description on the case of first one movie and then the next. He watched the girl out of the corner of his eye. She looked about the same age as his students, somewhere between eighteen and twenty-two. She was pretty, with rosy cheeks and wide-set blue eyes.

She finally settled on a romantic comedy, some schmaltzy holiday flick, and Ben grabbed a movie too, following not far behind her.

"It's under my boyfriend's name. Is that okay?" she asked the checker.

"Phone number?"

As she rattled off the number, Ben tried to burn the numbers into his mind.

The checker clicked the keys of the computer. "Mark Fitch?" the checker asked without looking at the girl.

"Yeah," the girl said.

"On South Beaver Street?"

"Yep." She smiled.

The checker scanned the DVD and placed it on the other side of the security gate. The girl pulled a crumpled five-dollar bill out of her back pocket and handed it to him. And then she was headed out the door.

Ben set the DVD case down and pulled out his keys with his rental card attached. He tapped his foot, repeating the phone number in his head like a song.

"Your credit card is expired on this account. Do you have your new card?"

Ben sighed, and pulled out his wallet. *928-555-0990.*

By the time they were finally done and he was outside again, the Mustang was gone. And snow was starting to fall. He pulled out the same piece of paper where he'd scrawled the license plate number and wrote down *Mark Fitch. South Beaver Street. 928-555-0990.*

He tried to think what houses were on South Beaver Street, what apartment complexes. If it was close to campus, he was probably some dumbass college kid. Though he might be local if he was staying in town for Thanksgiving. Most of the kids cleared out for the break, heading home to their parents' for the holiday.

But he had a name and a phone number and part

of an address. Now he would just need to be smart about this. He'd ask around first, see if anyone knew him. If the guy lived on South Beaver, he might hang out at the Brewery or at NiMarco's, the pizza place. If he lived downtown, chances are people would know him. The baristas at Macy's Coffeehouse, the waitresses at La Bellavia. If Ben knew one thing about people, it's that they tend to stick to their routines.

Ben knew that Sara was probably starting to freak out. He looked at his phone and saw that she had texted him three times. *Where r u @? Don't forget the Shiraz. U there?*

He pulled into their driveway and felt his stomach knot up again. The pain was sharp. He clutched his side. *Jesus,* he thought.

He unloaded the grocery bags from the truck, leaving them on the porch. The snow was coming down now in huge fluffy flakes. If this kept up, he'd probably be spending most of Thanksgiving morning shoveling the driveway so Sara's parents could have a place to park. Her father hadn't wanted them to buy this house because it didn't have a garage.

He opened the door, and Maude came running up to him.

"Hey, Maude," he said. "Hey, girl! Sara?" he asked.

She must have decided to take a nap. She was so exhausted after work most days, she went straight to bed for a couple of hours before forcing down some dinner. Lately he'd been eating alone in front of the TV while she slept. She'd get up just as he was starting to get tired. After a handful of saltines and a glass of milk, she'd curl up next to him on the couch, and he'd wait until she was starting to fall asleep again before gently nudging her up off the couch and back into bed.

He poked his head into the bedroom, and she was, indeed, burrowed under the covers. Her face was mostly covered, her hair fanned out across the sheets like corn silk.

He quietly closed the door and went to the kitchen, unloading the groceries into the fridge and cupboards, making a spot on the bottom shelf of the fridge for the turkey. When everything was put away and all of the dirty dishes were loaded into the dishwasher, he pulled the scrap of paper from his back pocket. He figured it would be safer to use his cell phone than his home phone. The home phone would probably show up on caller ID.

He opened the back door to let Maude out and followed behind her. He stood underneath the awning and tapped out the numbers.

"Hello?" a man's voice said.

"Hi, is this Mark Fitch?" Ben asked, realizing he probably should have come up with a plan first. Thinking maybe he should just hang up.

"Yeah, this is he."

"Hi, I'm, uh, Detective Bailey from the Flagstaff Police Department." Shit, what was he doing?

The man was silent on the other end of the line. *Shit, shit, shit.*

"Do you drive a blue Ford Mustang?" Ben asked.

"Yeah?"

Ben's mind raced. "Well, we got a call in with your tag numbers. Someone apparently saw you back into a red Chevy pickup in the Bashas' parking lot this afternoon and then take off. Were you driving your vehicle this afternoon, sir?" Damn, why did he describe his own truck?

It sounded like the guy was covering the mouthpiece of the phone. He could hear his muffled voice saying "Jessie!" or "Betsy!"

"Who are you talking to?" Sara said. She was standing in the doorway, rubbing her eyes.

Ben clicked his cell phone shut. His head was pounding, his ears were hot. "Work," he said.

"You don't have to go in *tonight,* do you?" she whined.

"No. Ned's covering for me."

"Good, because my parents will be here at noon tomorrow, and the house is just awful. I tried to pick up, but I got really sick. I threw up twice already. I don't know how I'm going to cook dinner tomorrow."

"It's okay," Ben said, ushering her back into the house. "I can do it."

Sara smiled and leaned into him. Then she took his hand and pressed it into her stomach. When she did, his own stomach twisted and he jerked with the pain of it.

Sara looked at him, her eyes narrowing.

"We'll tell them right after dinner," she said. "Mom is going to cry."

Long ago, when Ben's life was still whole, Thanksgiving was his favorite holiday. Every year, his mother started cooking the night before Thanksgiving. His father would take him and Dusty to the movies while she stayed at home rolling out piecrusts and prepping all of the casseroles and salads. By the time they got home, his mother would have flour-covered hands and flushed cheeks, and the entire house would smell like ginger and cinnamon and nutmeg.

The next morning, these smells would linger, but the stronger smell of sage and thyme and the cooking turkey would prevail. His aunt Catherine and uncle Woody from South Carolina would arrive by ten o'clock with their cousins, Jo-Jo and Peanut, spilling out of the back of their station wagon. Jo-Jo was Ben's age, and Peanut was the baby. While the grown-ups milled around in the kitchen, the kids would watch the Macy's Thanksgiving Day Parade, eating Krispy Kreme Doughnuts on the living room floor.

Later, when the football games came on, Jo-Jo and Ben would relinquish the living room to Ben's dad and Uncle Woody and disappear into the basement to play with Ben's collection of

Matchbox cars or the giant laundry basket full of LEGOs. And Dusty and Peanut would play with pots and pans in the kitchen while Ben's mom and Aunt Cathy gossiped and peeled potatoes and basted the turkey. Uncle Woody and Ben's dad would drink beer and snack on the sweet sugarcoated peanuts that came in a blue can. Ben would grab handfuls of them, and that sweet taste would linger on his fingers for hours.

If it was warm enough outside, he and Jo-Jo would play in the tree house his dad had built in the backyard, leaping off the wooden deck into the musty piles of leaves below. They were pirates. Soldiers. Indian warriors.

After Dusty died, Aunt Catherine and Uncle Woody kept coming for a year or two, but it never felt right. His mother would cry in the kitchen, and Jo-Jo and Ben forgot how to play. The floorboards of the tree house rotted out, and his mother said it was too dangerous. And then his aunt and uncle moved to Colorado and it was too far to travel.

In college, Ben spent Thanksgivings with his mom, but she didn't cook anymore. They usually met in the city at U-topia, eating crab cakes and seafood bisque. Sara had never cooked Thanksgiving dinner. Usually they went down to Phoenix to be with her family or stayed home and celebrated with friends.

So when Ben woke up on Thursday morning,

the smells confused him. Suddenly, he was six years old again, padding sleepy-eyed to the kitchen, woken by the pungent smell of stuffing and pumpkin pie.

"Hey," Ben said.

Sara was already dressed, a blue-and-white-checked apron tied tightly around her soft waist. There was a simmering pot on the stove with melted butter and sage and thyme. Her mother's cookbook, the one she'd given Sara last Christmas, was open on the counter.

"How are you feeling?" he asked.

"Actually good," she said. "I had some ginger ale and crackers, and I'm ready to go. Will you help me get the turkey out?" she asked, kissing Ben's cheek.

"Sure," he said.

"And thank you," she said. "The house looks great."

Ben had stayed up until midnight while Sara slept, picking up the clutter, scrubbing the counters and floors and toilet. The only thing he hadn't done was vacuum, because he didn't want to wake her. The trash was tied into neat bundles on the back deck. The muddy paw prints on the front window were just a memory.

Ben opened the fridge and pulled out the giant turkey, setting it into the sink.

"Wow!" Sara said. "It's huge!! We'll have leftovers for a month."

She peered at the open cookbook, tracing the poultry chart with her finger. "Okay, so this is a twenty pounder; it looks like we'll need about six or seven hours. That means if I can get it in the oven by ten, we'll eat around five. Perfect." She smiled at him, and he suddenly felt he'd done something right.

Sara reached into the sink and started to tear off the plastic wrapper, when she stopped.

"It's frozen," she said.

"Yeah?" Ben said.

Sara looked at him, her smile fading. "Ben, I said to get a *fresh* turkey."

"What's the difference?" he asked, knowing from her face that there must be a *big* difference.

"It's *frozen,* Ben. It won't thaw in time. It would take days for this thing to defrost." Sara started pacing the kitchen, wringing her hands. The butter on the stove top was starting to burn. "Ben, what are we going to do?"

"Can you put it in the microwave?"

"Does this thing look like it will fit in our microwave?" she said, gesturing to the microwave that had seen nothing but popcorn and pot pies.

"It's okay," he said. "I'll just go to the store and get a fresh turkey. No big deal."

"Have you looked outside, Ben?" Sara's voice was getting shrill.

Ben went to the living room. The shades were

still drawn. He pulled them back. It was a total whiteout. He couldn't even see his truck in the driveway.

"By the time you get the driveway shoveled out, it'll be too late."

"Well, maybe they won't be able to make it," Ben said, and was ashamed at how his heart thrilled at the prospect.

"They'll make it," she hissed. "They called from Camp Verde before you got up. They're on their way."

And Ben knew that nothing would stop this day from happening. Not a turkey that wouldn't defrost. Not a blizzard. Not his own sheer will.

Ben liked Sara's parents. Frank, her father, was one of those boisterous types, the exact opposite of his own father, who was always so serious. Quiet. Reserved. Frank was a friendly kind of guy, a man's man with a firm handshake. A man who always looked you in the eye, who always told you the truth. He was honest to a fault. He didn't censor himself, no matter the company, which, though it made Sara cringe and his wife blush, Ben found refreshing. And Jeanine. Jeanine was like Sara. Or like Sara used to be: easy, breezy, unconcerned. She was sixty but looked fifty, with butter-colored hair and smooth skin. She smelled like summertime all the time and listened when you talked to her. She had been a nurse when she met Frank, but she quit when Sara's brother was born, to stay home with the kids. Then Frank's business took off, and she never went back.

"Dr. Bailey," Frank said as he opened the door. His face was red, his eyes a bit bloodshot. He owned five car dealerships but no longer worked the floor. He spent most of his time golfing. He had a permanent sunburn and refused to wear sunglasses. He thought they made people seem shifty. "Helluva storm," he said. "If this keeps up, we might need to spend the night."

Jeanine was brushing the new snow off her coat, which Sara took from her. "Hi, Mommy," she said, squeezing her. Ben felt a pang as he watched Sara's eyes fill with tears.

"Well, we've run into a bit of a problem with the turkey," Ben offered. Might as well get this out of the way as soon as possible. "I screwed up and brought home a frozen one. And it's still frozen."

Sara winced.

"Oh no!" Jeanine laughed.

"Well, hell's bells!" Frank said. "Looks like you and I have got to go hunting!" he said, smacking Ben on the back.

Ben's eyes widened.

"What, you never been turkey hunting?"

Ben looked at Sara for help.

Jeanine hit Frank in the arm. "You're scaring him, Frank."

"I'm just joshing you," he said. "We'll go hunt us down a nice rotisserie chicken at the Safeway. Nobody'll be able to tell the difference."

Ben felt his shoulders relax. For a minute he'd actually tried to prepare himself to go out in the wilderness with Frank and the shotguns he kept strapped to the back of his truck. Alone. With Frank. And his guns.

"I've got four-wheel drive, chains if we need 'em," Frank said.

Ben grabbed his coat and followed him out the door.

· · ·

They could have gone to the Bashas' just down the street, but Frank had some issue with Bashas', the origin of which was probably forgotten, and he insisted they drive all the way into town to the Safeway. Snow was coming down now so hard and so fast it was almost disorienting. It was hard to differentiate the earth from the sky. The snow plows hadn't even been by to clear the parking lot, which was empty, save for a couple of cars that must have belonged to the employees. They slammed their doors shut and trudged through the snow to the store, which glowed like a neon oasis in a desert of white.

Inside, holiday music was playing, Christmas carols already, and there were signs of Christmas everywhere. Poinsettias and Christmas lights and mechanical Santas. Frank led the way to the deli and ordered up the biggest chicken they had.

"Not quite a turkey, but it's a bird," he said, taking the plastic container from the girl behind the counter. "Fowl's fowl."

Ben nodded.

In the checkout line, Ben got out his wallet to pay.

Frank shook his head and pulled his own battered wallet out of his pocket. "I'm sure Sara's already made you pay for this one enough," he said, chuckling.

Ben didn't know whether to laugh or not, so he just smiled and nodded his head.

"Women," Frank said. "Can't live with them, can't bury them in the backyard without the neighbors seeing."

Ben grimaced but smiled.

In the truck, Frank turned the ignition and sent the wipers flying through the inch of fresh snow that had fallen while they were in the store. He turned to Ben as they pulled into the driveway. Sara was standing in the doorway with her hands on her hips.

Frank leaned over and whispered, "I know you fucked up the turkey, but I've got some Wild Turkey in the glove box. I've got a feeling it's gonna be a long day."

Dinner was excruciating.

Sara was trying too hard, stumbling and bumbling, apologetically plopping huge spoonfuls of lumpy sweet potatoes onto everyone's plates, apologizing for her cooking, apologizing for their lack of matching dishes. And he could tell she was nauseous, that all of the smells that he loved were putting her pretty close to the edge. For the first time in a while, Ben actually felt sorry for her.

Jeanine piped up around midway through the meal, as if on some terrible cue, "Oh, honey, I completely forgot to tell you that Ginger is getting married this summer. Some guy she met in San Diego. I think he's in the navy."

Sara stared at the small piles of green beans and mashed potatoes and the rotisserie chicken on her plate.

"Sare-Bear," Frank said, nudging Ben, "I'm telling you, if you need me to lasso this one here, hog-tie him, and get him to the chapel, I know a rodeo guy or two."

Thanks, Frank.

Sara pushed her food around her plate some more. She was waiting for Ben. He knew this was *his* cue, and he had missed it. The stage was empty, and he was still standing in the wings. The audience was growing uncomfortable.

Sara looked up from her food, and Ben could see sweat beading up on her forehead. She took a deep breath and her eyes widened with panic. And then she was up and running to the bathroom, covering her mouth with her hand, gagging.

Jeanine excused herself and followed close behind. "Honey? You okay?" She disappeared into the bathroom with Sara, the door closing behind her.

Frank and Ben looked at each other.

"Guess the buns are in the oven?" Frank asked.

Ben sighed.

Frank winked and held up the empty bun basket. When he got up and went into the kitchen, Ben put his head in his hands.

After a couple of minutes, Frank came back

into the dining room and tossed a roll onto Ben's plate. He plopped down into his chair and reached for the butter. "Well, if that doesn't get you to the church on time, I don't know what will."

Later, with the cat now out of the bag and roaming quietly around the house, Sara napped in the bedroom and Jeanine cleaned the kitchen. Ben found the Arizona State game on TV, and Frank slapped Ben on the back, sitting down on the couch, gesturing for him to join him there.

"If you're worried about us being pissed off, don't be. I knocked up Jeanine before we got married too. And that was almost thirty years ago. Important thing is that baby. The wedding will happen in its own good time."

Ben cringed at how trusting Frank was. How little he knew. That Ben's very presence here was some twisted sort of miracle.

"Too much fuss made over one day if you ask me," Frank said. "Jeanine and I got married by the justice of the peace. Drove to LA for our honeymoon. And look at us."

Ben felt awful as Frank smiled and patted his back again. "You'll make a good dad, Ben. A really good dad."

B en's father. Ben hardly ever thought about his father anymore. He was living in DC still; he had gotten remarried when Ben was in college. He was teaching at George Washington still, and his new wife worked in the Human Resources Department. She had a shrill voice and candy-colored fingernails. She had three children, all younger than Ben, one of whom lived with them. During college, Ben and his father would meet for lunch once a month somewhere on the Foggy Bottom campus (his father never came to Georgetown), awkwardly catching up over overpriced risotto or Caesar salads. He paid Ben's tuition bills but never called him. Years later, when Ben's mother got sick, he'd ask about her but never once got in the car and went to Maryland to see her. Not even when she was in the hospital. And after she died, Ben had grown so angry with his father, for his absence while his mother, a woman Ben's father had spent fifteen years with, slowly fell apart, he could barely stand it. He couldn't reconcile the father he'd had, that he and Dusty had had, with this new man, this man who didn't cry at her funeral and only shook Ben's hand before driving away from the cemetery.

Ben preferred to hold on to the memory of the

father from his childhood. The father who was quiet but *present*. A fixture. He remembered sitting side by side in the living room at night, each absorbed in a book. He remembered his father silently tossing a baseball with him for hours in the street outside, even after the sun fell behind the trees, and streetlights clicked on. He remembered Sunday mornings when he and Dusty used to lie on the floor, poring over the funny papers while his father read the *Post*. He was there. On weekends, on cross-country road trips during the long summers when he wasn't teaching, across from him in the boat on Lake Accotink as they cast their lines into the water. There was something comforting in the predictability of him, in his hushed but certain presence.

His mother was the one who provided the sound track. The laughter, the music. The smell of coffee and strawberry pancakes, the gentle kisses on cuts and scrapes. She sang along with the radio in the car and listened to all of his and Dusty's silly knock-knock jokes. She was the one who sat with them at the kitchen table, helping Ben with his homework, coloring with Dusty in her coloring books. She was the one waiting to pick them up from school every day. She was the one who chose the dress that Dusty would wear when she was buried. The one who held Ben all night when he awoke dreaming of the accident, dreaming of Dusty still alive. And his father checked out.

He just slipped away. And he was so quiet about it, you might not have noticed at first. Maybe he'd been planning this the whole time he'd been with them, this disappearing act. Perhaps he'd been practicing his magic at night while they were sleeping. Because one Sunday morning, Ben woke up and he was just gone, and he might not have noticed if he hadn't seen the newspaper still lying on the lawn.

After he was gone, when Ben thought of his father, he liked to think about the slow grin when he reeled in a fish, the quiet chuckle at something he read in the paper, the sound of the ball hitting his leather mitt.

Ben couldn't understand then how you just walk away from a life, especially a life you'd made.

On Tuesday, after Ben's second class, he got in his truck and drove up to Sara's work to pick her up. Her first OB/GYN visit was scheduled for two o'clock.

"Hey, *Daddy*," Melanie said, winking and squeezing his arm when he walked into Dr. Newman's office. She hugged Ben and said, "Congratulations. I am so excited for you guys."

"Thanks," Ben said.

"Sara's in with a patient, but she should be out in just a sec. Go ahead and make yourself comfortable."

Ben sat down in one of the plastic chairs, next to a woman who was holding a toddler on her lap. The boy was half asleep, his hair matted. He convulsed with a rattly cough, and the mother pulled him in close, rocking him. "Shh, shhh."

There were two children playing with some blocks on the floor. A girl and a boy. The boy was banging the blocks against each other and the girl was constructing a multicolored tower. The boy smashed his block into the tower, sending it toppling over. The girl looked at him in disbelief, her bottom lip began to quiver, and then she started to cry. Ben looked around to see who the children belonged to, but no one seemed willing to claim either one of them.

There was a woman at the reception desk, cradling a baby on her hip, digging through her wallet for an insurance card. When the little girl on the floor began to squeal, the woman swung around and said, "Madison! Do I need to take you out to the car?"

The little girl sobbed and cried louder. The little boy kept banging the blocks. Ben's head started to pound.

When the child wouldn't stop crying, the woman left the reception desk and came over, scooping the girl up and plopping her into the empty seat next to Ben. "Here, read this," she said, handing her a *Curious George* book that was missing its cover. The little girl sucked in her next breath and opened the pages. The woman returned to the desk, apologizing to the receptionist, and the boy kept banging.

Ben leaned over and said, "That was a really cool tower."

The little girl looked up at him, wiping her runny nose with the back of her hand.

"Read this to me?" she asked, shoving the book into his hand.

"Sure," he said and opened to the first page. "Once there was a man in a yellow hat. . . ."

She leaned her head against his arm, and he stiffened. He looked up to make sure the mother knew he was reading to her, but she was still talking to the receptionist.

When he got to the last page, he closed the book and she said, "Read it again?"

"Hey," Sara said.

Ben looked up at Sara, who was standing with her purse slung over her shoulder. Her face looked a little green.

"I'm sorry," he said to the little girl. "I have to go. Maybe your mom can read it to you again." But the mother was across the room, feeding the baby now and trying to read a magazine at the same time.

"You ready?" Ben asked Sara.

"Uh-huh."

They sat in the OB's office for nearly an hour before the nurse came out and unapologetically told them it was their turn. She led them down a long hallway to a small room. She weighed Sara, took her blood pressure and temperature, told her to change into a paper gown. Then she left.

Sara started to pull off her clothes, and something about this made Ben feel embarrassed. He'd seen Sara undress a zillion times, but in this bright light, in this cold room, she seemed so vulnerable. Exposed. She quickly hurried out of her scrubs, slipping into the crinkly gown. Then she slipped off her panties and folded them into a tiny triangle. She handed Ben her pile of clothes. "Can you set those over there?" she asked, gesturing to the chair where her purse was.

She sat on the edge of the table, wringing her hands.

"Are you nervous?" he asked.

"A little," she said.

They'd gone onto babycenter.com and calculated how far along she was. If they were right, she was about seven weeks now. The due date calculator said the baby would arrive around the first week of July.

"I feel really sick," Sara said. "Can you get the crackers from my purse? There's a packet of saltines in there."

Ben riffled through Sara's enormous bag, finally locating the column of crackers. He handed her the whole thing, and she took out one cracker, nibbling the corner of it and handing the package back to him. She closed her eyes and swallowed.

"Do you want me to get you some water?' Ben asked.

She shook her head. "No, I'm okay."

It was another twenty minutes before the doctor came in, also without explanation or apology. He was a large man with pale skin and pale thinning hair and a pale smatter of freckles.

"Well," he said. "You're going to have a baby."

"That's why we're here," Ben snapped, and Sara shot him a look.

He looked at the clipboard with the information Sara had filled out in the waiting room and said,

"Okeydokey. It looks here like you're about seven weeks along. I think we'll do an internal ultrasound today, just to make sure everything's going smoothly and to confirm a due date. And then we'll get some blood work ordered and you'll be all set."

Sara nodded. He called the nurse back in and they all squeezed into the room.

"So, you work for Hugh?" he asked as Sara lay down on the table, putting her feet in the stirrups.

Sara smiled. "Uh-huh."

"Here, scooch your bottom down to the end of the table here."

Sara obeyed.

"Hugh and I were in med school together at U of A," he said. "I always tell him, if not for me he'd go out of business." He chuckled.

Sara raised her eyebrow.

"All of his patients are mine first," he said.

Sara smiled and looked at Ben.

"Okay, let's see what we've got here," he said.

The monitor by the table showed a grainy black-and-white image. The doctor tried to navigate, to explain, but it looked like it could just as easily have been tracking airplanes or submarines as it did the baby inside Sara.

The doctor wiggled the probe around, and Sara winced. Sara reached for Ben's hand.

"Sorry," he said. "I just wanted to be able to show you this," he said, gesturing to the monitor with his other hand. "See that little fluttering thing there?"

Ben leaned over Sara, peering closely at the blob on the screen.

"That's the baby's heart."

Sara and he stared at the screen, at the tiny flutter, and Sara squeezed Ben's hand. When he looked at her, he could see her cheeks were wet with tears.

Ben didn't tell anyone about the baby. Not Hippo, not Ned. He wasn't ready yet. He knew that as soon as he said the words, it would become real. At home it was all they talked about. Melanie and Sara were always at the kitchen table, poring over pregnancy magazines and baby name books. Sara's mother called at least once a day now, offering advice and comfort. The TV was always tuned into episodes of TLC's *A Baby Story*, and the giant bottle of prenatal pills on the dining room table was like a monument to gestation.

But at the bar, there was no baby. There was nothing but dirty glasses and peanut shells and a jukebox Johnny Cash all filtered through the dim amber light of the bar. Time stood still: afternoon passing into evening acquiescing to the pitch-black darkness of two A.M., each evening the same as the last.

He tried not to think about Shadi.

At home, this was easy. The world at home was pastel pink and baby blue; it was pages torn from catalogues with strollers and car seats and cribs. It was Sara, slowly beginning to crawl out of the first trimester nausea and exhaustion into the warm rosy glow of pregnancy. Her appetite was restored, her whole body starting to soften and yield.

He hadn't tried to contact the owner of the Mustang again; that had been stupid. He hadn't been thinking. He needed to just put it out of his mind. That was also easy at home. But here, at the bar, every Navajo face reminded him of Ricky. Every young rez kid shooting pool. Every asshole making racial slurs.

After Thanksgiving, it seemed that winter had decided to stick around. There was another storm that weekend that brought in six more inches of snow. Hippo was in heaven. The mountain had opened early, and he asked Ben to cover some of his weekday shifts so he could ski before the snowbirds flew up from Phoenix on Friday afternoon.

Ben had been grateful not only for the extra cash but also for the time away from home. It was hard to focus on school when he was working so much, but his heart had left the classroom since Rob took away his spring classes, and he was just biding his time now until the semester's end. His students sensed his lack of commitment and had responded in kind with a steadily increasing number of absences. He didn't even bother taking attendance anymore. But since word got out about his little episode, not a single kid had dared to send a single text message during class. They all looked at him with a mixture of terror and excited expectation. If he'd done this earlier in his career (to someone less likely to bring charges against him), he imagined teaching might have been a less aggravating experience all these years.

Weekday shifts were slow, just the regulars and a few college kids ditching class. He clocked out at four P.M. as Ned was coming in to take over.

"Dude, what happened to your truck?" Ned said as he tied his apron around his waist and lifted the gate to come behind the bar.

"Huh?" Ben asked. He was cashing in his tips, closing the drawer.

"Your truck. Looks like somebody keyed it."

Ben went outside without even bothering to put on his coat and sure enough, all along the side of the truck, from the cab to the tailgate, was a nail-size scratch through the clear coat and into the primer.

"Shit!" Ben said. "Goddamnit."

"You got some enemies?" Ned asked. A few of the bar patrons had come out to see what the ruckus was about.

"I do now," Ben said. "Listen, I'll see you tomorrow."

Ben got in his truck and turned the key. Nothing. He tried again, and the engine groaned but wouldn't turn over. For a minute he wondered if somebody had fucked with his battery too. Then he remembered that it had been snowing, dim, when he drove to work. He checked and realized he had, as expected, left the lights on. He hit the steering wheel with his hand. He had planned to get in the car and drive around town until he found that asshole Mark Fitch and his goddamn blue Mustang. It had to be him. Why the hell did he tell him what kind of truck he was driving? But he was stuck. Snow coming down. He looked around to see if somebody might be able to give him a jump, but the street was deserted. Ned had walked to work from his place on Aspen Avenue and didn't have a car. Ben was shit out of luck. He'd have to call Sara, either that or walk home. Goddamn.

He looked at his watch. Sara wouldn't be out of work for another hour. He figured he might as well grab a beer at Beaver Street Brewery and then call her for a ride. He closed and locked the truck, took one last look at the horrific scar, and then started walking down the street.

He had to wait at the tracks for a train to pass. It was cold out, the sun obscured by heavy clouds. He stood behind the bar at the railroad crossing, waiting for the train, feeling the rumble of it, the power of it emanating through the soles of his boots all the way up his body.

The whistle was deafening. It's funny how accustomed he'd gotten to the trains. He hardly noticed them anymore unless they were holding him up. Like now. When the last car had passed, he jogged across the tracks and stopped.

Standing in front of Macy's Coffeehouse was Shadi. She looked up, as if sensing him, and raised her hand reflexively in a hello.

He slowed his pace down, trying to slow his heart. Every step was agonizing. He tried to be cool. He tried to relax. His mind was racing with what he could say to her. With all the possible ways to say, *I'm sorry*.

I'm sorry," she said, reaching for his hands, tilting her head and smiling at him.

They stood there like this, studying each other's faces until Ben realized what he was doing and quickly let go.

He shook his head. "No. I'm sorry. This shouldn't have happened. I didn't want to hurt anyone."

"Can I get you a cup of coffee?" she asked, gesturing to the door.

He thought quickly about the alternative: her walking away, her *leaving,* and he nodded. Despite everything, he said, "Yeah. Of course." And he put his hand on her back, his fingers thrilling at the touch of her soft coat, and followed her into the warm coffee shop.

Inside, it smelled like baked goods and incense. It was another local hippie hangout, and Ben rarely came here unless he needed to pick up the carrot muffins that Sara had been craving lately. They were whole grain, flax-flecked, fibrous wonders, all health benefits of which were negated by the Pillsbury cream cheese frosting she smothered them with.

"Let's sit here," Shadi said, motioning to a table in an out-of-the-way corner. No one would see them here. This was a far cry from the picture window at Café Espress.

They ordered coffees and sat looking at each other again, each as if looking at a ghost.

"I didn't mean to be such a coward," he said. "Leaving a note. It was wrong. I should have come to see you."

She shook her head again. "You told me about her. You told me you had a fiancée. I should have listened. I shouldn't have . . . we shouldn't have."

He knew she was right. He shouldn't have slept with her, but he wasn't sorry for that. He had no regrets about sleeping with her. His true regret was that he'd fled. That he hadn't simply stayed.

"When is the baby due?" Shadi asked.

The mention of the baby felt like a brick being thrust into his chest. It nearly knocked the wind out of him.

"July," he said and looked hard into her eyes. She smiled, but her eyes were sad. "We saw the heart beating."

She brushed her hair out of her eyes and shook her head slowly. And then she reached across the table and touched his face.

He closed his eyes.

"You aren't happy," she said.

"No." It felt like such a relief to admit this. To tell someone.

The waitress came over with the sandwich he'd ordered. Shadi withdrew her hand as if his skin had burned her. He glanced at his watch. Sara would be out of work in five minutes. He would need to call her now, before she left, if he wanted her to get him.

He watched Shadi as she picked small pieces of her muffin off and put them in her mouth. He looked at his watch again, though only a few seconds had passed.

"You should go," she said.

He thought about his truck, about that thin white wound.

"I saw the Mustang," he whispered. "It belongs to some guy named Mark Fitch. Long story short, I think he knows I'm looking for him."

Shadi's eyes opened wide and she grabbed his wrist.

"I'll keep looking," he said and then left because he knew that if she touched him again he wouldn't ever leave. "And I'll be in touch."

Sara picked him up on the corner by Jack's. It was snowing again, and the Camry was coated in several inches of snow. He hopped in next to her and stared straight ahead through the windshield. He couldn't look at her; he worried that if he did, she'd know everything.

"I'm thinking Caroline," she said softly.

"What?" he asked. His mother's name was Caroline. But everyone called her Caddy.

"After your mother?" she said, and squeezed his hand. "If it's a girl. We could call her Caddy for short."

In his office at school after his last class, he graded the stack of papers he'd collected that morning. He thought about marking them all B and calling it a day, but he still had finals to deal with. He wouldn't be done with everything until close to Christmas.

He'd been working for a couple of hours, when he started getting antsy. His office didn't have any windows. He was starting to feel closed in, caged. He figured he'd take a break and stretch his legs, go see if anybody was hanging around in the break room. Maybe he could find somebody to go grab a bite with. He hadn't had lunch yet and his stomach was starting to rumble.

The main office was deserted except for Penny, one of the grad students who came in and helped out in the office a few times a week. She didn't look up from the computer when he came in.

"Hey, Penny," Ben said. "I'm headed to go grab something to eat. Can I bring you back something?"

"Nah, I'm good," she said, clicking away on the computer.

Ben shrugged. He checked the mail room, the break room. Nobody was around. Office doors were closed, up and down the hallway. Even Rob wasn't milling around, and Rob was always milling around. Jesus. Maybe he was the only one who hadn't already checked out.

He went back to his office and grabbed his coat. The stack of papers leered at him from his desk. "I'll be *back,*" he said, and then wondered if that was crazy.

He made his way across campus. By the time he got to the student union, he was starving.

The faculty may have been mysteriously absent, but students were everywhere. There was hardly any place to sit. Every single table had at least three students and all of their paraphernalia sprawled out across them. Coffee cups and textbooks, notebooks and laptops. With finals just a week away, all of the students who had been partying on weeknights, sleeping in, skipping class to go snowboarding were suddenly studious. Serious. He saw this every semester. There was something magical about the end of the semester; it made students believe in miracles. This is when they went into high gear, cramming in thirteen weeks' worth of information in the hopes that it would stick. It was when the bargaining, the pleading, the praying began. He'd been guilty of it himself to a certain extent as an undergrad. But he was pretty sure he'd never tried to make a deal with a professor, and already he'd had two kids who'd begged him to drop their lowest quiz grade so they could pass his class. He'd thrown up his hands and said, *Why not?* He really, truly didn't care anymore.

He stood in line at the Sub Connection, studying the illuminated menu.

There was a group of girls in front of him. They were all wearing flannel pajama bottoms and thick collegiate sweatshirts. Finals wear. Being in Flagstaff had been refreshing after DC. Here you were considered dressed up if you wore a button-down shirt with your jeans and boots.

He ordered his sandwich and was paying when he heard a loud voice boom above the din of clacking keyboards and muffled music: "Hey, Fitch!"

Ben spun around, trying to follow the voice, unsure if his ears were playing tricks on him or not.

Over by the main door, there was a table of guys, all wearing baseball caps and sweatshirts. And standing at the table, fist-bumping each of them, was a guy with blond hair.

Ben grabbed his food and quickly wound his way through the labyrinth of students and tables, finally making his way to a table near the guys, where a girl in glasses and sweats was clearing away her things.

"Are you leaving?" Ben asked.

"Huhh?" she asked, unplugging her iPod earbuds.

"You leaving?"

She nodded. "Yep, it's all you."

"Thanks," Ben said, and waited as she loaded up her backpack before he sat down and unwrapped his sandwich.

He was close enough to the table to make out a little bit of the conversation, their voices loud but muffled.

"You going up to the mountain this weekend?" one baseball cap asked the other.

"Nah, my mom's coming up from Phoenix."

"So?" said another cap.

"Dude, you're going to miss the party at Fitch's on Saturday, then?"

Fitch.

"No way," a new voice, *Fitch's* voice, said. "My girlfriend's getting a keg from work. You totally can't miss it."

Ben looked up from his sandwich.

The kid, Fitch, was sitting down now. He'd taken off his hat. His hair was the color of sand dipped in vanilla frosting. He recognized him right away as a California transplant. They all had the same hair. The same slow, easy way of talking. The same golden skin all winter long.

"Where's Jenny work at again?"

"Flag Brew. They've got a killer IPA," Fitch said.

Flagstaff Brewing Company. Jenny was probably the girl he'd seen at Bashas' driving the Mustang.

"Dude, you can always come out after your mom goes to bed. She staying at your apartment?"

"Yeah."

"Hey, give me those fries," a familiar voice said.

He'd know that voice anywhere. Ben looked up and watched as a kid grabbed a fistful of fries from the basket and opened his mouth to shove them in. Sure enough, underneath that baseball cap was Ben's old buddy, Joe Bello.

At the movies on Friday night, Sara ordered a large popcorn and M&M's. As they waited for the previews to start, she dumped the giant bag of candy into the vat of popcorn and held it out to Ben. "Want some?"

He shook his head.

"Mel?" Sara asked, offering the bucket to Melanie, who had come with them, and Melanie grabbed a handful.

"I am having the weirdest cravings," Sara said. "This morning for breakfast, I had scrambled eggs inside a peanut butter and cheese sandwich."

"You must need the protein," Melanie said.

"I hadn't even thought about that, but I bet you're right. That would explain why Burger King commercials practically give me an orgasm. I ate an Ultimate Cheeseburger for lunch yesterday at Jack in the Box, and I was still hungry, so I got another one."

By the time the lights dimmed and the speakers boomed with the previews, Sara and Melanie had made their way to the bottom of the popcorn. When the movie started, and Sara reached for Ben's hand, her fingers were slick with butter.

Earlier that day, while Sara was at work, Ben had gone to Flagstaff Brewing Company and sat down at the bar. He'd ordered a beer and some onion rings and chatted with the bartender a little bit. After they talked about how the Suns might do this season, he said, "Hey, does some girl named Jenny work here?"

"Yeah, I think that's the new chick's name," the bartender, Gus, said.

"She working today?" Ben asked, looking around.

Gus shrugged. "I think she's on tonight. She was here last Friday. You want me to check the schedule?"

"Nah," Ben said. "That's cool."

"You want me to tell her you said hey?"

"No," Ben said. "She doesn't know me."

Gus raised his eyebrow, waiting.

"Sara," he stumbled. "Sara went to school with her sister, I think."

Gus shrugged.

Now, at the theater, he kept checking his watch every time there was enough light from the screen to see. It was already nine thirty, and the movie didn't seem to be ending any time soon. It was a chick flick that Sara had wanted to see for a while now. She'd waited for a moment of weakness to ask Ben to take her. And then Melanie said she'd wanted to come, and now he wasn't even sure why he was there.

His plan was to drop the girls off at the house and then make some excuse to go into town.

Maybe he could say that Hippo had called him in for a couple of hours. That Ned had called in sick. Friday nights could be jam-packed, and Sara probably wouldn't think twice.

But then, as they were walking out of the theater, Sara said, "Hey, why don't we go out? You guys can get a drink and I can watch."

Ben said, "You're usually in bed by nine. You're not tired?"

"Ben, it's been so long since we've done anything, and I actually have some energy for a change. Come on. Just for a little bit. Go downtown somewhere?"

"Let's!" Melanie said. "There's some band playing at Charly's tonight. They're supposed to be pretty good."

"Please, Ben?" Sara said, putting her hands together and batting her eyelashes.

"Just for a little bit, and then you need to get some sleep."

"Yes, sir," Sara said mock serious, saluting him.

Ben bristled.

They parked across from the tracks and had to wait as a train barreled past. He couldn't help but wonder if Shadi might be waiting on the other side again as the caboose rolled past. What would he do then?

Sara and Melanie held hands like little girls, skipping across the street when the light turned green, and Ben followed behind reluctantly, dragging his feet. As they walked past Flag Brew, he glanced quickly into the window to see if he could see the girl. *Jenny.* The place was packed, and people were spilling out of the doors.

"Hey," Sara said. "Why don't we go here instead? I haven't been here in ages."

"Really?" Ben asked. "It's pretty crowded. We might not get a seat."

"I'm pregnant, not an *invalid,*" she said and yanked his hand, leading the way.

Ben prayed that Gus had left, but as soon as they got to the bar, he could see that he was still there. He must be working a double. Ben anxiously glanced around, looking for a free table. It was standing room only, except for two open spots at the bar. He could imagine the conversation already: Gus asking Sara how she knew Jenny's sister. Introducing them. Sara wondering what the hell was going on.

But Gus seemed pretty busy, probably too busy to even remember the conversation. At least that's what Ben hoped as they took the only open spots at the bar.

"Hey again!" Gus said. "What's up?"

"Hey," Ben said, shaking his hand.

Melanie and Sara were occupied with taking off their hats and mittens and coats.

"So Jenny *is* working tonight," Gus started. "I can call her over if you want."

"Who's Jenny?" Sara asked.

"One of my students," Ben said, looking at Gus, hoping he was getting it. Gus lifted his chin; he understood. "She's failing," Ben added for good measure. "I was going to try to talk to her before the final, but I don't want to bug her when it's this busy."

Gus nodded, slung his dishrag over his shoulder, and said, "So, what would you girls like to drink?"

"I'll have a vodka cranberry, and she'll have a cranberry cranberry," Melanie said, smiling, flirting a little, Ben thought. Melanie hadn't dated anyone since her fiancé, Doug, died. Doug was a helicopter pilot and had crashed in the Grand Canyon right before Melanie graduated from nursing school. He and Ben hadn't been close, but it had been nice to go out in pairs instead of this awkward threesome. And since Sara got pregnant, Melanie was always around. Ben felt extraneous. He kept wondering if Melanie might be a better father to this baby than he would.

They got their drinks and, because he had no place to sit, Ben stood. The girls gossiped and leaned in close to each other, until finally Ben figured they wouldn't notice if he slipped away for a minute. He wanted to see if the girl, Jenny, really was the girl he'd seen with the Mustang.

"Hey, I'm gonna hit the bathroom," he said and Sara brushed her hand, dismissing him.

He set his beer down on the bar between them and made his way through the crowded bar area to the men's room. There were only two waitresses in sight, and one was Asian. The other had brown hair, a short denim skirt, and pink Ugg boots. It was her.

He went to the bathroom, used the urinal, and then washed his hands, splashing water onto his face. This time he would be smart, actually think about what he might say.

When he came out of the bathroom, he saw the girl. It seemed to have slowed down, and she was just leaning against the bar, looking out over the crowd to see who might need her.

"Hey," he said. "Are you *Jenny?*"

"Yeah?"

"Hi," he said, reaching for her hand to shake it. "I think we might have met on Halloween."

She cocked her head at him.

He waited for her. For something to click. Anything.

"Oh! Were you the guy dressed up like the zombie salesman? At the Beta Beta Phi party?"

A frat party.

"That was me! You're Fitch's girlfriend, right?" he asked.

"Yeah," she said. "I'm sorry, I totally forgot your name."

"It's Gary," he said.

"That was an awesome costume," she said.

"The blood looked so real. And that gash on your forehead was so cool."

"Thanks," he said. "That was a wild party."

"Yeah, that's an understatement," she said, scowling.

And he knew then that whatever had happened that night had probably started at this party. His heart was beating hard. He took a deep breath and leaned close to her, speaking softly. "So, I heard there was a crazy fight. . . ."

Her smile dissolved, and she grabbed her tray. The glasses on it trembled. "I wasn't there when that happened," she said. "I got tired and I went back to my apartment."

"I'm sorry," he said. "It was just so . . ."

She turned to look at him again; her eyes were glossy with tears. "You better just pretend like we didn't have this conversation." And then she and her tray disappeared into the crowd.

Cold adrenaline surged through his body; he could feel its grip in his shoulders, spreading down each of his arms. He walked back down the length of the bar to Sara and Melanie.

"You tell her she's failing?" Melanie asked. "She looked super pissed."

"Yeah," Ben said, grabbing his beer. "She's in a lot of trouble."

He had to tell Shadi. Maybe this information would be enough to trigger an investigation by the police. And if they figured out what had happened to Ricky, then maybe this could all end. He could let Shadi go.

But telling her meant *seeing* her. And seeing her meant facing the overwhelming possibility that he'd made the wrong decision in staying with Sara. Seeing Shadi was seeing a future he would never have. Seeing Shadi meant being tempted to change his mind, to leave Sara and the baby.

But she had to know what Jenny had said. He couldn't let this go.

After proctoring his last final, he gathered all of his stuff from his office and put it into a banker's box. He took the few personal items down from the bookshelves and walls, rolled the posters up and tossed them in the trash. He had a feeling, no matter what Rob said, he wouldn't be back in the fall. He had looked a few times at the museum's Web site to see if they'd posted the job Shadi mentioned, but it still wasn't up.

He loaded everything into the truck and drove into town, stopping at Late for the Train for a coffee though he knew the caffeine was going to only make him jumpier, more on edge.

It was cold but sunny out, the sun reflecting off

171

of the snow, too bright. He searched for his sunglasses and then remembered leaving them on the table by the door on his way out of the house that morning. He squinted and pulled the visor down to shield some of the glare.

He turned into the RV lot and drove the winding path to Shadi's trailer. A woman walking down the road with a backpack and a walking stick waved at him as he passed.

Shadi's bike was leaning against the trailer.

His hands were sweating. He shouldn't be here. He could have sent her an e-mail, called. He could have made an anonymous call to the police department. But before he could do a U-turn and head back out of the lot, Shadi opened the trailer door and stepped out. She was wearing a dress, heels. Her hair was down around her shoulders. She had long silver earrings on.

He parked the truck and rolled down the window.

"Hi," he said.

"Hi." She took a deep breath and straightened her dress.

"Why are you so dressed up?" he asked.

"I have an interview."

"For a job?" He knew she was graduating in the spring, and she planned to try to get a teaching job at a local charter school.

"With a magazine."

"To work at a magazine?"

Shadi laughed. "No, they're interviewing me about my work. I have another exhibit coming up at the museum in a few weeks."

"That's great! Do you need a ride into town or something?"

"No, the woman is picking me up here and taking me out for a late lunch."

"When is she coming?" he asked.

"Any minute." She tucked a stray hair behind her ear and scratched her arm.

He was still sitting in the truck. He knew that if he got out, he might never leave.

"What happened to your truck?" she asked, running her finger along the scratch. He could almost feel her fingers touching the wound. She came closer to the window, put her fingers on the window frame.

"I have some information about what might have happened that night," he said.

She closed her eyes slowly and opened them again.

"There was a party, at a frat house. The kid, the one from the Laundromat, the one with the Mustang, was there. His name is Mark Fitch. His girlfriend was there too but won't talk about it. I think one of my students might have been there as well."

"Why would Ricky be at a frat party?" she asked. "It doesn't make sense. He didn't have any friends on campus."

"I don't know. I'm going to try to figure that out," he said. "In the meantime, I think you should call the police."

"And tell them what?" Shadi asked, sighing. "That some college boy is bragging about beating up a drunk Indian at a party? That his girlfriend won't talk about it?"

As she spoke, he realized how thin the information was. How insubstantial.

"Maybe it's time to let it go," Shadi said. "Let him rest in peace."

"You don't mean that," he said.

"Ben, *it's time to let it go,*" she said again, but this time he knew she wasn't talking about Ricky. She touched his face and then backed away from the window.

He heard a car idling behind him. He looked in the rearview mirror and saw a woman in a Volvo, waving at Shadi. "I have to go," she said, straightening her dress and backing away from the truck.

On Saturday, Ben and Sara drove down to Phoenix to get a crib. It seemed to Ben a little early to be buying furniture, but she was determined. She had been shopping for smaller items for weeks. Every day it seemed there was more stuff piling up in their room: pacifiers, tiny diapers, baby wipes and powder and stuffed animals.

They could have ordered the crib online, but Sara insisted on going to the Babies "R" Us in Scottsdale and picking one out there. Besides, this way they could have lunch with her mom, and she could come along to help them pick it out. They might even get a little bit of Christmas shopping done.

As far as Ben was concerned, the only bearable time to be in Phoenix is in the winter. But Phoenix at Christmastime was one of the strangest things Ben had ever experienced. Growing up in Maryland, they didn't always get snow for Christmas, but they always got cold weather. In Phoenix, it was like some Disneyland version of the holiday, twinkling lights on cacti, fake pine garlands strung around lampposts, Santas in sunglasses, sweating inside their suits on every street corner.

They pulled up at Sara's parents' house at noon,

and Jeanine came running to the front door. She hadn't seen Sara since Thanksgiving, and she immediately went for the belly. "Let me see, let me see!"

There really wasn't much of a difference in Sara's stomach. She'd rounded out all over, but the actual belly remained pretty much the same.

Sara put her hands on her hips, jutted her stomach out, and let her mother touch it.

"Oh my goodness!" Jeanine said. "We should pick up some maternity clothes while we're out today too. It won't be long before you won't be able to fit into your jeans anymore. How are you feeling? Still sick?"

"Better. It kind of comes and goes. Some days are fine, and other days I'm throwing up all day."

"Well, come in. I'll make some iced tea and we can sit out by the pool for a bit."

And then, as if just now remembering that Ben was also there, she stopped and said, "And how are *you,* Ben?" before she hugged him.

Before Sara, Ben had not seen this kind of wealth. His own family had been middle class, living in a neighborhood of modest brick Cape Cods, all built in the same year, identical except for the color of the trim around the windows. He'd had some friends at Georgetown with money, but the ones who were rich didn't talk about it much, and their families didn't live in DC, so he never saw their houses.

The house Sara grew up in could have held two or three of the houses in Ben's neighborhood. It was on the country club where Frank golfed, and looked liked something in a Southwestern version of *The Great Gatsby*. The front doors were enormous, with leaded glass windows, flanked on either side by thick-trunked palm trees and giant stone pots filled with flowers. Inside was the great room with vaulted ceilings, marble floors, and a double stairwell. Six bedrooms, five bathrooms, a library, and a billiards room. There were fireplaces in most rooms, despite the fact that they were almost never used. It was a ridiculously beautiful home; he knew it embarrassed Sara a little. Ben would never have guessed that she had grown up in a house with a gourmet kitchen and a garage that could hold five cars. She was driving the same Camry she drove when he met her.

Ben's favorite part of the house, the only part where he felt truly at ease, was on the back patio. It was a huge open area, both indoors and outdoors at the same time. With comfortable chairs, an outdoor fireplace, a glistening pool, and an outdoor kitchen fully equipped with a gas grill and refrigerator, Ben thought he could probably live happily on this back patio.

Jeanine busied herself with the iced tea in the

kitchen while Sara and Ben made their way to the back. Sara plopped down in a wooden deck chair and slipped off her flip-flops. "It is so beautiful today," she said, smiling. "God, I forgot how much I miss the weather down here."

Ben sat next to her and stretched. It *was* a beautiful day. Maybe he could convince Jeanine and Sara to go shopping without him, leave him there to drink Coronas by the pool all day.

"What's your dad up to?" he asked her.

"Golf tournament," she said. "He'll be back by dinner."

"Are we staying for dinner tonight?"

"I told you that," she said, exasperated. "Dad's grilling salmon."

Ben shrugged. Now that school was finally over, he had little on his plate. He had worked at the bar every day this week and gave his Saturday night shift to Ned. "It's fine," he said. "I just forgot."

Jeanine came out with the iced tea on a silver serving tray with a little white bowl of lemon slices.

"Well, where do you need to go to today?" she asked.

"I want to pick out our crib. Daddy said he'd buy the crib and changing table for us. I also want to start looking at strollers and car seats. If we have time after, I thought I might get started on some of my Christmas shopping."

Ben sighed. Sara hadn't mentioned that Frank would be footing the bill for the furniture. He didn't know whether he should be pissed or relieved. "Maybe I can wait here for your dad," he said.

Sara laughed. "I don't think so."

"Come with us, Ben," Jeanine said. "It'll be fun."

Four hours later, Ben sat in a glider in the furniture department of Babies "R" Us, listening to the Muzak wafting down through the speakers. He racked his brain, trying to figure out what it was. Prince. That's it. "When Doves Cry." Christ. At least it wasn't Christmas carols.

Jeanine and Sara, who had not lost an ounce of steam, were discussing the various types of mattresses available: pillow-top, vibrating, ones that sang the baby lullabies. Finally, when she had decided on the cherry sleigh crib that would later convert into a toddler bed, Sara pulled Ben out of the chair. They went to the service desk to arrange for delivery, and she gave the salesman her parents' address.

"Why are you having it shipped there?" he asked.

Sara waved her hand dismissively. "It's just easier. We don't need it right away. We can come down and pick it up when we're ready."

Ben shrugged and said to Jeanine, "Thank you. For this. It's very generous."

Jeanine made an identical gesture of dismissal. "This is my *grandchild*. I'd give him the moon. What's a place to sleep?"

"It might not be a boy, Mom," Sara said.

"But it *might* be," she said.

Back at the house, Frank was already outside at the grill, sporting flip-flops and his golfer's tan.

"Dr. Bailey," he said. "These ladies managed to drag you along today, huh?"

Ben smiled and eyed the fish, which was marinating in something that smelled really good. He patted Frank on the back. "You need some help?"

"You can help me drink this beer," he said, gesturing to a silver bucket full of ice and Coronas. "The limes are in the fridge," Frank said.

Sara and her mother disappeared into the house to go through the loot from the day. Ben had anxiously watched as Sara loaded up the cart with little clothes, a hundred-dollar ear thermometer, and zillion-thread-count crib sheets. He'd cringed a little when Jeanine got out her wallet to pay, but he also knew exactly how much was (and wasn't) in their checking account.

Ben opened up a beer, squeezed a lime in, and watched the foam rise to the top of the bottle. He stared through the pale-colored liquid. It made everything look golden.

"So has Sara talked to you about New Year's at all?" Frank asked.

"Not really," he said. "We'll probably be coming down here for Christmas again, I expect. But I don't think we have plans for New Year's yet."

The last few years, they'd spent Christmas Eve in Kachina with Melanie and then driven down to Phoenix the next day. Ben would have preferred to stay at home, but Sara had never been away from her family for a Christmas before. New Year's Eve was sacred, though. They went downtown and watched the giant pinecone drop off the balcony at the Weatherford Hotel and spent the next day watching football.

Frank nodded. "So she hasn't dropped the bomb yet?" he asked.

"What bomb?" Ben asked.

"Well, here comes the little missile right now," Frank said and winked as Sara and her mother came outside, each carrying a salad.

They sat at the table by the pool. The fish was incredible, and the beer tasted good as the heat of the afternoon fell around their shoulders. Ben waited.

"So Sara tells me you aren't going to be at the university next spring," Jeanine said, offering Ben some more potato salad.

"Yeah," Ben said. "I'm really burned out. You

can really only be an adjunct for so long before you start to lose your mind."

"Overworked and underpaid," Frank said.

"Well, I don't know about overworked, but you got the underpaid part right."

"Do you have any plans yet?" Jeanine asked, and Ben felt suddenly like a tennis ball, bouncing from one side of the table to the next.

"Well, I still have the job at Jack's. Business really picks up in the winter with all the traffic going through town from the mountain," he said. He didn't mention the job opening at the museum.

"Do you like working at the bar, Ben?" Jeanine served.

"Jesus H. Christ, why don't you stop pussy-footing around here?" Frank volleyed.

"Daddy," Sara said, her face clearly anxious about something.

"What's going on?" Ben asked.

"Sara?" Jeanine said. "I think you better tell him."

Sara stared at the gray skin of her salmon, at the wilted lemon rinds.

Frank clapped his hands together. "Sara's applied for a position at Children's. And if she gets it, I'd like you to come down here and work for me." There was the drop shot.

Ben looked at Sara, who would not look up.

"Sara?" he said. "What is he talking about?"

"It's a great job, and after the baby comes, I can

transition to part-time. And Daddy's opening a new dealership right near the hospital. A specialty shop dealing in imports and antiques. Isn't that great? And the best part is, you would be in charge. It would be *your* shop. It's opening right after New Year's."

Ben put his face in his hands and rubbed hard at his temples. "What the hell, Sara? I'm sorry," he said to Jeanine. "But Jesus, Sara. You wait until we're sitting here to spring this on me? Don't you think that we should be discussing this at home? Alone?"

"I thought you'd be happy," she said. "It's a great opportunity."

"I have a PhD, Sara. In *history*. I don't know the first thing about selling cars."

"You work at a *bar*," she said angrily. Her voice was rising into that angry octave above her normal speaking voice. "Good thing you have that PhD. You'd never be able to mix a screwdriver without that."

"Sara," Jeanine reprimanded.

"If you haven't noticed," Sara said, standing up, "we're having a baby. It's time to grow the fuck up, Ben. Sorry, Mom." And then she stormed into the house, leaving Ben alone with Frank and Jeanine.

"Well," Frank said, sitting back in his chair and stretching.

"How about some sorbet?" Jeanine asked.

The drive up to Flagstaff that night was silent. Sara pretended to sleep, using her jacket as a pillow against the window, and Ben fumed. Sara was a lot of things lately: bitter, sarcastic, moody. But he'd never seen her be dishonest or underhanded before. He thought about her covertly submitting her résumé to Children's, making plans with her dad. For all he knew, they'd picked out a house for them. Probably right next door. That's why she didn't bother having the crib shipped to Flagstaff. And then, as the landscape began to change—saguaros replaced by Ponderosa pines, desert assenting to snow-covered ground—he was hit with a horrific realization. Maybe she'd planned *all* of this. Maybe the pregnancy hadn't been an accident at all. He couldn't believe he hadn't thought about this before: the possibility that *this* was her way of getting what she wanted. That maybe it wasn't dumb luck or a blessed life at all. Maybe she was just a manipulative liar.

He looked at her, curled into herself and leaning against the passenger door of the truck. He turned the radio on, to a station she hated, and waited to see if she'd stir. Nothing. He thought about slamming on the brakes, jarring her out of her pretend dreams. He thought, though briefly, of smashing the truck into a tree.

Finally, as if reading his mind, she sat up and turned to him. She said softly, "You know, I might not even get the job."

"What?"

"I didn't tell you yet because I don't even know if I'll get the job. It's pointless to get all worked up when I don't even know if they're going to want me."

She sat up straighter and pulled her coat on. Ben could feel the air growing colder, but he didn't turn on the heat.

"What on earth makes you think I would agree to move to Phoenix and work for your father?"

"That's the good thing, Ben. You wouldn't be. You'd be running the place. It would be your shop. And you love antique cars. You could keep the truck. We'd be close to my folks, so my mom could watch the baby while I work."

She had clearly been formulating this argument for a while now.

"I think a better question is why you *wouldn't* want to do this," she said.

"What the hell does that mean? I hate Phoenix. I hate the heat. I spent five years getting a degree I might never use again if we do this. There are a zillion reasons why I wouldn't want to do this."

Sara rolled her eyes.

"What?" he asked, staring at her.

"Keep your eyes on the road." She gasped, gripping the dash.

He had drifted over into the next lane and had to yank the wheel to correct.

"I'm just wondering if maybe there's something else keeping you in Flagstaff," she said quietly.

"Like what?"

Sara looked at Ben, her face angry, but her eyes wet. "I don't know, Ben. I don't know. But ever since Halloween, you've been so weird. At first I thought it was just finding that guy, you know? How awful that was. But it's different. It's like when you're with me, you're not really with me. It's like your body is walking around doing stuff, and you're saying stuff, but your mind is on something else." She paused and looked down at her lap, touched her stomach with her hand. "Or some*one* else."

"Christ," Ben said, gripping the wheel tighter. They were pulling into town. "What are you accusing me of? Exactly?"

"Nothing," Sara said. She stared at her hands.

Ben felt a sharp pain in his temples.

She reached and touched his leg. "I just . . . I just miss you. I miss *us*. And it's even worse now because of the baby. I just want everything to be normal and okay. I just want for you to be happy. For us both to be happy. Why is that so hard?"

Ben thought about waking up in Shadi's trailer, about the softness of her blankets against his naked skin. About the sunlight filtered through the dark veil of her hair. He thought about the smell of coffee lingering from the night before. He thought about the geometry of her collarbones, her hips. *Happiness*. That was the last time he'd felt happy, felt the promise of a life about to begin.

Sara lifted her hand from his leg and turned to face the window. They didn't speak the rest of the way.

At home, Sara ran straight to the bathroom and slammed the door. He could hear her vomiting, the awful sound of her gagging and then spilling and splashing into the toilet. He knocked gently on the door when it was over.

"Go away, Ben," she said.

"Sara."

"Just let me be."

At work on Wednesday night, Ben tried to imagine what a life living in Phoenix would be like. He thought about getting up every morning and putting on a suit and tie. He thought about the sun beating down on him as he made his way to his sedan. (The truck did not fit into this picture at all.) He thought about car lots, about the barren desert beyond. Golf with Frank on Saturdays. Sara. *The baby*.

But no matter how hard he tried, he could not imagine the baby. He had dreamed about it once, about Sara in the hospital, holding the new baby in her arms. But when he looked down to see its face, there was nothing there; it was just a blanket wadded up into a swaddled mess of flannel.

He saw himself and Sara piling into a minivan and driving across the desert to Disneyland. He imagined backyard barbeques, sitting in the bleachers at soccer games in the scorching heat. He imagined the sweaty auditoriums of dance recitals and piano recitals. He dreamed of hot metal swing sets and blistering monkey bars. But he couldn't imagine the child. It was like the vapors rising off of hot pavement. Distorted, unreal.

"Hey," Hippo said, coming out of the kitchen with a fresh basket of hot French fries. "Want some?"

"Not hungry," Ben said.

"You okay?"

"Yeah," Ben said. He still hadn't told Hippo about Sara being pregnant.

"Hey," Hippo said. "I was just thinking about that kid you asked me about, the one you found. You said his name was Ricky, right?"

"Yeah," Ben said, snapping out of his reverie.

"Remember he used to play pool with this other kid from the rez sometimes?"

Ben tried to remember. Ricky was always shooting pool. He couldn't remember him hanging out with anyone in particular. He didn't remember him having any friends. Shadi hadn't mentioned any friends.

"I only remember because the other kid had a tattoo of an eagle on his arm, and I asked him where he got it. I thought maybe Emily did it; it looked like her work."

"And?"

"Well, he came in the other day and I asked him if he remembered seeing Ricky on Halloween night. At first he looked spooked, but then he said that he did see him on Halloween. He ran into him at the Monte V. Ricky came in with some frat guy who talked them both into going to some party. He said he thought they might be trying to hustle another fraternity, and they wanted him and Ricky to be their ringers. I don't know if that helps at all," Hippo said.

"Jesus," Ben said. "That proves that he was

there. There must have been a fight at the house. Was he there with Ricky?"

"I don't know. You know how those rez kids are. Super quiet."

"Do you remember his name?"

"He calls himself Lucky," he said. "He washes dishes at Beaver Street too. I think that's how he and Ricky knew each other."

"Listen," Ben said. "Is there any way you can cover the end of my shift?"

"I think I can handle it." Hippo laughed, gesturing to the empty bar. It had been dead since school let out. They'd even been closing early.

"Cool," Ben said. "I appreciate it."

As Ben walked down San Francisco toward the tracks, he thought about what Shadi had said about just letting go. But if she knew that he was so close, would she still want him to stop? If he could just get one person who saw what happened to speak up, then he could go to the police. Somebody had to crack.

He knew the Beaver Street kitchen staff hung outside the door by the parking lot for cigarette breaks. When he got there, three guys were sitting on upturned pickle buckets, smoke curling up into the night air.

He approached them and they stiffened.

"Hey, do you guys know a kid named Lucky?" he asked.

"Yeah," one guy with a greasy baseball cap said. "He's in the kitchen."

"Do you think you could ask him to come out?"

"What do you want with him?" the other guy asked. Ben wondered how much other people knew, because this guy sure was acting like a mother hen.

"I just wanted to talk to him for a minute."

The guy sized him up and then said, "You a cop?"

"He's not a cop," the kid with the baseball cap said. "He's a history prof. I had him last semester."

Ben squinted; the exterior light was bright in his eyes. "Hey!" he said, offering the kid his hand. The kid ignored him. This was clearly not one of the front-row students.

"Hey, Lucky!" the guy yelled into the open doorway of the kitchen, and the kid appeared.

He was about half Ricky's size, maybe five foot five. He had a wild mess of hair and a filthy apron tied around his waist. As he approached, the other guys slipped back into the kitchen, leaving only a hazy fog of cigarette smoke in their wake.

"Are you Lucky?" Ben asked.

The kid nodded and sat down on one of the buckets. He motioned for Ben to do the same. The kid pulled a pack of cigarettes from his pocket and held it out to Ben.

"No, thanks," Ben said, shaking his head.

"What do you want?" he asked.

"I knew Ricky," Ben said.

The kid nodded.

"And I know that something happened at that party. I'm the one who found him."

The kid took a long drag on his cigarette and blew a long, skinny stream of smoke into the air, aiming it away from Ben. "Nobody's gonna do nothing about it," he said.

"Were you there?"

Lucky looked at Ben, as if trying to figure out if he could trust him or not. It was the same look Shadi had first given him at the hospital.

Ben continued. "Hippo, from Jack's, told me you guys were playing pool that night. Did you go with Ricky to the party?"

"Man, I told you it don't matter. Nobody cares what happened."

"*I* care what happened. His sister cares what happened. If you were there, we can go to the cops. If there's a witness, we can get the guys who did this to Ricky."

Lucky took another drag on his cigarette and closed his eyes. It looked like he might just fall asleep.

Ben sighed and threw up his hands. He stood up from the bucket and was about to walk away, when the kid said, "Wait."

Ben turned around, waiting. The air was quiet, the air heavy with the promise of more snow.

"You want to know the worst part?" Lucky asked.

Ben nodded. He could feel every inch of his

skin tingling. It was cold out already, but it felt as though he'd been doused in ice water.

"After it was over, they locked the doors. Kept on partying. We didn't even have our coats."

"Why didn't you call 9-1-1?" Ben asked. "The police?"

Lucky smiled again. "You think the police gonna help two kids from the rez saying that a bunch of college kids picking on them?"

"He was totally beaten up!" Ben said.

"He was bloody." Lucky nodded. "But he was walking, standing up. He said he was okay. He said he was gonna walk to his sister's house and she would take care of the cuts. He said he would be fine."

Now it made sense. Ben couldn't imagine what had brought Ricky to his neighborhood. It was miles from campus. But it was just down the road from Shadi's. He must have gotten lost in the blizzard, passed out in the snow. Only feet from Ben's door. Only steps from help. From him.

"We have to tell the cops," Ben said. "Somebody's got to know this happened."

Lucky tossed his cigarette down on the ground and stomped it out with his Doc Marten.

"Don't you think Ricky deserves justice?" Ben asked.

Lucky smiled and shook his head. "You just don't get it, do you? There ain't no such thing as justice."

Sara made lists. This was always how she had organized her life, and now this was how she communicated with Ben. In bullet points: hierarchical directives and enumerated edicts. *Take the trash out. Call cable company. Get milk.* They didn't talk about the job at the hospital. They didn't talk about the move to Phoenix. What Sara did was make lists. To-do lists. Grocery lists. Lists of pros and cons for the move. Lists of things they might need in Phoenix. They hung under magnets on the refrigerator. They were stuck to walls, the insides of cabinets, to the dash of the truck. The self-adhesive instructions inserted like a scavenger hunt leading nowhere.

Today he had the Christmas shopping list.

- *Mom—new cashmere scarf (blue)*
- *Dad—new barbeque utensils*
- *George—leather attaché*
- *Melanie—gift certificate to salon (mani/pedi)*
- *Birdy—gift certificate to salon (pedi only)*
- *Veronica—Godiva chocolates and a pound of coffee beans (ground) from Late for the Train*
- *Dr. Newman—Home Depot gift card ($50)*

His name was not on the list.
He told her that he would take care of the

shopping. That all she needed to do was wrap the gifts. She was particular, a perfectionist when it came to wrapping presents, so he knew it wouldn't help to offer to do this too.

He went to Home Depot first, got the gift certificate and found a nice set of barbeque tools for Frank. He went to the salon next and got the gift certificates. At the mall, he found a scarf at Dillard's and the chocolates. The only thing left was the attaché case for her brother, George, and the coffee beans. It was only noon.

He grabbed a cheeseburger to go at the food court and figured he'd drive back into town to look for a case for George. They might have something at Gene's Western Wear. Last would be the coffee beans.

He hadn't planned on going to the antique store, but then he drove past the shop on 66 and his heart nearly stopped. He yanked the wheel and pulled the truck into the lot. A smile spread across his face. There, outside, next to an iron bed frame and a Ms. Pac-Man machine was an old drive-in movie speaker on a stand.

The speaker looked almost as if it had grown there, an errant sunflower, a chrome weed sprouting from the dirt.

He went inside the little shop, the sleigh bells on the door jingling. He had to search through a labyrinth of junk to find the saleslady, who was crouched on the floor next to a box inside of which was a black Lab that, Ben soon realized, was in the middle of giving birth to a litter of puppies.

"Excuse me?" he said.

The woman looked up, startled. "Hi. I'm so sorry. Molly just started whelping her pups, and she's having kind of a rough time. Would you mind putting the CLOSED sign up in the window?"

"Sure, sure," Ben said and went back to the front of the store. He flipped the OPEN sign around to CLOSED and locked the dead bolt.

"Do you need anything?" he asked.

"I'm going to need some towels. They're in my car," she said, handing him a large set of keys.

He went back out to the parking lot. He walked over to the speaker to see if there was a price tag. He had exactly a hundred and fifty dollars left, with which he was supposed to get everything left on the list. Sara had swiped his credit card after he told her that he wouldn't be teaching next semester. There wasn't a tag; he'd have to ask the woman inside. He opened up the trunk of her car, grabbed the towels, and went back into the shop.

Inside, the mother dog had pushed out the first puppy. She was clearly suffering, whimpering and moaning, ignoring the puppy that slithered and wriggled on the cardboard beneath her.

"Looks like she's going to need some help," the woman said and grabbed one of the towels from him. She broke the sac and started rubbing the squirming little pup. And then the next one came out.

"Holy shit," Ben said. He'd never seen anything like it in his life.

He got down next to the woman. She handed him the blanketed bundle with the first puppy and started to repeat the procedure with the next. He rubbed the puppy, looked at its sealed eyes, marveling that this life had literally just begun before him. It wriggled in his hands, its heart beating hard against his chest.

He'd gotten Maude when she was nearly seven months old, halfway grown. She was a rescue dog, brutalized by her owner. She had welts on her belly, a bullet hole in her ear, though remarkably, she wasn't afraid of people. She never barked, not even at other dogs. Not when people came to the door. He'd never seen her as a puppy. Not like this.

The puppies kept coming and coming, and Ben and the woman kept rubbing the life into them until the mother, at last, lay back panting. Then, as if realizing for the first time what had happened to her, she began to take care. She nudged and licked, prodded and poked each puppy into place until all of them were finally snuggled in a furry row, nursing on her swollen teats.

"This is her first litter," the woman said. "Sometimes they don't know what to do the first time."

Ben watched as the puppies sucked, and the mother closed her eyes. Contented. Exhausted.

"I am so sorry," the woman said, wiping a hand on her jeans and then reaching out to shake his. "Not very good customer service."

"Oh no, I totally understand," Ben said. "Wow."

"Was there something in particular you were looking for?"

Ben stood up, his knees resisting after having sat on the floor for so long.

"Actually, yes. I was wondering if you knew where that drive-in speaker was from."

The woman stood up as well, and stretched her back. She was wearing jeans and cowboy boots. Her hair was the color of vanilla pudding, all spun into an elaborate hive. Her chest was freckled and tan. Her eyes were a shocking blue.

"I believe it's from the Tonto Drive-In. They tore that place down in 2002. It's not the original stand, of course, but I'm pretty sure it still works."

The mother dog was making noise again.

"She's lucky they all lived. I've had eight mama dogs, and almost every litter has had a pup that didn't make it. No runts this time, though."

"You said the Tonto Drive-In? Where was that?" he asked.

"In Winslow. I never went there, but my husband, God rest his soul, grew up there. He used to talk about going there as a kid."

198

Ben thought about Shadi and Ricky in the back of that pickup, staring up at the pale white screen, waiting for the movie to start. The speaker hooked to the window of the truck. Buttery popcorn, and the air growing cold as the sun went down. He thought about the crackly static of the speaker, about the old mattress in the back. About their grandfather sitting in the front of the pickup, tuning in to the right station.

"*Hush,* Molly," the woman said to the dog as she whimpered in the corner. "It's not rocket science, it's just feeding time."

"How much are you asking for it?" Ben asked.

"Well, I think I was asking a hundred bucks, but I can give it to you for fifty. A thank-you for helping out today," she said. "And of course, if you find yourself in need of a puppy in about six weeks, you just come on back."

Fifty bucks. He wondered if there was any way he could get the rest of the stuff on Sara's list with only a hundred dollars. He tried to think if he had any tips stashed in his drawer or in the pockets of his coat.

"You mind me asking what you're gonna do with it?" the woman asked.

"It's a Christmas gift," he said. And then, just to try the words out, just to imagine for a stolen minute this glistening impossibility, he added, "It's for my wife."

• • •

As Ben drove past the turnoff to his neighborhood and kept going to deliver the speaker to Shadi, his phone buzzed on the passenger seat next to him. He looked down as it shook across the seat. A text message. He picked it up and clicked OK.

9-1-1. COME HOME ASAP.

He did a U-turn on Fort Valley Road and pushed the accelerator. The speaker rolled across the bed of the truck. His mind raced with all of the possible scenarios. Something was wrong with Frank, a heart attack or worse. A car accident. Maybe the house was on fire. Had he turned off the Christmas lights this morning when he left? The baby. God, no.

He thought about the mother dog, about those tiny little puppies. About how small and fragile they were. About the tiny beating hearts beneath the thin skin of their chests as he rubbed them to life.

He pulled into the driveway, grateful to see that the house was intact, and the screen door opened before he could even get out of the truck.

Sara was still in her scrubs. He glanced at his watch. It was two o'clock, too early for her to be home. But she looked okay. Nothing was wrong with her, or the baby, as far as he could tell.

"What's going on?" he asked. *Shit, don't let anything be wrong with her folks.*

Her eyes were wide and bright, and a slow smile crept across her face.

He ran up the steps to the porch. "Why are you home so early?" he asked.

"I got the job, Ben. The hospital called today. I applied for a position in Rehab, but something opened up in Oncology and they want me. I know it's going to be tough, but I think this is what I'm meant to do, Ben. I really think I can be good at this. They want me to start right after the new year. I left work early. Please? Can we celebrate this?"

YELLOW WORLD

Ben dreamed the sunset colors of Shadi's woven blanket: the amber, gold, and rust. The mahogany sky and golden mountains. In the dream, he was parched, walking across a barren desert spotted with cacti and shrubs. The ground scorched his feet, and the air burned his lungs. The air before him was thick and distorted, making mirages. He was lost. He was thirsty. But in the dream, he knew that if he could just find blue, he could drink. Yellow. Gold. Orange. Not a drop of blue in sight. And he knew, as his feet blistered and his chest burned, he would die of thirst.

He woke up sweating, his legs twisted and tangled in the sheets on Sara's childhood bed. It took a minute to orient himself. Sara slept peacefully next to him. Oblivious. He went to the bathroom and splashed cold water on his face, stared at the wreckage in the mirror. His cheeks were hollow, his chin nicked with cuts from the last shaving attempt. His eyes were swollen, with dark shadows looming beneath.

It was Christmas Eve, and they were in Phoenix. It was Christmas Eve, and in less than five hours they would be the owners of a brand-new town house in a brand-new development only two blocks from Sara's parents' place. It was a modest home with three small bedrooms, one and a half baths, a kidney-shaped pool out back, and a sprinkler system already installed. Every house on the street was the same, only some of them flip-flopped, their architectural plans mirror images of each other.

A week before, Ben had walked through the empty shell and tried to fathom living there. Tried to imagine coming home to that white kitchen, those white walls, the white carpet.

Sara had gone to the never-used refrigerator, and leaned into the cold, clean air. "It's beautiful, isn't it, Ben?" Sara asked. "It's so new!"

Their house in Flagstaff was a 1920s bungalow. The hot water heater didn't work very well, the dishwasher was always on the fritz, and some of the windowsills were starting to rot. But it felt like home, like a real home. It had a smell, like ash and musk. It had a history.

"It's so . . . *white,*" Ben said.

"We can *paint,* silly," she said. "Look." And she pulled a folder out of her purse, full of paint chips, shades of yellow and gold and peach. She pressed a chip against the wall.

"The baby's room is up here," she said, pulling him by the hand up the stairs and down a short hallway. She opened the door to a small bedroom with two windows and pale yellow carpeting. "Can't you picture it?' she asked, touching her stomach.

And he tried. God, how he tried. But there was

nothing but white, a blank space where the crib and changing table and glider should be. The air conditioner whirring through the vents, and the distant sound of a lawn mower, were like a pale suburban lullaby.

Frank had offered them the down payment as a Christmas gift. He said that when the house in Flagstaff sold, they could take the equity and put it in an account for the baby. He was with them at the signing, standing at the white tiled counter in the kitchen, going over the papers with his realtor as Ben and Sara watched and waited to be asked for their signatures. Frank was dressed for golf. He planned to take Ben out for a quick nine holes after the signing while Sara and her mother prepared for Christmas dinner.

"Thank you, Frank," Ben said, handing him the pen. "This is very generous."

Frank smacked Ben on the back and said, "S'my pleasure."

It was a hot day for December. Almost eighty degrees, and Ben was sweating. They were on the last hole and Ben had been playing like shit.

"Didn't bring your 'A' game today, huh, Benny?" Frank asked as he parred. Ben had duck-hooked, shanked, and trapped his ball twice on number 9, which was also, unfortunately, the number he posted.

"Jesus," Ben said, wiping his forehead with his golf towel.

"Let's finish up and go to the clubhouse. Get ourselves a little Christmas cheer."

It took another fifteen minutes for Ben to hole his ball, and he was relieved afterward to be in the golf cart, headed off the course and to the bar.

In the clubhouse, Frank ordered a couple of drinks for them while Ben went to use the restroom. He figured he'd check in with Sara while he was in there, make sure she and her mother were doing okay. Her brother and his wife weren't due to arrive from Tucson until tomorrow. There were no messages from Sara, but there was a text message from an unfamiliar number. He scrolled quickly through the message:

Lucky contacted me. Took your advice, called PD. Need to talk to you. P.S. Thx for the gift.

Ben's hands started to shake, and he shoved the phone back in his pocket.

Ben had brought the drive-in speaker to Shadi's house the morning after Sara told him about the job in Phoenix. Luckily, she hadn't seen it in the back of the truck. He'd hoped to find Shadi there, so that he could at least say good-bye, but she wasn't home. He'd set the post up by the door to her trailer and slipped a note into the chrome grill: *Found this treasure from the Tonto Drive-In in Winslow and couldn't resist.* There were a thousand other things he wanted to say, but he knew it would only make it worse, and so he just wrote, *Merry Christmas.—Ben*. As he drove away, he looked at the speaker in the rearview mirror and knew that this would be, *had* to be, the last time he drove away. He was going to be a father. A husband. He would not fuck this up. He would not ruin any more lives.

Now, in the cold, clean restroom of the country club, he felt a rush of heat through his body and he started to sweat. He used the restroom and then pulled his phone out and looked at the message again. If she contacted the police, then the investigation might be reopened. If this were the case, the police would probably want to talk to him. He couldn't believe that Lucky had sought out Shadi. Ben smiled at the thought that his conversation with him had made any sort of impact. Maybe this meant he was ready to talk to the cops about what happened that night. If he did, it could mean they might catch that asshole Fitch and put him away for what he and his buddies did to Ricky.

Tomorrow was Christmas. He and Sara weren't moving their stuff out of the house in Flag until New Year's Eve. In the meantime, he was supposed to get started with Frank at the new shop. Sara was starting her job at Children's right after the new year. Their new life was supposed to begin. Right now.

He looked at the message again, and thought about Shadi's fingers tapping out the words. About the way her fingers had traced the line of his jaw, the trail from throat to chest to belly button and lower. He thought about her fingers intertwined with his and neither of them wanting to let go.

He glanced around the empty restroom and looked back at his phone. And then he hit REPLY and wrote: *In PHX for X-mas, will be back ASAP. Promise.*

When he got back to the bar, Frank was slapping some guy on the back.

"Ben!" he said loudly. "I want you to meet somebody."

The guy, who looked like an aging Ken doll in a yellow golf shirt and duck pants, thrust out his hand and shook Ben's firmly.

"This is my future son-in-law," Frank said. Proudly, Ben thought. "And this is the future governor of Arizona."

"Ah, Frank, don't get ahead of yourself," the guy said. "I haven't even officially announced that I'm running yet."

"Mister Modesty," Frank said, shaking his head. "He's been like this since college. How about some ice cream with that humble pie?"

The guy laughed heartily.

"Ben Bailey." Frank smiled. "Marty Bello."

B en's mind was racing.

Sara went to bed right after Christmas Eve dinner, and not long afterward, Frank and Jeanine excused themselves as well.

"Get some sleep so Santa can come," Jeanine said. She'd been hitting the eggnog pretty hard and her words were slippery.

"Mind if I take a swim?" he asked. He needed a few minutes to be alone, to think things through.

"Enjoy," Frank said. "And the Christmas lights are on a timer, so you just need to turn out the overheads."

"Merry Christmas," Jeanine said, and stumbled as they made their way upstairs.

Ben changed into his swim trunks and went out to the back patio. He walked around to the diving board and climbed the ladder. He walked to the edge of the board and dove into the pool. The water enclosed his body in a cold liquid embrace. When he emerged, he blinked the water from his eyes and flipped onto his back. Christmas lights were strung in all of the palm trees and birds-of-paradise. They twinkled like constellations as he stared up at the sky. His skin prickled.

Luckily, Martin Bello hadn't recognized Ben's name. He didn't realize that he was the guy who had chucked his son's cell phone at a wall. And thankfully, Frank didn't bring up anything about his job at NAU. Instead he'd said, "Ben's going to be running the new shop. Make this a real family business." And Martin Bello had nodded approvingly.

Apparently, he and Frank had met at ASU when they were getting their MBAs. They'd both been in the same fraternity, at different schools, as undergrads. Ben wondered if Martin Bello had any idea what an ass his son was. About the assholes he was friends with. He wondered if he knew anything about what happened that night, though he doubted it.

Ben knew that most kids at school kept their parents pretty insulated against their collegiate activities. Just a year ago, a girl had died from alcohol poisoning after some party off campus. Her parents were fundamentalists and had no idea, until they saw her MySpace page, how very bad their good little girl was. He knew from his own experience that the stuff that happened behind closed dorm room doors was not usually included in the phone calls to Mom and Pop. And something of *this* magnitude was not something to write home about.

As he bobbed and dipped in the cool water, he thought about how he could possibly meet Shadi in the short amount of time he had left in Flagstaff. He'd promised he'd be there. He imagined the investigation would be under way by now. He wanted to know if they were making progress. But he and Sara weren't going back to Flagstaff until New Year's Eve Day to pack up, and they were moving on New Year's Day. One week from tomorrow. Now that the decision to move had been made, Sara seemed hell-bent on spending as little time in Flagstaff as possible.

Ben pulled himself out of the pool and dried off. He quietly went into the house, locking the doors behind him, and made his way to Sara's room.

The Flagstaff house was empty, the U-Haul full by five o'clock on New Year's Eve. Ben walked through the bungalow, with Maude at his heels, looking at all the empty spaces. Sara and Melanie were sitting in the kitchen on two folding chairs. Sara was crying. Their voices sounded hollow, echoing in the empty room.

"Maybe we're making a mistake," he heard her say. "I don't have a single friend down there anymore."

"You'll have your mom and dad," Melanie comforted. "And *Ben*."

Sara cried some more, and Ben lifted up a box labeled *Bathroom*.

"I'll be down every other weekend," Melanie said. "I'll be there so much, Ben will want to kick me out," she said and laughed as Ben came into the kitchen.

Sara's face was streaked with tears, and Melanie was holding both of her hands.

"She okay?" he mouthed to Melanie and she nodded.

"Listen," Ben said. "There are only a few boxes left. Why don't you girls go into town and get some lunch. I'll finish up."

Melanie nodded. "Good idea. What are you craving?" she asked, squeezing Sara's hands. "What does the baby want to eat?"

Sara shrugged.

"Crystal Creek sandwiches?"

Sara shook her head.

"Beaver Street's Southwest chicken pizza?" Melanie tried. It was like watching a mother negotiating with her child.

Sara smiled and wiped her tears with the back of her hand. "And lemonade."

"Okeydokey," Melanie said. "Ben, you want to meet us at Beaver Street when you're done? I'll buy you a pint?"

"Sure," Ben said. "Give me about a half hour."

"Just a half hour, Ben," Sara said. "We'll be waiting."

They were going to watch the midnight pinecone drop at the old Weatherford Hotel one last time and then drive down to Melanie's in Kachina for the night. The next day they'd drive the U-Haul down to Phoenix and move into their new house.

After Melanie and Sara drove away in Melanie's car, Ben picked up his cell phone to call Shadi. He scrolled through the messages, looking for the text he'd gotten down in Phoenix. Nothing. It wasn't there. He clicked up and down through the list. It was gone. Had he erased it? Shit. Jesus, what if Sara had seen it? He took a deep breath and cracked his back. What had it even said? Something about Lucky. Something about the gift. It's not like it was anything incriminating. Crap. Sara wouldn't have looked at his messages, would she? He wasn't sure what she was capable of anymore.

Regardless, the message was gone. Her number was gone. Now if he wanted to talk to her about Lucky, he'd have to drive up to her place. She didn't have a landline, so he couldn't look up her number. But this also meant that he'd have to see her again. And as much as he wanted to see her, he knew it would just make all of this that much harder. He shouldn't go. He should just go to the police and tell them what he knew. On the morning after Halloween, he had found a man dying in the snow in front of his house. Later he heard a rumor there was a kid from the university who was bragging about beating him up. There was someone who saw what happened, who watched the kid, Mark Fitch (who drove a blue Mustang), beat Ricky up and throw him out into the cold. There was a witness. His name was Lucky and he worked at Beaver Street. Ben could remain anonymous. Because Ben had no place in this. Not anymore.

"Come on, girl," he said to Maude as he glanced around the house one last time.

When he and Sara moved into this house, they were so in love with each other. Every time Ben saw her, a surge of happiness had pitched inside of him. It was October. The first night in the house, they hadn't unpacked anything yet. They had no furniture except their mattress, nothing in the fridge except a bottle of wine. It was autumn and cold. He'd tried to make a fire in the woodstove. He hadn't known what he was doing though, forgetting to open the damper first. And so the small fire he'd managed to light went out, leaving the house freezing. They'd found the box labeled *Linens* and pulled out every blanket they had to stay warm. They drank the bottle of wine and curled around each other, skin to skin, the heat of their bodies its own furnace. He remembered thinking then that he had never been more content. That if he could hold on to just a fraction of this feeling, he would always be happy.

Now something panged in his chest. Something primitive and vivid. He used to *love* Sara. His blood and skin once felt for Sara the way it did now whenever he allowed himself to think of Shadi. But over time, that feeling for Sara had dulled at the edges. Softened. Sometimes it slipped away entirely. And if this dissolution were possible, maybe it was possible that one day these feelings he had for Shadi could disappear too. They could fragment, until there was nothing left but slivers that would scatter and be lost. Though, while this should have comforted him, should have given him hope, it didn't. Instead it made an ache that started somewhere deep in his gut and spread through his limbs.

He got in the U-Haul and drove to the end of his street. If he turned right, he would be headed into town, to Sara and Melanie and a waiting pint of beer. If he turned left, he would be headed to Shadi's. He sat in the truck for five minutes until someone drove up in a car behind him and gently tapped on its horn. He glanced in the side-view mirror and waved an apology. Then he signaled left and pulled out onto the road.

A half hour later, Ben pulled the U-Haul into the parking lot at Beaver Street Brewery and sat for a few minutes before cracking the window for Maude and opening the door. He was shaky, unsteady, as if he had the flu or a bad hangover.

When he got to Shadi's, she had come out of the trailer and held both of her hands up, as if in surrender, shaking her head.

He'd gotten out of the truck, slammed the door, and gone to her, even as she backed away from him.

She shook her head over and over again.

"What's the matter?" he said. "Shadi, what's wrong?"

"You can't be here," she said. Her soft, deep voice cracked.

"I just wanted to talk to you about Ricky. About what happened that night. If Lucky goes to the police, then they can get that kid. Isn't that what you want? He can't get away with this."

"Ben," Shadi said. Her voice was suddenly stern.

"I can make a statement about what I heard. And Lucky, if we can convince Lucky to talk, then they can arrest him, Mark Fitch."

By then, Ben had come close enough to Shadi to touch her. She pressed both open palms against his chest and the mere contact, the simple pressure of her hands against his body, was enough to bring him to his knees.

"What's the matter?" he said, feeling something hook into his heart like a fishing lure. Snagging and pulling, sharp and painful. "Shadi, what is it?"

"Sara," she said. It was the first time she had said her name. It made Ben catch his breath.

Ben shook his head. *Sara. Sara.*

"Sara *called* me, Ben. From your cell phone. And I thought it was you."

Ben stepped back. *Sara.* She had seen the message. She'd *read* his messages. And she'd called Shadi.

"I thought it was *you,*" she said angrily, hitting him now even as he backed up. Her hands curled into fists and she hit him hard against the chest. "What are you doing to her, Ben? What are you doing to *me?*"

"What did she say?" Ben asked softly.

"She didn't say anything. I just kept saying your name, waiting for you to say something, and then I heard her crying."

Now, at the Brewery, Ben locked the U-Haul and walked briskly across the parking lot, glancing quickly at the restaurant's kitchen door, which was open. There were two guys sitting on buckets, smoking cigarettes. Neither one of them was Lucky. Ben took a deep breath and opened the front doors, the warm air coming at him in a rush. Enclosing him. He concentrated on every step. He couldn't let Sara know that he knew what she'd done. If he did, she would know that he had gone to see Shadi. She would know that it wasn't over.

He said to the hostess, "I'm meeting my fiancée and her friend?" and the words were bitter in his mouth.

And then he saw Melanie waving her over and Sara sitting at the table, smiling knowingly, expectantly, at him.

On opening day for Frank's new dealership, *Ben's* new dealership, Sara was up at five A.M. making pancakes in the kitchen. It was her first day at work too; she would be working the seven-to-three shift until the baby came. She had the radio on and was singing softly to some pop song. Ben came out of the bedroom bleary-eyed and still exhausted. He'd been tossing and turning all night, unable to get comfortable, disoriented by the new sounds, the new silence, of the house. Maude was also uneasy and refused to leave the foot of the bed, the sheets and blankets weighted down by her warm body.

They hadn't talked about what happened, though what they each knew hung in the air between them like a ghost. But Sara had won, and she must have known this, because there was a certain smugness about her now, as she flipped the pancakes in the frying pan and put the syrup in the never-used microwave. She had busted him, and now, without a word exchanged between them, she had him completely under her thumb.

"Are you nervous for your first day?" she asked Ben.

He stretched and yawned, shook his head.

"Daddy's going to be with you this week, right?"

She knew Frank would be there. And he couldn't help but wonder if he would ever be alone again, or if what he had done now meant that someone would always, always be watching him.

"Yeah, he's got to show me the ropes, I guess," he said.

The microwave beeped and she pulled the hot syrup out. She handed him a plate stacked high with pancakes and bacon and pointed to a seat at the counter separating their dining area and the kitchen. There was a cup of coffee waiting there, a glass of juice.

"I'll get spoiled if you keep this up," he said, but his attempt to be lighthearted fell flat.

Sara frowned and came to him. She kissed him on the forehead and then on the lips. When she pulled back, she seemed to be waiting for his response.

"I love you, Ben Bailey," she said, her voice quivering a little.

"You too," he said and looked down at his plate. He could feel her eyes, could feel her expectation and disappointment. He lifted his face and looked at her. "I do," he said. And he reached for her to come closer. He willed his arms around her, and as he did he felt, for the first time, the soft swell of her belly. Just the smallest bump, so small he might not have noticed it if he weren't absolutely familiar with every nuance of her body.

She pulled away, satisfied it seemed, and he

reached his hand out and touched her stomach. She looked down at his hand, hesitated, and then covered it with her own. She squeezed her eyes shut tight for a second and then opened them wide.

"Well," she said and straightened herself up. She was wearing a pair of scrubs he'd never seen before. They were blue and littered with tiny little trucks and cars. She had brand-new white Crocs on with crisp white socks.

"Are you nervous?" he asked.

He tried to picture her working in the Oncology Department of the hospital and couldn't. Her job at Dr. Newman's was tame: checkups and shots, nothing worse than chicken pox and strep throat. The children here would be sick. Really sick. She assured him she was ready for this. That she was a nurse, a professional.

"I am," she said. "Nervous. But it was time for a change."

He nodded. "Are you going to eat?" he asked.

"Too queasy," she answered. "I'll get something at the hospital. And I'll be back by four or so to make dinner."

"Sounds good," Ben said and wondered if she'd taken this shift to make sure he was never at the house alone.

The dealership was beautiful. Glossy and bright. The air conditioner blew cold air across the onyx floors, and everything gleamed.

"What do you think?" Frank asked.

"It's gorgeous," Ben said. "Really, I had no idea it would be so . . . so spectacular."

Most of the cars on the showroom floor cost more than Ben had made in his entire working life.

The morning was spent orienting Ben to the facility and the staff. As far as he could tell, his job would be behind the scenes. There was a sales team, a finance team, a service team, and then the administrators. He was in charge of them all, though what this meant exactly was ambiguous. He had an office with a comfortable chair, a computer, and a view of Camelback Mountain. There was a water cooler in the corner that glug-glug-glugged and a flat-screen TV suspended from the wall like a dream. There were papers to process, databases to maintain, and calls to take. Frank rattled off his daily tasks and Ben scribbled furiously on a yellow legal pad.

By noon, his brain was full of information, overloaded with car talk.

"Let's get some chow," Frank said.

They got into Frank's car and drove across the street to Chili's, where the hostess winked and flirted. They ordered burgers and beers, and Frank wolfed down an entire basket of onion rings before Ben had even started his meal.

"You think this is going to work out for you, Dr. Bailey?" Frank asked.

"Frank, I really do appreciate this. I know it's not my area of expertise, and you're taking a real chance with me," Ben said.

Frank stopped eating and wiped the corner of his mouth with his napkin. "As much as I love you, Ben, this isn't about you, and you know it. Sara is my only daughter. She's my baby. And she deserves to be happy," he said. "If being with you, making a life with you, makes her happy, then I'm on board. And I will do whatever it takes to make sure that life is a good one. A comfortable one. I have no idea if you can do this job or not. And I have no idea if you'll be happy working for me. But I do know that it's *my* job to take care of my little girl. And this is the best way I know how."

Ben nodded. And felt like a total shit.

"And if you can just hang in there, there are perks. Free lunch is one," he said when he got the bill that had charged him only for the two beers. "And there are others. I'm thinking in particular about a certain vintage Mercedes I saw you looking at. You give me the old college try for a full year and it's yours."

Ben shook his head. "That's not necessary, Frank."

"Shut up," Frank said. "Don't look a gift horse in the mouth."

The rest of the day went smoothly, and everyone Ben met was very friendly. He actually started thinking this job might not be so bad. It sure was a hell of a lot less exhausting than the bar, and not nearly as dirty. And unlike teaching, when he pulled out of the lot, he had no work to come home with him. He was pretty sure this kind of job would not keep him up at night. And it was so far from the life he'd had in Flagstaff, it almost seemed like he'd woken up in someone else's body. In someone else's life.

He pulled into the driveway of the town house at six thirty. The sun had already gone down, and the air was cooler. He went into the front door and could smell marinara. Garlic and oregano.

"Sara?" he called, setting down the new attaché case Sara had bought him for Christmas. It was almost exactly like the one they'd wound up giving to George. He figured now she'd been planning all along to see what kind of bag he wanted by having him pick one out for her brother. Little did she know he had just picked the cheapest one after blowing fifty bucks on the drive-in speaker.

"I'm up here," she said.

He slipped off his loafers and went up the stairwell to the bedroom. The door was closed. "Sara?"

"Just a minute."

When she opened the door, he barely recognized her. She was wearing a dress and heels, her hair was down, and her eyes were made up. She smelled good too, the tea rose perfume she used to wear when they first met.

"You look so pretty," he said.

She blushed a little. "Come with me," she said, taking him by the hand and leading him back down the stairs and through the kitchen to the sliding doors. She pulled back the accordion shades and slid the door open.

When they bought the house, the only appealing thing about the property, for Ben, was the backyard and pool. He used to swim in high school and thought he might get back into shape doing laps in the morning before work.

Sara had clearly been busy since she got home. The outdoor table was covered in a pretty tablecloth, and the entire fence was strung with twinkling lights. There were candles floating in the pool, and soft music coming through the radio she'd brought outside. The table was set, and there were candles there too, and a bunch of heady-smelling roses cut from the bushes in the backyard and stuffed into a pickle jar.

"Take your tie off and sit down," she said. "I'm going to give you the meal of your life." She spun a little on her heel, smiling, and went back into the kitchen.

She had not only made homemade lasagna, but also picked up a bottle of Ruffino Chianti, the kind of wine they always ordered at Pasto in Flagstaff. The kind they were drinking the night he proposed.

"What is all this?" he said, squeezing her hand.

"Ben, I want to start over. I want everything to be new. I want . . ." she started but her voice was trembling. "I want you back."

"Hey," he said.

She leaned into him, and her tears soaked through his collared shirt to his shoulder.

"Hey, it's okay. Sare . . . it's okay."

And there was that snag, that sharp hook. It punctured somewhere smack-dab in the middle of his chest and pulled.

"I'm sorry," Sara said, laughing. "God, enough with the hormones already. Let's eat."

After dinner they left everything on the table, and Sara led Ben to the bedroom. In the cool, quiet white of the room, Ben made love to her for the first time in a month. And afterward, as they both caught their breaths and lay staring at the ceiling fan above them, Sara said, "There's a little girl at the hospital. Emma. She's five, and she has leukemia. But she is the brightest, happiest child I have ever seen."

Ben rolled over to face her, propping himself up with his elbow.

"Her mother had to quit her job when she got sick. Then the dad left, and I get the feeling he's not doing much by way of support. But her mom is the most optimistic person I have ever met. She's at the hospital all day every day. She does puppet shows for the kids, and she reads to them. She brings in homemade cookies and today she helped some of them start a window box garden in the atrium. She's really managed to make a home there for Emma."

There was a tear rolling down her cheek.

"And all day while I was doing my rounds, I kept thinking about how lucky we are. That this baby is healthy. That we are healthy. That we have each other." She turned to look at him. Her eyes were sad, wet. "I know this isn't what you wanted, Ben. I know that. I'm not stupid. But I promise I'll make a home for us. For the three of us."

Ben reached and touched the tear that had snuck onto her earlobe. Then he leaned over and kissed it; it was cold and salty. Her neck still smelled of tea roses. Sara smiled.

"Hey," she said, sitting up suddenly, hitting the pillow with her hand. "I have an idea."

"What is it?" he asked.

"Just come."

The fence around their backyard was only six feet high; somebody could see in, and Ben was self-conscious as they climbed into the pool, still naked. The air was cooler than the water, and it felt good against his skin. They both floated on their backs, looking up at the sky. As the water filled his ears, he listened and could hear his heart beating in his temples and he thought about this life. About how clean and bright it was. About how shiny it all was. How golden.

It could have ended here, with this strange bliss: of never-ending sun and impossibly blue skies. With Sara's unspoken forgiveness and Ben's gentle assent. But nothing is ever as easy as it seems. And nothing is ever truly clean. Like a fractured bone improperly set, the healing can be slow and incomplete, and, in the worst cases, infection can set in, sending sickness traveling slowly, silently through the rest of the body.

In February, Sara was scheduled for the ultrasound that would reveal whether they were having a boy or a girl. At first they had wanted to wait, to be surprised. But as the date drew nearer, Sara started getting antsy. She didn't want any more surprises, she said. She wanted time to prepare for whatever their future held in store.

Ben left work early to meet Sara at Children's. He checked in with the receptionist, who asked him to have a seat in the waiting room. He was anxious; he hadn't been in a hospital since Ricky died. This hospital, unlike the one in Flagstaff, was terribly cheery inside: with cartoons on the TV and candy-colored floors. It felt more like a playground than a hospital.

Their appointment was at four, and Sara was running late. By the time she finally came into the waiting room, she was harried.

"Can we still get there in time?" she asked Ben, glancing at the Cinderella watch Ben had bought her for Christmas, the one he thought the kids at the hospital would like.

"I think so. If we don't hit any rush-hour traffic," he said.

In the truck, Sara was quiet, staring out the passenger window.

"You okay?" Ben asked. Her silence made him anxious.

"Huh?" she said, distracted.

"Everything okay?"

She shook her head and looked back out the window.

"They're having a hard time finding a bone marrow match for Emma. And every day she just gets sicker and sicker. And the real kicker is, she's just so damn grateful for everything. We threw her a birthday party yesterday, and I'd never seen a kid so excited about cupcakes and balloons. You'd have thought she was at Disneyland."

"I don't know how you do it," Ben said. "I really don't."

"I dream about the kids, Ben. Every single night. Of course, sometimes it's just like I'm at work, administering meds, doing my rounds. But then other times the dreams are so bad." Sara shook her head. "I never stop thinking about them."

They pulled into the parking lot at the imaging

center and rushed inside. They were ten minutes late.

"Have a seat," the receptionist said after she got their information.

They sat down and Ben looked around. There was an elderly woman and another couple, the young woman looking as though she might give birth any minute.

Sara went to the magazine rack. "You want one?" she asked Ben. He shook his head. She picked out a magazine for herself and sat back down.

Ben got up and got a paper cone filled with water, drank it, and then filled it again. It probably held only about two ounces and he was thirsty. In Phoenix he was always so thirsty.

"Hey, Ben," Sara said. "Come look at this."

She had folded the magazine's cover over and was pointing to an article. "This woman is from Flagstaff. She's a Navajo artist, a weaver. It says her last name is Begay. Wasn't that the guy's last name? The one from Halloween?"

Ben gripped the fragile paper cup. He took the magazine from Sara.

In the photo, Shadi was standing next to a tree, with the Peaks jutting up into the sky behind her. Ben scanned the article. *Shadi*. His entire body was trembling.

"Huh. I wonder if they're related," Sara said.

Ben shook his head and handed her back the

magazine. "Begay is a really common Navajo last name."

Sara nodded her head. "Her work is beautiful. My parents have been looking for something for that wall in their family room," she said. "I'm going to see if I can keep this article. Maybe we can see where she sells her work the next time we're in Flagstaff. It might make a nice thank-you gift, for everything they've done."

He ran his hand across his face, felt the sharp stubble of late afternoon. *Christ.*

"Sara Harmon?" the nurse said, appearing with a clipboard.

Sara set the magazine down. "Here we go," she said, and they both stood up to follow her. "Wait a second," she said. And she grabbed the magazine and tore the page out, stuffing it into her purse.

The technician asked Sara to pull up her scrubs and then squirted jelly over her stomach, which was rounded now, a noticeable swelling. "Sorry if this is cold."

Ben sat down in the chair next to the table and looked at the screen, trying to shake the image of Shadi, of the mountains, out of his head. The technician probed and recorded. "The baby is measuring at exactly twenty weeks," he said.

Sara squeezed Ben's hand. Her palm was hot and moist.

"This is the foot," he said, pointing to the screen. "Kicking away! A little soccer player, maybe. See, and here is the spine, and a nice profile shot for you."

He took a thousand measurements, moving the probe and then freezing the image. Clicking and tapping information into the computer. Sara let out an audible sigh every time he confirmed that the baby was developing appropriately.

"Now, did you want to find out the baby's gender?" he asked.

"*I* do," Sara said. "Ben?"

Sara looked at Ben, and Ben said, "Sure."

"Okay, let's see if we can get the baby to give us a peek." He prodded Sara's belly, and the baby on the screen kicked and moved.

"Must be shy," the technician said, laughing.

"You can't see?" Sara said, sounding the slightest bit panicked.

"Let me try one more thing," the technician said. "Why don't you roll over onto your side here. This works sometimes."

Sara turned over onto her side, facing Ben. She was really sweating. He brushed a damp piece of hair out of her eyes. "You okay?" he asked.

She nodded quietly.

"Well, *there* we go!" the technician said, and Ben glanced toward the screen. The technician fiddled with the buttons on the computer and the image froze. "Look at this," he said and Sara rolled back over. "See," he said, pointing at some lines on the screen. "These lines that look like an equal sign?"

Ben leaned forward, looking to see what he was talking about.

The technician smiled and said, "I'm ninety-nine percent sure you've got yourselves a baby girl here."

Sara's hand flew to her mouth and she sucked in her breath. "A girl? *Really?*"

"You got it."

"Ben," Sara said, starting to cry. "We're having a baby girl."

When Ben's mother came home from the hospital with Dusty, he thought she was a birthday gift for him. They were born almost exactly five years apart, and because his mother went into labor on his birthday, his party had been delayed. Her arrival came at the same time as the balloons and the cake and the rest of his presents. At the same time as the candles and wishes.

"Mine," his mother said he exclaimed, reaching for the little bundle in her arms. And when she shook her head and said, "You need to wait, Benny. Let's get you on the couch so you can help Mommy hold her," his face had fallen in disbelief. *"My* baby," he said.

Looking back now, he'd always had a proprietary feeling about Dusty. She was his in the same way his Matchbox cars and LEGOs were his. She had come, was there, for him. To tickle and push on the baby swing. He was the only one who could make her giggle. The one she cried for when she was hurt. She was *his*. His sister. His responsibility.

Dusty, with her long blond braids and freckles. With her green eyes and tiny hands. Dusty, who could sing every single song on the *Grease* sound track and could do back handsprings across the whole length of the park. How do you fit that into a box? How does that just end? At the cemetery, Ben stood between his parents and watched as the minister said a prayer over the tiny white coffin. The leaves were turning gold and red in the trees, but summer hung on. The thick heat filled his lungs. He felt like he did sometimes when he got water up his nose in the pool. As though he were drowning. Dusty, who liked to cut words out of magazines and tape them to her door. FABULOUS. AWESOME. GOOD MORNING. Dusty, who hated chocolate milk but loved chocolate cake. Dusty, whose breath smelled like peppermint.

At home that afternoon, Ben went to his room and lay down in his bed. He looked around at all of his stuff: the model airplanes hanging by threads from the ceiling, the basketball shoes in the corner, the stack of CDs. Did any of this stuff belong to him? Did this house, did his school, did his family belong to him? If Dusty could disappear, couldn't just about everything else too?

B en held on tight.
He held on to every single moment, because he knew how things could vanish. Wasn't this what had been happening his whole life? One gift given, something taken away? Hadn't he been waiting for the other shoe to drop his entire life?

They went to Home Depot and picked out the paint for the baby's room. And now, he lifted the lid to reveal the color Sara had chosen. It was called Peaceful Princess. Purple. She'd chosen sheets for the crib, tiny violets, and curtains as sheer and light as a whisper. The crib was still in its box; he planned to put it together after the paint dried. They'd been to the Container Store for bins and boxes. The bureau they'd bought was already nearly full of tiny little onesies and pajamas. When he opened the closet, there was already a neat row of miniature dresses hanging from tiny little hangers.

There was something calming about painting. Ben had always loved the rhythmic monotony of the roller, the concentration required for edging and painting trim. Now, as he stood on the stepladder and applied the first brushstroke to the baby's wall, he wondered if he'd missed his calling. Maybe house painting would have been a more fitting vocation.

By the time Sara returned from IKEA, where

she'd been looking for a small bookcase and a rug, he had finished the room, assembled the crib, and hung the hardware for the curtains. She came into the room and started to cry.

"Ben, it's so pretty."

He put his arm around her and held on. Held on tight as she hugged him.

"I got the sweetest little bookcase. We can put it over there. Make a little reading corner."

"Did you find a rug?" he asked.

"I think I want something more custom," she said, pulling away and walking over to the crib. "Remember that artist I read about, the one in Flagstaff?"

Ben stiffened, felt a shiver running like cold water down the ladder of his spine.

"The one from the magazine at the ultrasound place?" she persisted.

Ben scowled. "I don't remember."

"Of course, you do."

He stole a look at her face but couldn't read anything in her expression.

"Oh yeah," he said. "I remember. The Navajo woman. The weaver."

"The one with the same last name as the boy we found." Sara was smiling, touching her belly absently. "I was thinking we could get something for Mom and Dad and maybe commission her to do a rug for the baby too. Something with purples and pinks."

"She might be hard to find," Ben said, reaching. Grasping. "And she might not even do that sort of thing."

"I'd actually completely forgotten about her, and then I found the article in my purse when I took out my wallet to pay for the bookcase. So I contacted the gallery where she shows her work, and they gave me a phone number for her. She had left a business card." Sara was still smiling.

"I can call," Ben said. "Just get me the number." He wondered if she'd written down Shadi's number before she erased it from his cell phone. Jesus Christ. What the fuck was she doing to him?

"That's okay. I'll call," she said, smiling. "I just wanted to make sure it was okay with you. I don't know how much it will cost, but it will definitely be more than IKEA."

The sunlight was coming through the curtainless windows, and Ben had to shield his eyes against the glare. He waited, waited for everything to detonate; he anticipated the explosion, the wreckage of its aftermath.

But instead, she just sat down in the new glider. "It would mean a lot, to have something from Flagstaff for the baby," she said, putting her feet up on the matching ottoman. "Boy, my feet really are starting to hurt."

"Can I get you something?" Ben asked, grateful for the shift in the conversation. His heart clanked against his chest. He could feel himself beginning to sweat. "Something to drink?"

"Nah, but could you bring me my phone? I want to give her a call right now. I'm excited, Ben. I think this is exactly what this room needs."

At work on Friday, Ben couldn't focus on anything. Frank had business to attend to at another dealership and had left Ben alone for the first time. He'd left behind a whole checklist of things to do, but the harder Ben focused, the more blurry the list became.

Sara had tried to no avail to get in touch with Shadi, but she was determined to get through. She'd left at least three messages, and Ben figured that Shadi had probably figured out who she was. She was probably wondering what sort of cruel joke this was.

Ben knew he should contact her. Should let her know that all of this was just an awful coincidence. That he had planned to do as she had asked. To leave her alone. But he also knew that contacting her was dangerous. Not only because of Sara.

By noon, Ben had managed to make his way through about half of the list. He'd checked in with the sales folks during their weekly meeting and he'd drafted the newsletter that Frank had put Ben in charge of. He'd updated the customer database and made some follow-up calls to recent customers.

He decided to go get a bite at Chili's, see if Frank's discount would apply without Frank there. He took a newspaper from the machine out front; he'd overslept and hadn't even had time for a cup of coffee on the way out of the house, never mind read the paper.

The lunch hostess, the one with the big breasts and bleached teeth, seated Ben at a small table by the kitchen. While he waited for his order, he opened up the paper and scanned the headlines. He flipped to the local section and looked for Flagstaff news. Though he settled into his new routine in Phoenix, he missed Flagstaff, and reading about what was going on up north always made him feel just a bit less disconnected.

A longtime business was closing down, another victim of the economic disaster. A story about the record-breaking snowfall's effect on tourism at Snowbowl. And the investigation into the death of a Navajo man found dead in the Cheshire neighborhood on November 1.

The waitress set down his plate. "Can I get you anything else?"

Ben shook his head, skimming the brief article. Anxious.

Victim believed to have attended a fraternity party near the university's campus that night, though he was not a student himself. No suspects, but the fraternity brothers had been questioned by the police based on an anonymous tip. The victim's blood alcohol level was .08, the legal

244

limit, and no autopsy was performed at the family's request. The cause of death was exposure. The victim was from Chinle, AZ, survived by his sister, Alice "Shadi" Begay, a local artist in Flagstaff.

Ben pulled a twenty-dollar bill from his wallet and left it on the table. He needed to get home, to get rid of the newspaper sitting on their kitchen table. Sara always read the paper after work. If she knew there was a connection between Shadi and Ricky, she wouldn't let up. She might even begin to piece things together, if she truly hadn't already. It was just a matter of time until everything blew up.

Ben figured he could just swing by the house and grab the paper and then get back to work before the hour was over. He could pretend that none of this was happening. He could convince Sara to find another rug.

Ben pulled into the driveway and unlocked the door. Inside, he grabbed the newspaper, which appeared not to have been touched, sighing with relief. He knew he would be starving if he didn't eat something, so he took an apple from the fruit bowl and noticed the light on the answering machine was blinking.

"Hi, we're not here right now; please leave a message!" Sara's voice chirped.

"Hi, this is Shadi Begay. I'm returning your

*call about the rug you'd like to commission? I'd
be happy to talk to you more about this. I think
you have my number; just give me a call."*

Ben glanced quickly at the door, his finger
hovering over the DELETE button. But he wanted
to hear her voice just one more time. It sounded
like winter, the sound of a fire, the sound of snow.
This would be it. And then he would let her go.
Let all of this go. The police were investigating
Ricky's death. She didn't need him anymore. He
hit REPLAY, and as Shadi's voice echoed through
the kitchen, Sara walked in the door and started to
cry.

The little girl, Emma, passed away while Sara was working that morning. Emma had been sick, but stable, all week. A donor had been located, and her transplant was scheduled. They put her in ICU that morning because she was running a high fever and they were worried that she had an infection. And then, while her mother went out to get coffee for herself and for the nurses, Emma closed her eyes and didn't wake up.

"What happened?" Ben asked.

"I don't know," Sara said. Her whole body was trembling. She was pale, ghostly.

"Sit down," he said, guiding her to the couch. She sat down and put her head in her hands. It sounded like she was hyperventilating.

"Do you need a paper bag?" he asked.

"I can't do this, Ben," she said, looking up and shaking her head. "I was her *nurse*. I'm not supposed to let this get to me. It's not professional at all. I'm probably going to lose my job."

"No," Ben said, sitting down next to her. "She's the first patient you've lost. Of course you're upset. This is an adjustment. They have to understand."

"The charge nurse sent me home. Told me to get it together. I have to be back in an hour."

"It's going to be fine," he said, putting his arm across her shoulder, cradling her. Rocking her.

"Why are you here?" she asked suddenly.

Ben's eyes went from the counter where the newspaper lay to the light that still flashed on the machine.

"I came home for lunch," he said. "Listen, what I want you to do is go lie down. Just for a little bit. I'll call work and tell them I'll be back a bit late."

"I can't, Ben. I have to go back to work."

"You have plenty of time," he said. And then he added, knowing this was the one thing she would listen to, "It's not good for the baby. This stress. Just rest. Just for a few minutes."

And, like magic, she listened, shuffling up the stairs to their room. When the door closed, he shoved the newspaper into the bottom of the trash can, covering it with coffee grounds and a banana peel.

Shadi didn't need him anymore, but Sara did. This baby did.

He looked at the blinking light and clicked DELETE.

B en tried not to think about the snow. He tried not to think about the way it felt to walk out into the cold and to feel winter all the way through to your bones, about the way it sparkled, about the infinite prisms. He tried not to miss the purity of it, the baptismal chill every time you went outside. But when Sara said she wanted to go up and see Melanie for the weekend, the first thoughts that came to mind were crystalline and white.

"Do you want me to come with you?" he asked.

They were sitting outside by the pool, having breakfast before Sara went to work.

She shrugged. "Doesn't matter," she said, pushing a perfectly symmetrical ball of honeydew around with her fork.

"I'd love to stop by Jack's, see Hippo and Ned."

Sara seemed elsewhere. Since Emma died, there was a pall about her, something heavy and dark. Ben didn't know whether it was losing Emma or some hormonal shift that made her so quiet, so sullen. She was still in her second trimester. These were supposed to be the golden months of pregnancy from what he'd read in the books that lay splayed open or dog-eared on every flat surface in the house. He avoided the very good possibility that it wasn't Emma or the pregnancy, and that maybe it was him. Whatever it was, it felt like the calm before the storm.

"I'll come with you. It'll be great," he said cheerily. "That way you don't have to drive. And I'll leave you girls alone. I promise."

She looked up from her bowl of fruit and said, "Have you seen my prenatal vitamins?"

Ben shook his head.

She looked distracted, tired.

"You okay?" he asked.

The sun sparkled on the surface of the pool, the aquamarine refracting the early morning light. He'd started swimming in the mornings, disappearing into the blue just as the sun was coming up. The water was cold and clean and made his skin tingle into life.

"Yeah, come with me if you want," she said. "It's supposed to snow, and I hate driving in the snow."

They left after work on Friday and sat in traffic for nearly an hour just trying to get out of Phoenix. The traffic was bumper to bumper, and as they inched forward, Ben could feel Sara's frustration growing. It was palpable. As thick as this heat.

They were driving the Camry because the truck didn't have AC, and Ben was glad not to be miserably hot on top of it all. Sara usually kept a clean car. A little trash bag hanging from the back of one of the seats. No old coffee cups in the cup holders, no soda cans. She brought the Camry to the car wash once a week and had it detailed once a month. She bought air fresheners in packets of three and hung them from the rearview mirror like Christmas ornaments.

But today, as they crawled through the heat toward I-17, Ben glanced around the car and saw it was a disaster. An empty Pringles can rolled back and forth across the floor beneath her feet, and a dirty pair of scrubs was stuffed into the space between them. There were crumbs on the floor, and the windshield was filthy. In the backseat, he'd had to make room for Maude among a dozen shopping bags from baby stores. The items inside seemingly forgotten.

"What do you and Melanie have planned?" he asked.

Sara was looking out the window. She shrugged.

"She must really miss you," he offered.

"She wants to plan my baby shower," she said.

"That'll be nice," he said. "Will it be in Flagstaff?"

"Well, I don't have any real friends in Phoenix," she snapped.

The cars, which had been creeping steadily at ten miles an hour for the last twenty minutes, came to a stop. Sara put her face in her hands and groaned. "Maybe we should go back home," she said. "We're never going to get there."

"It's okay. Once we get onto 17 it should thin out," he said.

"Not if all these assholes are headed to Flagstaff too," she said.

Ben stared out the window at the sea of cars. There must be an accident, something blocking a lane or two of traffic. At this rate they might get to Flagstaff by the end of the weekend. And, unfortunately, Sara was probably right. After all the snow they'd been getting at the Peaks, probably every Phoenician and their brother had decided to go skiing this weekend.

"My back hurts," she said. "Really bad."

"Can you take anything?" he asked.

She looked at him like he was an idiot. "Tylenol. Why, do you have any?"

"You all right?" he asked again.

Sara sighed and leaned her head against the window, positioning the air-conditioning vent so that it was blowing on her. And she closed her eyes.

He was grateful that he didn't have to try to make conversation anymore. He hoped he didn't have another four months of this to look forward to. He'd been trying; he really had. But she wasn't making it easy for him. When Sara was sweet, when she was bubbly and happy, he could love her again. He could remember that old feeling. He clung to that. But when she was like this, he could feel the anger spilling through his veins. Quiet toxins flooding his veins and arteries. Poisonous and bitter.

Finally, Ben could see what was holding everyone up. There had been an accident near the exit for the Loop. It looked as though two cars had collided; one was accordianed against the guardrail and the other was up on the median. Ambulances had arrived, and there was a cop directing everyone to the far left lane. As Ben merged into the single lane of cars, he, like every other looky-loo, craned his neck to gauge the damage. And while he didn't see any people, he did see a small sneaker lying in the middle of the road. Just a single child's shoe. His stomach turned. He was glad Sara's eyes were closed.

Beyond the accident, the traffic picked up and then they were on 17 headed north. If there weren't any more delays, they would get to Melanie's house by nine or so.

At some point, Sara stopped faking sleep and actually fell into a fitful slumber. Her head kept slipping from the window to her chest, startling her awake for a moment before she fell back asleep again. In the first few months, she'd been able to sleep anywhere. Now sleep wasn't as easy, and he figured some of her crabbiness was from sheer exhaustion.

He knew it was going to be difficult to be in Flagstaff; he knew that it was risky too. In Phoenix, he was able to put thoughts of Shadi out of his waking mind, though she did visit him in his dreams. There was nothing he could do about that. But in Flagstaff, he knew he not only ran the risk of thinking about her (about second-guessing everything), but he also ran the risk of running into her. Flagstaff was small. Too small. He hoped that Sara would want to stay in Kachina with Melanie, and wouldn't want to go into town. Ben knew that Shadi no longer needed him or wanted to see him. She'd told him so in no uncertain terms. And now that the investigation was open again, he didn't need to play amateur detective. He'd done what he could, and now it was time for the professionals to take over.

As they approached the exit to Kachina, Sara woke up, stretching. She smiled at Ben and leaned her head against his shoulder. "I must have been tired." She yawned.

"You slept the whole way," he said. "We're almost there."

Maude yawned and stretched in the backseat too.

He hoped that Sara had left her misery back in Phoenix somewhere. He was pretty sure he couldn't take a whole weekend of sarcasm and senseless irritability. If she was going to spend the weekend being crabby, she could be crabby with Melanie. He'd be at Jack's.

"Oh," Sara said, clapping her hands together. "I totally forgot to tell you. I finally got in touch with that woman about the rug. I was supposed to meet with her on Sunday to discuss the design we want. Now we can both go."

Ben gripped the wheel of the car. He stared straight ahead, pretending to concentrate on the road. The pavement *was* icy, the air outside freezing. If he wasn't careful, they might have an accident, go off the road, down an embankment. They might not be found. They could die out here.

The second that Melanie opened the door and Sara saw her, she fell to pieces.

"Come in, come in," Melanie said, motioning for them to come inside. "Oh, honey," she said, hugging Sara tight. Without letting go of Sara, who was a bumbling mess, Melanie caught Ben's eyes and gestured for him to go to the kitchen. "I bought some Sierra Nevadas. That's your beer, right?"

"Thank you," he said, putting his hands together in gratitude.

In the kitchen, he grabbed a glass from Melanie's cupboard, ran the water in the sink until it was ice cold, and then drank the whole glass in a series of desperate swallows. He could feel the icy water making its way down his esophagus and into his stomach. His gut felt like a chunk of ice.

He had to come up with a plan, and quick. The ridiculousness of the situation mocked him. How on earth did this happen? He could see Sara somehow accidentally bumping into Shadi if they still lived here, but they were a hundred and forty miles away. She hadn't heard about Shadi on the street but in a goddamn magazine. What were the chances? It was as though the world were conspiring against him. Spilling his secrets into

256

the universe. He knew the answer was simple. He knew there was only one way to avoid absolute disaster. He needed to talk to Shadi, to explain that Sara Harmon was *his* Sara. That the baby was *his* baby.

The baby.

The evidence of the baby's impending arrival was everywhere: in the black-and-white filmy ultrasound printouts on their refrigerator to the fully furnished room (the still mobile, the expectant stuffed animals perched in the corners of the crib). Even in the growing bump of Sara's belly. He hadn't felt the baby move yet, but Sara had. She'd pressed his hand against her skin, hard, waiting for him to feel what she did. Frustrated when he didn't.

When he came out of the kitchen with two beers, one for Melanie and one for himself, Sara had stopped crying and was sitting on the couch. Melanie's hand was pressed against Sara's stomach, and her eyes were wide with disbelief.

"Did you feel it?" Sara asked.

"I did!" Melanie squealed. "I really did. It was like a little flutter, like little wings or something. Like a little bird!"

Sara nodded knowingly. She touched her stomach, rubbing the skin in soft circles. "She wakes me up sometimes at night. And I'll be all confused, and then it will hit me. There's a *baby* in there!"

"It's really happening," Melanie said. "Ben, you must be so excited."

Ben nodded and smiled, but it felt as though he were hovering somewhere just outside of his body. It was like those movies where someone dies and you watch the soul rise up and stand there watching as the doctors try to revive the corpse. He watched himself nodding and laughing. He listened to his voice talking about the nursery, about the plans to build a playhouse for the backyard someday, about the middle names they'd considered. He saw a man, a father about to be born, while the real Ben, the vaporous man he was supposed to be, was already far away.

In the morning, Sara slept in, and Melanie asked Ben if he wanted to take a walk. Ben checked on Sara in the guest bedroom before they left and kissed her. "Mel and I are taking Maude for a walk," he whispered.

"Okay," she said. She was curled up on her side, smiling, and asleep again before he walked out the door.

For as long as Ben had known Melanie, he was pretty sure they'd never been alone together. When Doug was still alive, he and Ben always paired off when the couples got together. And afterward, when Doug was gone, it was always Melanie and Sara, and Ben alone.

They both pulled their boots on, hats and mittens. The thermometer said thirty degrees, but the sun was bright.

"Ready?" she asked.

Melanie's house, like a lot of the houses in Kachina and Mountainaire, backed up against the Coconino National Forest. Ponderosa pines as far as the eye could see. It was peaceful and quiet in these woods. A good place to clear your head. They walked silently for a while, just listening to the sound of the birds and the wind in the tops of the trees. The snow crunched beneath their feet.

"Sara seems sad," Melanie said.

"Yeah?" Ben asked.

"I don't think the job at Children's is the right place for her," she said. "It's got to be awful being around so many sick kids while she's getting ready to have a baby."

Ben nodded. "She was really upset when that little girl Emma died."

"She's a terrific nurse, but she gets *attached*. I've seen her cry her eyes out after giving shots. It's like she feels all of their pain."

Ben nodded. He didn't know this about her. She never really talked much about work, and when she did, she was always lighthearted about it. It made him feel weird to be learning something new about Sara.

They stopped when they got to a small frozen pond. Melanie sat down on a fallen tree trunk, looked out across the frozen expanse.

"I miss her a lot," she said. "Everybody at the office misses her too. I really wish you guys could come back up here."

"Yeah?" Ben asked. He sat down next to her. "Do you think Sara would want to come back?"

Melanie turned to face him, and cocked her head quizzically.

"Because I'd move back in a heartbeat. I'm sure I could get back my job at Jack's. Maybe teach at Coconino Community College. I know it wouldn't pay as much as Frank does, but at least we'd be home. I heard there might be an opening coming up at the museum." Ben hadn't considered this before. Maybe Sara wasn't as happy in Phoenix as she thought she would be. Maybe he could convince her to come back.

Melanie laughed a small, sad laugh. "I don't think that's going to happen."

"Why not?" Ben asked, though he knew exactly why not. Jesus. What had Sara told Melanie? What did she know?

"You made your bed, Benny," Melanie said, patting his back and smiling at him with eyes full of pity. "And I think now you're all lying in it."

After Sara finally got up, they all went to MartAnne's Burrito Palace for brunch. It was a cramped restaurant, with only a handful of tables and one cook working behind the small counter. There was art by local artists hung crookedly on the deep red walls. It smelled like refried beans, like cilantro and onions. After brunch, the girls were going to go get pedicures at the mall and go shopping for maternity clothes.

Melanie and Sara both ordered huevos rancheros, but Ben wasn't hungry. He ordered coffee, drank cup after cup. The wait was long; they had been sitting at their table for nearly an hour by the time the waitress brought them their food. Maude was outside, napping on the cold pavement. Ben kept bringing her water while Melanie and Sara caught up. He hadn't seen Sara this happy in a while. She missed Melanie; he knew this.

"Hey, do you mind if I run up the street to Jack's while you guys eat?" he asked.

Sara was telling Melanie about the hospital, about Emma. She looked at him as though she'd forgotten he was there, and tucked a piece of hair behind her ear. She nodded, though he knew this meant she was worried. That she didn't trust him. He took her hand. "I promise I'll be right back."

He drank the last swallow of his coffee and put his coat back on. He kissed the top of Sara's head and went outside. He untied Maude from the bike rack and said, "Come on, girl, let's go see Hippo."

Jack's was empty except for Leroy from upstairs, who looked like he'd already tied one on. "Hey!" he grumbled at Ben.

"Hey, Leroy!" Ben said, smacking him on the back.

"Where you been?" Leroy said.

"I'm down in Phoenix," Ben said, sitting next to him at the bar.

"Whatcha wanna go and do that for?" he said, scowling at Ben.

Ben laughed. He looked around the bar; nothing had changed since he left.

Hippo came through the swinging kitchen doors with a giant breakfast burrito, which he put down in front of Leroy.

"This ain't got no goddamned guacamole, does it?" Leroy asked.

"No guac, Leroy," Hippo said and shook Ben's hand across the bar. "Bailey! How's P-town?"

Ben stretched and yawned. "Hot."

"How's Sara?" he asked. "When's she due again?"

Ben had waited until he gave his notice at the bar before he told Hippo and Ned about the baby. He'd felt then like he had to have some sort of explanation for ditching his life in Flagstaff. Surprisingly, neither one of them had seemed shocked.

"July," Ben said. And then smiling, he said, "It's a girl."

"Right on," Hippo said. "You still waiting on the wedding?"

God, the wedding. With all of the fuss about the baby, Sara had barely mentioned the wedding. They'd set the date for the end of August, but they hadn't done anything beyond setting the date and reserving Hart Prairie Lodge.

"End of the summer. I'll let you know."

"Emily and I are getting hitched too," Hippo said.

"You are?" Ben said. Emily and Hippo had been together for ages. He figured they'd be one of those couples who lived happily ever after without ever getting married. "That's great!"

Hippo turned around and poured three shots of tequila, lined them up on the bar: one for each of them. "Well, cheers all around!" Hippo said and they all held up their shot glasses. It was ten o'clock in the morning. Shit. But the tequila felt warm and good. Maude curled up at Ben's feet and fell asleep.

"You read the news about that kid?" Hippo asked.

Ben's chest tightened. "I saw something that said they're questioning the frat guys at that party. Looks like Lucky might have tipped off the cops."

"Damn, you *have* been gone," Hippo said.

"Huh?"

"Lucky got the shit beat out of him. He's been at the hospital since last weekend."

"What?"

"He was leaving work last Friday night and got jumped in the parking lot. The produce delivery guys found him a couple of hours later behind the Dumpster."

"Jesus Christ," Ben said. The tequila had made his chest hot, his head thick.

"Guess somebody didn't appreciate his tip," Hippo said. "One of the kids in that fraternity has a dad in politics. Probably some of his fucking goons."

"Bello," Ben said. "The kid's name is Joe Bello."

Somehow, Ben convinced Sara that he needed to stop by school to deal with some paperwork in Human Resources, tax stuff, while she and Melanie were at the mall. Despite what Melanie had alluded to during their walk, neither one of them seemed remotely suspicious as he dropped them off at the mall entrance.

"Just call when you want me to come get you," he said through the open window. "It shouldn't take me more than an hour."

"You sure you don't need a pedi? A manny mani?" Melanie asked, smiling.

"I probably do, but maybe the next time," Ben said, laughing. He rolled up the window and pulled out of the parking lot.

He knew he couldn't call Shadi from his cell phone. He was pretty sure his cell had become public domain, and any calls, especially calls to an unfamiliar cell number, would sound the alarms.

Before this, his plan had just been to get Shadi to cancel the appointment with Sara. It would have been simple enough. A call from a pay phone, a message left on her voice mail.

But as he drove back through town, he thought about Lucky walking out of the restaurant, not suspecting anything and then getting pummeled. Anyone who could do that, or have that done, probably wouldn't hesitate to do it again. To anyone who knew more than they should about that night. To him. To Shadi.

He needed to go to her, to let her know that she might be in danger. He needed to warn her. He needed to make sure she was safe. That was all. And then he would go.

Traffic was slow on Fort Valley Road. Melanie had said there was some sort of festival going on at the museum. And a zillion skiers were headed to the mountain. He was behind a pickup truck with about five guys in full Native costume sitting in the back with several large drums. One of the men, wearing a feathered headdress and knee-high moccasins, beat slowly on his drum. Ben rolled down his window and listened. They were chanting, singing. It was haunting, beautiful. The San Francisco Peaks rose up ahead of them like monoliths. As the cars crawled, Ben closed his eyes for just a moment, listened to the slow, aching music.

He felt something buzzing in his pocket and remembered he'd set his phone to vibrate when he and Melanie went out for their walk. He pulled the phone out. It was Melanie's number. Shit. He'd just dropped them off twenty minutes ago.

"Hello?" he said.

"It's Melanie. You need to come pick us up."

"What's the matter?" he asked.

"Ben, just get here."

Ben pulled up to the front entrance to the mall, and Sara and Melanie were sitting outside on a bench. Melanie ran to the car and Ben opened the door. "Come help me," she said.

Sara's face was colorless, her eyes wide and terrified. She stood up slowly, and Ben's stomach dropped. There was blood on her pants. Not a lot, but it was a bright red blossom.

"Here, sweetie, get in the backseat and just lie down," Melanie said.

Ben got in the driver's seat, and his head started to pound, blood rushing in his ears like the sound of drums.

In the emergency room, they whisked Sara away into triage, and Melanie and Ben stayed behind in the waiting room.

"Was she having any pains?" Ben asked, pacing.

Melanie shook her head, glanced at the TV that was blaring from the wall mount. A basketball game. She scowled at the man who had turned the volume up, and he clicked the remote to bring the volume back down.

"Do you think the baby is okay?" Ben asked. Melanie was a nurse. She would know. She'd probably seen this before. He waited for her to assure him that everything would be okay. With the baby. With Sara.

"She's only twenty-three weeks. It's too early," she said. Her voice was cracking. "If she loses this baby, it'll kill her."

The nurse came into the waiting room and said, "Mr. Bailey?"

Ben and Melanie both stood up.

Dr. Chandra, a soft-spoken Indian woman with tiny hands, sat Ben down in the room where Sara was now in a hospital gown, lying on a bed with an IV attached to her arm.

"Usually what happens during pregnancy is that the placenta moves away from the cervix as the uterus grows. If it doesn't happen, the cervix can become blocked by the placenta. We call this *placenta previa*."

Sara's hand fluttered near her mouth.

"In your case, Sara, the cervix is partially blocked. Your OB/GYN in Phoenix is going to need to monitor your pregnancy very closely, because there are a lot of complications that can arise from this, including premature birth. He may want to put you on bed rest until your due date. Because you've had some bleeding, I am going to keep you overnight to make sure we've got it under control. And I want you to see your doctor in Phoenix on Monday morning so that he can begin to monitor your condition."

Ben reached for Sara's hand and squeezed it. Her skin was cold.

"Am I going to lose the baby?" she said quietly.

The doctor frowned. "This is serious, but the good news is that now we are aware of it. It's most dangerous when it goes undiagnosed. We know you've got the problem, so we can take all the necessary precautions before you go into labor."

"You didn't answer my question," Sara said.

"We're going to take good care of you and your baby. It's important for you to understand that this can be just as dangerous for you as it is for the baby. Your only job is to rest."

Melanie drove the Camry back to Kachina to get pajamas and Sara's toiletry bag, leaving Ben with Sara at the hospital.

Sara was restless, fidgety. "I'm scared, Ben," she said.

"It's going to be okay. Everything will be fine. We just need to do what the doctor said. When we get home, you'll rest. We'll set you up by the pool for the next few months. Just think of the tan you'll have." He smiled at her.

"What if we lose her?" she said, her voice breaking as she stared at her hands, which were folded across her belly.

"We won't," Ben said. And suddenly, for the first time it struck him: The baby might not survive. Even Sara might not survive this. "I won't let anything happen to either of you. I promise."

Sara looked up at him, her face worried and pale. He stood up from his chair and went to her, lay down next to her in the bed and held on to her. After a while he pulled away and pressed his hand gently against her stomach.

It felt like a wave, like some slow-moving current beneath her skin. He pressed his palm just a bit harder, thinking he must have imagined it. His heart was in his throat.

"Did you feel her?" Sara asked, her eyes brightening.

"I don't know," Ben said. He leaned down and pressed his cheek softly against her belly, and closed his eyes. Like a current of electricity, like a shiver. He turned his face so that his lips were grazing the cool cotton hospital gown. "Hi, baby," he said and felt his throat swell. "I love you, little one. Everything's going to be okay."

B en stayed.

He didn't leave Sara's room even to get dinner. Melanie brought some Mexican food from Ralberto's and he ate while Sara slept. He was ravenous and devoured the chili relleno burrito in just a few bites. The nurses set him up with some blankets and a reclining chair, and surprisingly, within moments after Sara closed her eyes and drifted off to sleep, Ben felt his own eyelids grow heavy as well.

He dreamed a game of hide-and-seek. A memory pushed through the narrow tunnel of sleep, distorted and compressed, but vivid. Twisted, but real enough to make his hands twitch, his eyes dance behind closed lids.

During the school year, the bus would drop Ben and Dusty off at home an hour before his mother got home from work. They, and all the other latchkey kids, would go straight from the bus stop to the woods by the creek, dropping their backpacks on their respective porches on the way. In the winter, the woods seemed small; in the absence of leaves, you could see all the way through the plot of land to the main road beyond. But in the late spring, when the foliage grew in, dense and green, it became larger, deeper, both disorienting and enormous. It was a place with a thousand spots to hide.

The air smelled of summer: honeysuckle, grass, breeze. The sun was hot, and his T-shirt stuck to his back. Ben was in the fifth grade and Dusty was in kindergarten. It was June; school was almost over for the year.

Before Dusty had started school and their mom went back to work, Ben played with Charlie and Ethan, dragging big sticks around, pretending they were swords or light sabers. They'd dig holes in the dirt, looking for treasures, like Indiana Jones. They built forts out of the trash they found: hubcaps and car doors and cardboard boxes. Now, Ben was in charge of Dusty after school, and so she came along.

Dusty loved the woods. She loved the gnarled roots and twisty trees. She was a good climber, a real monkey. She could shinny up the flagpole at school, up the doorways at home. She was tough, as tough as Ben. She never cried when she got hurt; she picked herself up when she fell down, brushed herself off, and kept playing. While the other neighborhood girls played with their Barbies at the edge of the creek, Dusty only wanted to play hide-and-seek with Ben and his friends. And because it was Ben's little sister, because it was Dusty, they relented.

Dusty pressed her hands against her eyes, and her whole body against the trunk of a tree, and counted. *One Mississippi, two Mississippi . . .*

And they scattered and hid. Dusty was good at hiding but terrible at seeking. It always took her forever to find the boys who disguised themselves in the limbs of trees, behind giant rocks, and inside bushes. "You're it!" she'd squeal at Ben, who inevitably had to give himself away to somehow end her turn.

Today, Ben counted extra slowly to give Dusty time to find a good spot to hide. *One Mississippi . . .* he drawled. *Two Mississippi . . .* When he got to *Twenty, ready or not, here I come . . .* they were all gone.

He found Charlie first, who had gotten distracted by an anthill behind a tree. It took longer to find Ethan; he was in the upper limbs of a giant oak tree, his face hidden by the leaves.

"I wonder where Dusty is," he said loudly. "I can't find her anywhere. . . ." He pretended to look under rocks and behind twigs, just in case she was watching.

"Dusty!" he hollered after he'd looked in all of her usual spots. "Come out, come out wherever you are!" He waited, anticipated her popping out from behind a tree, swinging down through the branches, bounding through the brush, gleeful that she'd managed to elude him. "Come out, come out wherever you are!" he yelled again. Ethan and Joe had gone onto other things, tossing a Frisbee, smacking it against the trees.

"Dusty!" Ben hollered again as he retraced his

footsteps, searching all of the spots he'd already found empty.

The air was humid, thick. He was really sweating now as he ran deeper into the woods. His mother had said they were allowed to play in the woods as long as they stayed away from the creek and the place where the woods opened up to the main road. "Dusty!" he cried out, the faint trace of fear starting to spread through his arms and legs, slowing him down. He didn't know which way to go: to the creek or to the road. Bad things could happen at both places. His throat was swollen.

"I give up!" he yelled. "You win!"

The air was still and heavy, but there was so much noise. He listened for her voice, but all he could hear was the racket the birds made, the rushing water of the creek, the remote hum of the traffic in the distance.

Now that he'd stopped running, his heart was thudding in his chest like beans in the coffee can shakers they made in music class. It felt as if his heart had come loose and was rattling around inside his torso.

He started running again, toward the creek first to see if she'd gotten bored and found the other little girls who had set up their Barbies at the edge of the creek to pretend it was the beach. He imagined how he'd reprimand her for going where she wasn't supposed to. But the twins,

Amy and Anna, shook their heads when he asked if they had seen her.

The road. His sneakers pounded against the earth like drums, the air whooshed in his ears, and his temples pounded with each footstep. His mind began to race, shuffling the possibilities like cards. She'd broken a leg, encountered a bear, gotten trapped under a rock. She was lost. She was stolen.

His class had gone to the "Stranger Danger" assembly early in the year, but the kindergartners didn't go. She didn't know about strangers yet. He blinked the sweat out of his eyes and wiped his forehead with the back of his hand. His vision blurred again, and he pictured a man, the Stranger. When he thought about Strangers, they wore dark hooded sweatshirts, masks over their faces, even though Principal Pendergast told them that strangers look just like everyone else. Dusty wouldn't know not to get in someone's car. She wouldn't know to scream as loud as she could.

By the time he got to the far end of the woods, it felt as though his head might explode with all the bad thoughts. His lungs ached. His heart ached.

Then he heard her. It could have just been a bird, the sound was so small.

"Ben," it said. *She* said.

And Ben started running toward her.

"Look," she said as he saw the flash of red of her T-shirt. "Look what I found."

She was standing near the edge of the woods, and cars were rushing past them just beyond.

She held out her hand as he ran toward her, and he could see that she was holding a tiny pink pebble in her hand. "Look, Ben, isn't it pretty?"

Ben was shaking now, with relief and happiness and anger.

"You're so stupid!" he yelled at her. "Mom said we're not supposed to go this far in the woods. See those cars there! A stranger could have taken you in their car and we'd never see you again."

Dusty looked up at him from the tiny pink pebble. Her bottom lip trembled, and tears started to roll down her cheeks as Ben continued to yell.

"I looked everywhere for you! Mom is going to be so mad. God, you're so stupid." But even as he yelled at her, the buzzing current of anger and fear shorted out.

"I'm sorry, Benny," Dusty said. And then she extended her hand out to him, opening her palm with the little pink stone, offering it to him. "You can have this if you want. Just don't be mad at me anymore."

Even as Ben's heart pinged with happiness and relief, he grabbed her hand and pulled her behind him all the way back home. She cried and stumbled and tripped, and he just kept pulling. By the time they got to their backyard, her face was streaked with tears, and they were both drenched in sweat.

"Don't you ever, ever scare me like that again," he said.

"I won't, Benny. I promise," she said, crossing her heart. "Hope to die. Stick a needle in my eye."

The next morning, when he woke up, rubbing the sleep from his eyes, the first thing he saw was the pink pebble sitting on his nightstand next to his geode from the Natural History Museum and his baseball mitt. *Hope to die.*

Ben awoke with a neck so stiff he could barely turn it to either side. He rubbed his hand along the taut muscle and turned to the hospital bed where Sara lay curled up like a child. The blinds were closed, but he could see that it was still dark outside. The bright lights from the parking lot cast a strange haze.

He went to Sara and stroked her face with his hand. He leaned over and kissed her cheek, his neck screaming with the effort. She didn't stir.

He opened and closed the door softly, his boots squeaking on the linoleum floor. He turned back to make sure they hadn't woken her, and she remained in the same position. She was exhausted, he figured. Her body, the baby, needed to rest.

He'd spoken with Frank the night before, and Frank had offered to drive up from Phoenix in the morning. Ben told him they would be heading back down to the valley by Sunday night; it wasn't necessary, but Frank had insisted. "We can drive her back home in the Range Rover. It'll be a lot more comfortable than the Camry."

Ben glanced at his watch when he reached the hallway. It was four thirty A.M. He suspected Frank and Jeanine were probably already on their way.

"Can you tell me how to get to the ICU from here?" he asked one of the nurses staffing the station.

"Ms. Harmon isn't in the ICU," she said. Confused.

"I know," he said. "I have a friend I need to check in on."

"If you tell me his name . . . her name?" the nurse asked, wriggling the mouse of the computer.

"It's okay," he said, realizing as he spoke that he didn't even know Lucky's real name, his last name. "I'll find him."

Hospitals during the day made Ben uneasy, but hospitals in the middle of the night were something else entirely. The pale light and green walls made him feel as though he were underwater, swimming through some murky netherworld.

He navigated the dim labyrinthine corridors of the hospital, arriving finally at the ICU waiting room where he'd first met Shadi. He almost expected she'd be waiting there in her paint-splattered overalls. But the room was empty except for a nurse who sat quietly reading in the half-light behind the desk.

"Excuse me," he said. "I was wondering if you could tell me if there's a patient here named Lucky?" he asked. "A young Navajo kid? I think he was admitted about a week ago."

The nurse nodded. "Mr. Yellowhawk was only

in ICU for a night, and I believe he was discharged this morning."

"He's okay?" Ben asked, feeling the pain in his neck lessen.

"Well enough to go home." She smiled sadly. "His father took him back to Tuba City."

Ben felt a sharp pang. He nodded. "Thank you," he said and started to walk away. He stopped and turned around. The nurse had returned to her book. "Do you know if the police know who did this to him?"

She shook her head. "I'm sorry, I don't know."

Ben stretched his neck from side to side as he made his way back through the hospital to Sara's room. He had really hoped he would be able to talk to Lucky. To hear his side of the story, to find out, if he could, who might have done this to him. From what Hippo had said, this didn't sound like some stupid frat-boy prank. This sounded serious. Somebody really didn't want him talking to the police. Now he was back on the rez, and chances were he wouldn't be talking to anyone about what happened. Without Lucky, there was no witness, at least not one willing to talk, to what happened to Ricky.

By the time he got back to Sara's room, Jeanine and Frank were already there. Jeanine was sitting next to the bed, holding Sara's hand. Sara was awake, sitting up. Frank was standing at the foot of the bed doling out to-go cups of coffee.

"Honey," he said, handing Jeanine a cup.

He checked the label. "Decaf vanilla latte for my girl. And regular coffee, black, for the doctor," he said, handing Ben a cup.

"Thanks, Frank," he said.

"What time are they setting you free?" Frank asked Sara.

"I think as soon as I'm ready to go," Sara said. "Ben, we still have that appointment with the artist today. Can you just meet with her? I have the fabric swatches from the crib bedding. You know what I'm thinking about."

The muscles in Ben's neck throbbed. "Forget about that," he said, and shook his head. "I'll follow you guys home, make sure you're okay."

"It's okay," Sara said. "I'm *fine*. Mom and Dad can stay with me at the house until you get home."

Ben rubbed his temples.

"We were supposed to meet her at La Bellavia at ten o'clock," Sara said, reaching for her purse. She pulled out the magazine article and an envelope of paint and fabric samples. "This is what she looks like," Sara said. "So you can find her."

Ben nodded, rubbing and rubbing his neck.

"I'll be *fine*," she said and motioned for him to come to her.

He leaned over the bed and kissed her eyelids as she closed her eyes.

La Bellavia was busy. Sunday morning brunch always meant a good twenty-minute wait, the line snaking outside. At least it was sunny today, the air frigid but the sky clear and bright. Ben could feel every single nerve ending as he stood on the sidewalk, waiting for Shadi.

He had considered telling Sara that Shadi had canceled, and just not showing up to meet her. He thought about taking a hike on Mount Elden with Maude, disappearing into the forest until it was time to go home. But Shadi would probably call Sara, would wonder why she hadn't shown up. They could always reschedule, and then it would start all over again. On top of that, Lucky was gone. And someone had made sure that he wouldn't be coming back. He needed to make sure Shadi was safe. He had to do this. He would meet her, and then he would go home. He wasn't doing anything wrong.

He tied Maude's leash to a bike rack and squatted down to pat her head. "If you're good, I'll give you my leftovers," he said, rubbing the backs of her ears.

When he stood up again, he saw Shadi riding down the street on her bicycle toward him. Sunlight in her hair.

She stopped the bike just short of him.

"Hi," he said.

She shook her head and glanced around as if Sara might be around the corner.

"She's not here," he said.

"What are you doing here? I thought you moved."

"Sara is the one who called you about commissioning the rug. I tried to get her to stop. I was going to call you yesterday, but then she was in the hospital, and shit. I'm sorry." He moved toward her, his body having a will of its own.

She stepped back. "Is everything okay? With the baby?"

The baby. "Yes." He nodded. "She's okay. They're okay."

"That was *your* Sara?" she asked, sighing. "The answering machine didn't say your names. I didn't know. God."

"I know," Ben said. "I'm sorry."

"Should we go inside?" she asked as the line crept forward.

"Yeah," he said. "I really need to talk to you."

They were seated at a small wooden table near the front door. Every time someone came into the restaurant, a blast of cold air engulfed them. They both kept their coats on. It was loud: dishes clanking, people talking, the pale din of music. After the waitress took their orders, Ben said, "Did you hear about Lucky?"

Shadi nodded and looked down. She was fiddling with a packet of sugar. "I went to the hospital to see him."

"You did?" Ben asked. "Was he okay?"

She nodded. "They broke his collarbone, and his arm. He was only in the ICU for a night. For observation. He had a concussion. I saw him after they put him in a regular room."

"Did he tell you who did this?" Ben asked.

She shook her head. "He said he couldn't remember much. The guys had masks. There were three of them, and they had bats. He said they told him he'd better keep his mouth shut."

"Was it Mark Fitch?" Ben whispered.

She shook her head again. "Lucky said they were older guys, big guys. It sounds crazy, but he thinks somebody must have hired them. He's scared, Ben. He went back home to the rez. He said he didn't want to wind up like Ricky."

Ben watched Shadi's hands; she was folding the corners of the sugar packet, tearing at the edges. She was trembling. "I'm scared too. I'm thinking of going home."

"What?" he asked. "To Chinle?" He watched as his hands reached out and enclosed hers. "You can't go."

He let himself look at her face then; he'd been avoiding it since they sat down.

Shadi's eyes darted nervously, as if she were trying to figure something out.

"You know, Ricky used to trust everyone. Someone would tell him something and he would believe them. He was gullible. The other children, when he was in school, could always play tricks on him. He always wanted to believe what they said was the truth, and they knew they could fool him. But me, I never believed anyone. I never trusted anyone. I know how cruel people can be."

Ben waited.

"You're not a bad man, Ben, but you're doing bad things. Sara trusts you, believes you, and you keep betraying her."

Ben started to shake his head. "You don't understand. I just want to help you."

"The only way you can help me now is to leave me," Shadi said. "You don't *get* it. You're so selfish, you don't even know you're breaking *two* hearts."

The waitress came then with their breakfast; both had ordered the Swedish oat pancakes. The smell was too sweet, too heady. Ben looked at his plate and then out the window.

"Can I get you anything else?"

"No, thank you," they both said.

They ate quietly, the heavy pancakes settling like stones in Ben's stomach. He took a sip of his coffee, which was hot and bitter.

"When would you go?" he asked. "To Chinle?"

"I don't know. Probably as soon as school gets

out in May. But I'm really only working on my thesis now. I have two classes that meet once a week. I could commute if I had to, borrow my uncle's car."

"But you have the exhibit at the museum," he said.

"I know."

"What would you even do there?" he asked.

"I'll keep making my blankets and rugs," she said. "I could teach at the high school."

Shadi looked out the window. Her eyes looked tired.

"You can't let them make you leave," he said.

"What?"

"You can't let these assholes force you out of your home. You can't let them win." He reached for her hand and held on tight.

The front door of the restaurant opened, letting in another cold blast of air.

"Hey," the kid said, smirking. "Professor Bailey."

Any other time, the kid's name would have escaped him. It would have been lost in the deep folds of Ben's memory. But not today.

"Joe," he said, nodding, quickly letting go of Shadi's hand.

Joe Bello came over to the table and pulled off his baseball cap. His mop of blond hair had grown since Ben had last seen him.

"What's up?" Joe said, extending his hand to Ben.

Ben reluctantly shook it.

"And this is?" he asked, cocking his head and extending his hand to Shadi.

"Shadi Begay," she said before Ben could stop her.

Joe shook her hand really slowly, studying her face. If Ben didn't know better, he'd think he was just appraising her, just flirting. Ben could almost hear the gears clicking inside his brain. *Begay. Begay.* "Pleased to meet you," he said to her.

Turning to Ben, he said, "Hey, I wanted to say I was sorry for what happened last semester. My dad can get a little crazy." That sly smile never left his face. "I heard they let you go."

Ben shook his head. "I got a job in the valley."

Joe nodded. "That's cool."

A rush of cold air came in as the door opened again.

"Hey, dude!" Mark Fitch slapped Joe on the back.

"Fitch," Joe said. "I want to introduce you to somebody. This is my old prof, Ben Bailey. He's the guy with that red mint '52 Chevy pickup." He nodded at Fitch and then said, "Hey, where's your truck? I didn't see it outside."

Fitch held out his hand to shake Ben's; Ben felt the cold all the way into the hollows of his bones. He imagined Mark Fitch digging his key into the side of his truck. He imagined him smashing his fist into Ricky's face, his boots into Ricky's ribs.

Shadi kicked Ben hard under the table, and the pain radiated up his shin like an electric current.

"And this," Joe said, his smirk spreading into a sinister smile, "is Shadi. Shadi *Begay*."

At work the next morning, Ben closed the door to his office and turned on his computer. It took forever for it to come on, and he paced back and forth, listless and listening to the hums and clicks as it came to life.

He'd been reeling since breakfast at La Bellavia. After Joe Bello and Mark Fitch got a table, the color had left Shadi's face.

"Can we please go?" she'd asked.

He'd pulled a twenty from his wallet and put it on the table, not even bothering to wait for the check. Outside, he'd walked with her to her bicycle, but her fingers had been shaking too hard to unlock it.

"Damn it," she said.

"Here, let me. What's the combination?" he asked. "Are you okay?"

"Ben, go *home*. Just forget about this. About me. About Ricky," she said. Her eyes pleaded with him. "Can't you see it's just getting worse?"

She leaned into him then as if to give him a quick hug, but when their bodies touched, Ben couldn't let go. He buried his face in the sweet darkness of her hair, could feel the heat of her skin on his nose. And the longer he held on, the less she resisted. He felt her body yield, felt her beginning to return the embrace. His lips grazed the leather choker on her neck, and she trembled. She pulled away and got on her bike.

Her eyes were wet, but her face was stern. "Promise you'll stop."

Ben closed his eyes and nodded. "I will. But you have to promise me you won't leave. That you won't let them win. This is your home. They can't take that from you."

Shadi laughed and shook her head sadly. "For a history professor, you certainly don't know your history very well, do you?"

Ben felt like he'd been punched.

"Good-bye," she said, more an order than a farewell.

And then she was riding away on the bicycle, becoming smaller and smaller, until she turned the corner and was gone.

It took every ounce of strength that he had not to follow her. He got in the Camry and revved the engine against the cold. Now he barely remembered the drive down to Phoenix. He was on autopilot, his body remembering how to shift and brake and steer while his mind was otherwise engaged.

He didn't remember parking the car in the driveway, or the conversation with Jeanine, who was cleaning their kitchen while Sara slept. He barely remembered whispering, "Good night," into Sara's ear before he lay down next to her to sleep.

Now he was wide awake, his mind ticking off what he knew.

It wouldn't take much for these guys to put it all together, if they hadn't already. Ben Bailey, *Detective Bailey—Jesus—*, who'd called Fitch about the truck. Shadi Begay, Ricky Begay's big sister. Even the girlfriend, Jenny, might put two and two together about their conversation in the bar that night. One call to daddy (*sorry, my dad can get a little crazy*), and who knew what might happen?

He was in danger. And now so was Shadi.

The computer prompted Ben for his password, but he was typing too quickly and made a mistake. He willed his fingers to slow down. The computer came to life, and he opened up a browser, went to Google, and entered slowly: *Martin Bello Arizona.*

It didn't take long to find him. He was all over the Web. The Arizona State House of Reps. The charity 10Ks and even the Bello family home page with pictures of the whole clan. The image search yielded a number of photos, and in all of them he looked almost exactly the same. Tan skin, white hair. A wide, square face with small, deep-set brown eyes. Thin lips. The same smugness he'd seen in Joe's face.

He kept searching. *NAU alumnus and major donor. MBA from ASU.*

Ben returned to the state site. There he was

again, an older version of his son, red tie, black suit. From what Ben could gather as his eyes darted through the paragraphs, and his mouse scrolled down through the pages, Martin Bello was an Arizona native, born and raised in Prescott. After business school, he'd stayed in Phoenix and became a real estate developer. He was responsible for the development of more than one hundred condominium and town house complexes in the Scottsdale and Paradise Valley area. He was a Republican, serving his third term in the Arizona State House of Representatives. Three years ago he had put in a bid for state senate but had lost. His ambitions now were of the gubernatorial sort.

Frank hadn't been dicking around. He *was* running for governor. Christ.

Ben left the site and Googled Bello's name again. More political stuff, including a campaign site. Some real estate pages. And then here, a transcript of a public meeting regarding the development of a condominium complex near the Snowbowl in Flagstaff. Ben vaguely remembered this from years ago. It was back when the Snowbowl had first started talking about using reclaimed water to make snow. The Native Americans had been fighting it ever since, arguing that the San Francisco Peaks are sacred to their religion and that the use of reclaimed water was a desecration. He remembered someone comparing it to asking Catholics to use toilet water as holy water. The opponents argued that without snowmaking, the tourism industry in Flagstaff would die.

Ben knew how a bad snow season could affect the economy in Flagstaff. There had been several barren winters in a row when Jack's was virtually empty every night. Just the locals buying their cheap beer and well drinks. Without snow, there were no skiers. Without skiers, there was no tourism. Without tourism, there was no money coming through town. And without tourism, there would certainly be no need for a bunch of brand-new condos. From what Ben could glean from the transcript, Martin Bello had a huge interest in snow-making at the Snowbowl.

He Googled the words *snowmaking snowbowl flagstaff* and found a zillion sites discussing the controversy: article after article after article.

The Snowbowl, though privately owned, is on national forest land, making this anyone, *everyone's* game. The Navajo and Hopi, who performed religious ceremonies on the Peaks, claimed that the use of reclaimed water to make snow disregarded their rights as defined by the Religious Freedom Restoration Act. The environmentalists were worried about the safety and environmental impact of using treated sewage water to make snow. But for the business owners, people like Martin Bello, it all came down to money.

Ben searched for *Bello* on this page and sure enough, there he was: "As my voting record shows, I have the utmost respect for the Native population in Arizona. I have consistently voted in favor of the rights of indigenous people. However, it seems to me that the decision of the 9th U.S. Circuit Court of Appeals to overturn its original denial of the Snowbowl's right to make snow is for the greater good of this city. And an appeal to the U.S. Supreme Court seems inappropriate."

Bello had a hell of a lot more to worry about than selling condos. It certainly wouldn't help his campaign for governor if his son were arrested in the beating death of one such *indigenous* person.

Despite the cool blast of air from the AC vent, Ben was sweating. He closed down his browser and went to get a cup of water from the cooler. Bello was clearly a powerful guy, well connected, with a lot at stake. Ben had no idea how far he was willing to go to keep all of this quiet, but if what happened to Lucky was any indication, then Ben knew that Shadi was probably wise to return home to Chinle, and, if he was smart too, he'd just pretend this had never happened.

But Ben's stomach roiled at the thought of letting go. Acid rose in his throat, and he swallowed more water to make it go back down. He needed to do something, but he had no idea what. This wasn't about Shadi anymore, no matter what she thought or said. This was about corruption and greed. *Murder*.

Ben felt his chest swell with purpose. He would make everything right again. Even if it meant breaking his promise to Shadi. To Sara.

BLACK AND WHITE WORLD

Sara slept. Like a Grimm's fairy-tale princess, she lay prone, flitting in and out of sleep. During the day, she rested by the pool, a pitcher of ice water sweating beside her. In the afternoons, when the sun became too hot, she moved to the living room, where she lay prostrate on the couch. Then, by early evening, when the sky turned orange and pink and the air cooled, she retired to the bedroom, where the ceiling fan spun lazily above her.

It was a life of strange repose.

But while Sara rested, Ben schemed. While she lay in languor, Ben found himself restless. Wide awake and buzzing with a renewed sense of purpose. He had started getting up at five and swimming for an hour every morning. In the pool was where he did his best thinking. The cold water cleared his head, and the rhythmic strokes were meditative. In the cool green depths of the water, he was formulating his plan. As he did the back stroke, the side stroke, the breast stroke, he was ruminating, contemplating, planning. Every morning for the last two weeks he had slipped into the pool, and as his arms and legs and lungs worked, his mind was free to strategize. He knew he could not be rash. He would not make the error of impatience, of impulsiveness again.

He could not go to the police, not yet. Clearly, they had made little to no headway with their investigation, and when Lucky had tipped off the police, he'd wound up in the hospital. Shadi had told him that Lucky did not plan to press charges. At this point, Ben was pretty sure that Mark Fitch and Joe Bello both knew that he was involved somehow, and he was also certain that one false step on his part might have devastating consequences. For him. And for Shadi.

He knew that ultimately what he needed was to find another witness, someone else who had been there. If he could find just one person at the party to speak up, one of *them,* to come forward, then maybe the police would listen. Maybe then everything would be exposed. He had to believe that Lucky had been wrong, that justice *was* possible, even for someone like Ricky. He had to believe that there was someone at the party who had a conscience. Someone else who wasn't sleeping at night because of what they knew. He just had to find that person.

"What are you doing?" he asked Sara. "Shopping?"

Ben had told Sara that Shadi had a family emergency and had to return to the reservation. She would not be able to make the rug. Sara had been shopping for one online ever since.

She was lying on a lawn chair, clicking on her

laptop, as he emerged from the pool and grabbed his towel. Her skin was turning a soft gold from all of the sun. Her hair bleaching out to a pale butter color. Her belly was a small bump now, like half of a basketball inside her bathing suit.

"Just chatting," she said.

"With?" he asked, rubbing the towel across his head and then wrapping it around his waist.

"This girl Laney," she said, looking up at him. "She's due the same week that I am, and she's on bed rest too."

"Huh," Ben said. "Where does she live?"

"California somewhere. Sacramento, I think."

"What do you talk about?"

"I don't know." She shrugged. "Baby stuff. Other stuff. She's having a rough time because her husband just got deployed to Iraq. She's living with her sister, but her sister works sixty hours a week, and she's all by herself all day long. She's got preeclampsia, and she's really scared. I just try to distract her, I guess." Sara shrugged again. "Keep her company."

As difficult as working at the hospital had been for Sara, he knew she missed it. For the first week after she was mandated to stay in bed, she talked about the hospital all the time. She talked about Emma. She was still in touch with Emma's mother, who had invited Sara to the memorial service. He knew she had wanted to be there. He'd brought flowers to her that day after work:

a bouquet of pink roses that had since shrugged off their petals and sat wilting in a vase on the kitchen counter. Without nursing, and stuck in bed, Sara was at a loss as to how to bide her time. All the energy that went into taking care of people had nowhere to go.

Her mother brought her books by the dozen from the library and an armload of magazines, but she soon grew bored with the stories and tired of the tabloids. Melanie came the first weekend and tried to teach Sara how to knit, but she was frustrated when the stitches slipped and gave up as soon as Melanie went back home, the scarf unraveling into a fuzzy purple mess. She watched movie after movie but usually fell asleep before they ended.

Finally, when her birthday came a week later, her father had wrapped up a pretty pink laptop in a pretty pink ribbon, arranged for wireless service to be installed in the house, and it was like a prince's kiss. Now she shopped for baby things online, squandered hours on Facebook, and chatted in virtual rooms with other women who were lying in their own beds all over the world. He imagined a network of these sleeping beauties, all lying in wait as the babies inside them incubated.

"You should start your own Web site or something, a blog maybe. There must be a lot of women on bed rest."

"That is a *great* idea," she said, her eyes widening. She looked at him in disbelief. "I mean, a really, really good idea. I could call it . . ." She clapped her hands together. *"Bedtime Stories!"*

Ben shook his wet hair and wiped his feet off before stepping through the sliding glass doors into the kitchen. He could hear Sara's fingers furiously tapping even after he slid the doors closed.

Now they both had a project. And Sara would be occupied while he figured out where to go from here.

Frank had handed the reins over to Ben at the dealership but still came by every Friday afternoon to check in on him and the rest of the staff and then take Ben out for a long lunch. Most Fridays they got back so late, Ben just had time to grab his stuff and head back home. This week, Friday could not come soon enough. Before Ben did anything, he wanted to get more of a sense of exactly who he was dealing with, what sort of man this Martin Bello was, though he certainly had his suspicions. Ben knew that Frank was in the know in Arizona politics. He and Jeanine had been huge supporters of McCain throughout the years and, according to Jeanine, Cindy even called her once for advice on flower arrangements after attending a fund-raiser hosted by the Harmons at their house. Getting the dirt on a little guy like Bello would be nothing. If he could just figure out how to slip it into the conversation.

"Dr. Bailey," Frank said, ushering him ahead of him into the restaurant. Usually they went to Chili's, but today, Frank had insisted on driving all the way to the Pointe Hilton at Tapatio Cliffs. He said he was craving their shrimp scampi, and a plate of Texas cheese fries would not cut it.

The resort was breathtaking. Like Disneyland

for grown-ups. Frank and Jeanine had taken him and Sara here once before, to the Different Pointe of View, the hotel's restaurant, which teetered a couple thousand feet up a mountaintop with a vertiginous view of the city below. That was two years ago, after Ben had proposed to Sara.

They were seated at a two-top, and Frank ordered them each a martini.

"What's the occasion, Frank?" Ben asked. He knew this had to do with more than the scampi.

Frank laughed a hearty laugh and said, "Cut to the chase, right, Dr. Bailey?"

Ben smiled.

"Listen, Benny, I know you and Sara have reserved the lodge up at the Snowbowl for the wedding, but I've been thinking that maybe, now that you've moved down here, it would be easier to plan a wedding at home."

Home. Ben wasn't sure he would ever think of Phoenix as home.

"We put a deposit down," Ben said.

Frank waved his hand dismissively. "I'll reimburse."

Ben suddenly felt uncomfortable. The waitress brought them their drinks and he took a big swallow of his. The gin was warm and thick going down.

"What did you have in mind, Frank?" Ben asked. He thought maybe the country club. Or perhaps their backyard. Jeanine had hosted some pretty spectacular events at their home, including Sara's brother's wedding.

Frank motioned for the waitress to come back. "Can I get some extra olives, please?"

Ben waited.

Frank cleared his throat. "Did you look around much when we came in?"

"The hotel?"

"Pretty nice place, huh? Might be a spectacular venue for a wedding." Frank winked.

Ben raised his eyebrows. "Frank, this might be a little on the extravagant side, don't you think?"

"Just think about it, Benny. They've got indoor and outdoor facilities for the wedding and for the reception. They've got a bridal suite, and our out-of-town guests could stay here as well."

"Frank, I really don't think Sara and I can afford this. I've only been working for you for a couple of months, and now that Sara's on bed rest . . ."

"Consider it done," Frank said. "Sara is my baby girl. And this is only going to happen once. Nothing would make me happier than to be able to give her, give you both, this day."

Ben shook his head and sighed. He looked at Frank and wondered if someday he'd be sitting across from his own daughter's fiancé, making a similar offer.

"What does Sara think?" Ben asked. He was pretty certain he was the last to hear the proposal.

"Sara thinks a sunset wedding might be nice."

By the time their lunch arrived, all of the plans, which clearly preceded him by at least a month, were spelled out. Terrace reception, outdoor ceremony at sunset, Grande Ballroom reception, and a night in the bridal suite before they flew to Puerta Vallarta (or Cabo or Jamaica—because, really, the honeymoon was up to them). The menu was still up in the air, as was the music, but Frank had a friend who owned a DJ company and owed Frank a favor; Ben and Sara would just need to make the playlist. Ben didn't ask how much any of this would cost, because he knew the answer didn't matter. All that mattered was that Ben showed up.

"How many guests?" Ben asked.

"Well, I think if we can keep it to three hundred or so, we'll be good."

Ben was pretty sure he could count his invitees on two hands. That left approximately two hundred ninety from Sara's side.

Frank rattled off the details: the available dates, the name of the nanny who could accompany them on their honeymoon to watch the baby, the option of having an in-house wedding planner.

After the second martini, Ben's head was swimmy, his neck tired from all the nodding. He wanted nothing more than to go home early and sink into the pool.

"We're good, then?" Frank asked.

"Sure, Frank."

Emboldened by the booze and ready to talk about anything other than the wedding, the plans for which had unfolded before him like some intricate origami bird, Ben said, "Hey, Frank, who do you think the next governor's going to be? If you had to make a wager. Your buddy Bello really throwing his hat in?"

"Funny you should ask that," Frank said, spearing a jumbo shrimp with his fork.

"Why's that?"

"I was just talking to my buddy Chester McPhee, ran into him at the country club the other day. He's spearheading Marty Bello's campaign, and I think he's courting me for some campaign contributions. Marty would never ask himself, too much class for that." Frank popped the shrimp in his mouth and chewed slowly. He swallowed and pointed his fork at Ben. "Listen, I know you lean a hell of a lot farther to the left than I do, Benny, but Bello's got a good head on his shoulders. I'm thinking we might be able to put together a fund-raiser. Get together the really big dicks in the valley. Get the ball rolling for him. He could do a lot for this state." Frank popped another shrimp in his mouth and said, "And besides, he's a Beta Beta Phi. Brothers need to stick together."

Secrets. Like tiny little toads in your pocket. You can't ever forget they're there because they're always moving, wriggling, trying to flee. You know that any moment, one of them might break free and leap from your pocket, announcing itself with a shrill croak. And the harder you try to contain them, to conceal them, the more adamant they become about their escape.

Ben had called Shadi five times since his return to Phoenix. He called from work, from pay phones, from borrowed phones at shops and restaurants. And each time when she picked up, he felt relief like a flood of warm water. She was okay, okay. He listened to her voice as she demanded, "Hello? Who is this?" and felt his eyes sting. He didn't want to scare her, but he needed to know that she was okay.

True, Sara was preoccupied with her new endeavor, consumed even, but she was already developing that heightened sense that only mothers have, that ability to know what's going on not only right in front of her but also behind her back.

When Ben said he planned to go to Flagstaff the following weekend, he saw her stiffen, imagined the hackles on her neck bristling.

"Remember? Hippo and Emily's wedding is

next weekend. It's just a small ceremony, but he wants me to stand up for him." This was actually the truth. Hippo had called and said that Emily and he had finally set a date to tie the knot, and would Ben be a witness. And Ben knew, as much as Sara probably didn't want him in Flagstaff alone, she grew soft at the very mention of weddings. And she liked Emily. She'd actually considered going to her for a small tattoo for a while, though she'd never gone through with it.

"I *forgot,*" Sara said. "Shoot. And next weekend my parents are going to be at George and Angela's in Tucson."

"So?" Ben asked. As far as he knew, Frank didn't want them to come along.

"So, that means I'll be here all by myself for the weekend."

"Oh," he said. "What about Mel? Is she planning to come down?"

"No," Sara said. "She's going to Vegas."

"Oh," he said. "Well, I'll only be gone two nights. I figured I'd head up after work on Friday. The wedding is Saturday morning, and the reception is Saturday night. I'll leave first thing in the morning on Sunday. I can be home before you even wake up. Maude will keep you company."

She frowned and sighed. "Where are they having the wedding?"

"That old stone church? Our Lady of Guadelupe, I think," he said.

"I wish I could go," she said sadly. "I feel so *trapped*."

Ben nodded. He couldn't imagine being stuck in bed like this. Her patience so far had been remarkable. He was actually surprised by how little she had complained.

"I'll bring you back some carrot muffins from Macy's," he said, sitting down next to her on the couch. He reached and touched her belly. "Does baby girl want some carrot muffins?"

Appeased, she said, *"Fine."*

The week went slowly. Work was quiet, the minutes and hours dragging. The clock on the wall announcing the slow passing of each moment with a hollow tick. It gave Ben plenty of time to think, though, about what he needed to do. His plan was, indeed, to leave right after work on Friday. Since Frank was out of town, he wouldn't be meeting him for lunch. He could probably leave a couple of hours early to dodge some of the rush-hour traffic.

Ned had invited him to stay at his place. He would check in with Ned and then go to Flag Brewing Company to find Jenny as soon as he got into town. He thought that if he could just talk to her, just let her know how serious all of this was, that she might reconsider talking to the police. It was a long shot, he knew. She was Fitch's *girlfriend*. The chances of her speaking up were small. But if Ben didn't try, if he didn't at least make an attempt, then he would never forgive himself. And he had sensed something when he spoke to her the first time. She'd teared up even as she denied being at the party that night. She clearly knew something. She was the key. And she might be his only chance to finally put this behind him. And there was an urgency now to all of this. The fact that Joe and Fitch knew that Shadi was in town terrified him. Even with the reassuring sound of her voice each time he called, he couldn't put out of his mind the way Joe had said her name. *Shadi Begay.* And now, beyond all that, Frank's connection to Martin Bello made it seem even more important to set things right. He didn't want Frank connected in any way to this business. To that man. To that night.

Ben stopped by the house after work to get his suitcase and to say good-bye to Sara. She was outside by the pool, on the laptop, sipping a glass of lemonade.

"Hi," he said.

She set the glass down and motioned for him to come to her. He sat down next to her on the lawn chair, and she put her arms around him.

"Do you *have* to go?" she said.

He nodded and squeezed her hand. "Listen, I want you to order something to eat tonight and tomorrow, Chinese or pizza or whatever you want. Do not get up to cook," he said. "I picked up a couple of movies for you. I've got my cell phone in case you need me, and I'll be back Sunday morning. I promise."

She nodded like an obedient child.

"I mean it about dinner," he said. "And don't do anything else you're not supposed to do."

"Yes, sir," she said, saluting. When she kissed him, her breath was musty.

He didn't like the idea of leaving Sara by herself, but he also knew that she would not take any chances. He knew that she was bored, frustrated, and that the prospect of another fifteen weeks of this was excruciating. But Sara, if nothing else, played by the rules. He knew he could trust her.

When Ben stood up to leave, Sara pulled his hand. "Couldn't you just leave early tomorrow morning?" she said.

"I promised I'd be there tonight. To help get ready," he said.

By the time he got to Flagstaff, the sun had set, and the blue-black sky was flecked with pinpricks of light. He pulled into Ned's driveway. Ned's Honda was parked there, and so was Hippo's truck. There was a warm yellow light through the drawn curtains, and he felt happy as he knocked on the door. The air smelled like snow. Like home.

"Well, look what the cat dragged in," Ned said

when he opened the door. He threw his arm over Ben's shoulder and ushered him into the living room. Hippo was sitting on the couch.

"Here's a man enjoying his last night of freedom," Ned said, shaking his head at Hippo, who was drinking a can of Pabst Blue Ribbon and watching a Suns game on Ned's small black-and-white TV. "Really living it up."

"Hey, dude," Hippo said, standing up and giving Ben a handshake and hug.

"You ready for tomorrow?" Ben asked.

"Ready as I'll ever be. It's really not a big deal. Just about a dozen people. Neither one of us wanted to make a fuss."

Ben thought about the Pointe, about the ballrooms and china and crystal goblets. He thought about parquet dance floors and itchy tuxedoes and squeaky shoes. He thought about filet mignon and duck à l'orange and chalky candy-covered almonds tied into neat little bundles. Calligraphy and taffeta and moaning violins.

"So what's my job?" Ben asked. "Some sort of toast? Do you guys have rings I need to hold on to?"

Hippo flicked up his ring finger to show what looked like a fresh tattoo: an intricate Celtic knot encircling his finger in ink.

"Nice," Ben said. "Em get one too?"

"Yep."

"You want a beer?" Ned asked, disappearing into the kitchen.

"Please," Ben said and sat down next to Hippo on the couch. "Who's winning?"

They decided to go celebrate Hippo's last night of bachelorhood at Brews & Cues: shoot some pool, have some drinks, and then get to bed. Emily said he needed to be at the church by nine. She had also insisted that she and Hippo spend the night apart. "A real old-fashioned girl," Ben had said with a laugh. Emily with her serpentine tattoos and multiple facial piercings. Emily, who spent the first ten years of her life on a commune in New Mexico and who had worked as a carnie for six years after dropping out of college.

"Why are you guys having a church wedding?" Ben asked.

"For the grandma. She's like ninety-nine. Em promised her she'd get married at Guadelupe. That side of the family's all Mexican Catholics," Hippo said. Ben remembered Shadi's grandmother, all the velvet and silver of her.

"And they're letting *you* in the church too?" Ned asked.

"Hey, man, I've been taking Pre-Cana classes for the last two months."

"Wow," Ben said. "That's love."

And it *was* love. Ben had watched their relationship unfold, watched Hippo unfold. When he first started working at Jack's, Hippo was always irritated. Sarcastic and grumpy. Ben had avoided him for the first six months at the bar. But then Hippo met Emily, and it was like watching a fist unclench. Like watching a dry and hardened sponge soften in warm water.

He'd never seen such an easy couple, a couple so simply happy to be around each other. Emily was smart and cute. She had a great unrestrained laugh. When she and Hippo were together, they both couldn't stop smiling. They were so *content*. Ben envied this. They loved Flagstaff. They loved their jobs. They loved each other. The life they were making made sense.

"Rack 'em up," Hippo said as a table finally opened up, and Ben complied.

Ben was just an average pool player. He'd never played before he moved to Flagstaff. He'd somehow made it through college without learning. But everyone in Flagstaff seemed to play pool. He'd even seen little kids shooting pool with their dads during the day at some of the bars.

"Hey, anything ever come of the police investigation about that Indian kid you found?" Ned asked. "I heard that kid Lucky got out of the hospital and went back to the rez. But I haven't seen anything in the papers."

Ben felt his skin prickle. He took a sip from his beer bottle. It had grown warm while he was playing. "I think you were right about one of the frat boy's dads being involved. He was actually one of my students. That kid Joe Bello. Real asshole. His dad is running for *governor.*"

"Shit," Hippo said.

"There's a girl, though, who I think was there too. The girlfriend of one of the guys. If I could just get her to talk to the police . . ."

"Why the hell would she do that?" Ned asked as he made a bank shot. "You think after what happened to Lucky, anybody's going to say anything?"

Ben tensed. *Shadi Begay.*

"Never mind that it's her boyfriend," Hippo said.

Ben shook his head. She was his last chance, and he needed to believe that there was still the possibility of making this right. For Ricky. For his sister.

"Well, how do we find her?" Ned asked.

"She works at Flag Brew," Ben said, and smiled.

They made their way across the tracks and up the street. It was starting to snow, but it was a listless snow, directionless, light. It landed on their shoulders and quickly melted. It wasn't cold enough to stick.

It was a quiet night at Flag Brew, early still. They sat down at the bar, and Hippo ordered them all drinks. "Is Jenny working tonight?" he asked the bartender, a girl Ben didn't recognize.

"She'll be in at eight thirty," she said.

"What time is it now?" Ben asked.

"Eight," Ned said.

"Why don't we go sit outside for a bit?" Hippo said.

"In the snow?" Ned asked.

"It's my fucking party," Hippo said and smacked Ned on the back.

Fifteen minutes later, the girl came walking down the sidewalk. Ben might not have recognized her if not for the pink boots. Her hair was cropped short now, to her chin. When she came into the light, Ben also noticed that she had a nasty black eye.

He stood up, willed his legs to hold him.

"Jenny?" he asked.

She squinted and cocked her head.

"Yeah?" she said.

"We met a couple months ago." He put his hand out and she shook it reluctantly. "I was asking you about Halloween night. My name's Ben. I'm the one who found Ricky. The Indian guy, the one who got beat up."

"You said your name was Gary," she said. She shook her head and dropped his hand.

Ben sighed. Ned and Hippo sat watching.

"I lied," he said. "And I know what happened that night."

The girl looked around nervously. "Listen," she said. "I'm supposed to work in, like, ten minutes."

"What happened to your eye?" he asked.

She was quiet, seeming to appraise the situation. She started to walk to the door and then stopped. She came back and said, "Listen. Why don't you meet me tomorrow? I'm working lunch, but I'll be out by four. But don't come here. Meet me at the Zane Grey Room. You know, the bar upstairs at the Weatherford Hotel? And you can leave these guys at home."

Ben nodded. Jesus, he hoped this wasn't some sort of setup. He hoped to God she wasn't going to go give her boyfriend a call and let him know that somebody was sniffing around, asking questions. It didn't matter. He'd just have to take his chances.

"I'll be there. Four o'clock," he said.

And he felt light all of a sudden. As she disappeared inside the doors, he looked up at the sky and closed his eyes, let the snow land and melt on his eyelids. This was it. This was all he'd hoped for. For someone to speak up. For someone to tell the truth.

"The next round is on me," Ben said, returning to the table where Ned and Hippo were waiting. Then he remembered Sara at home, figured she was probably making her way to bed, and texted her: *Sweet dreams.*

• • •

That night, Ben dreamed about snow. In this dream, he was in Phoenix, at their town house, but when he pulled back the blinds, there was nothing but snow as far as he could see. An avalanche had enclosed the house. Every window was filled. The skylight in the bathroom was obscured. When he turned on the faucets, snow came pouring out. The cupboards were filled with it. The refrigerator and stove and drawers. He awoke shivering.

He was sleeping on Ned's couch. He looked at the clock on the cable box by the TV. It was only four A.M. He was thirsty and got up to get a glass of water from the kitchen. He flicked on the kitchen light and took a glass from the cupboard; as he turned on the faucet, he looked out the window and there was nothing but snow. Another blizzard. He smiled.

The wedding was short and simple, an abbreviated version of the other Catholic weddings Ben had attended. Emily looked so pretty in a vintage white minidress, like a '50s pinup girl with her black bangs and red lipstick and long legs. Hippo cleaned up well too, in a black suit and purple paisley silk shirt. There were only a dozen or so guests: her parents, her grandmother, and Hippo's mom in from Vegas. Ben and Ned stood up for Hippo, and Emily's girlfriends, Tia and Loretta, stood up for her. Emily clutched a bouquet of dark red roses that matched her lips.

As they exchanged their vows, Ben tried to imagine standing up next to Sara in a few months. Tried to think about the baby girl that would be there too. About the words he might say to her. Tried to think about that life that felt as distant to him as someone else's dream.

Emily cried, her false eyelashes fluttering. And Hippo's voice cracked as he recited the e. e. cummings poem he'd scratched onto a piece of paper, which he pulled out of his suit pocket. When they embraced, Ben felt his throat grow a little thick. And he felt both happy for them and so disappointed. So sad for everything he did not have, would never feel.

After the ceremony, they all piled into Loretta's Thunderbird and made their way to Jack's to celebrate.

About halfway through the party, Ben excused himself, patting Hippo on the back. "Congratulations, man. I am so happy for you. I'm going to go meet that chick over at the Zane Grey Room."

"If you're not back in an hour, I'll send reinforcements," Hippo said.

When Ben laughed, Hippo shook his head. "I'm not kidding."

• • •

It was warm and quiet in the old Weatherford Hotel. He went up the winding staircase, dizzied by the patterned carpet and wallpaper. The Zane Grey Room was empty except for the bartender and the girl, Jenny, who was sitting by herself at a table near the bar. Ben's shoulders relaxed.

"Hi," he said, going to her and sitting down when she motioned to the chair opposite her.

"Why are you so dressed up?" she asked.

"I had a wedding this morning," he said.

"Oh."

"Thanks for seeing me," he said, feeling suddenly awkward in his suit and tie.

"Now, we have to make this really quick, okay?" she asked. "He's watching me like a fucking hawk."

"Fitch?" he asked.

She nodded, her eyes darting across the empty bar.

"Did he do that to your eye?"

Her face was plain but pretty. But her eye was a disaster. Whoever did this wasn't messing around.

"I told him I wanted to break up," she said. "I can't take this anymore. The police have been asking questions. Nobody will say a fucking thing. The *brothers,* they'd do anything for each other. It's scary." Her hands were trembling. He could see her nails were bitten to the quick, pink polish chipped down to the cuticles.

"Did they question you?" Ben asked.

She shook her head. "The guys told them there weren't any girls there."

"You *were* there, though, right?"

She nodded, looked down at the table. "I didn't know he *died*. There wasn't anything in the paper."

"Have you gone to the police?" he asked.

She shook her head. "It was awful," she said, looking up. "The things they were saying to him. He was just a kid trying to have a good time. They totally let loose on him."

"How did the fight start?" Ben asked. "What happened?"

Halloween night, before the snow, before winter came. Ben had forgotten, but the moon had been so bright, like a burning white hole in the sky. Jenny said it lit up the night, that while she sat out on the porch with her girlfriends, waiting for Joe and Fitch to get back from the store with food and Solo cups, it looked almost like twilight.

There were gauzy spiderwebs strung along the porch railing, a jointed cardboard skeleton hanging at the door. They didn't have candy for the trick-or-treaters, but they did have tons of booze. The girls were drinking frozen margaritas, had brought the blender out onto the porch, the electrical cord snaking through a window they had cracked open. Jenny was dressed up like a fairy: short skirt, body glitter, a pair of diaphanous wings attached at her shoulder blades. Joe's girlfriend, Lissy, was Cat Woman.

Fitch and Joe had arranged for a pool tournament with some guys from a rival frat. This was a Halloween tradition. Last year, Fitch won six hundred bucks. This year, he said he wanted to go to sleep with a grand in his pocket. When they got back at around nine, they called the guys from the other frat. They were at Jack's getting a buzz on; they'd get there when they got there.

A bunch of people started showing up, stopping by on their way to and from the bars. One guy with a really awesome zombie costume brought Jägermeister. *Gary.* The party was rocking; Jenny almost completely forgot about the pool tournament.

The guys from the other frat didn't show up to play pool until almost eleven. The party had fizzled out at that point, everybody heading downtown to the bars. Only Jenny and Lissy had stuck around; their other girlfriends had bailed.

"Oh, *great,*" Jenny had said, answering the door, pissed and feeling a little drunk already. She hated this guy Higgins. He was an idiot. She hated his girlfriend too. A total slut.

"Chill-ax, chica," Higgins said to her. His girlfriend, *Simone,* was hanging on his arm, drunk and swaying.

"Dude!" Fitch said, coming up behind Jenny and fist-bumping him.

"Hope you don't mind, we brought a couple of pledges along," Higgins said, gesturing to two guys who stood at the foot of the porch with their hands shoved in their pockets. One of them was wearing an ogre mask. The other one's mask looked like a rotten scarecrow.

"Whatever. We are so ready to kick your ass."

Inside, Simone bumped into Jenny, making her spill her drink. "Oopsy," she said, and laughed. Jenny was worried that Fitch had seen. She didn't want him to start a fight. If he'd seen, he'd be pissed. Stupid girl. Dressed up like a fucking cowgirl with her boobs hanging out all over the place. Sequined vest and red cowboy boots with fishnet stockings.

Take a picture! Take a picture of the cowgirl and the Indian.

So the guys started playing pool in the big room off the kitchen. The three girls went inside and watched from the counter that separated the kitchen from the rec room. The cowgirl kept pouring herself drinks.

Jenny couldn't believe that Fitch and Joe didn't notice right away. It was obvious even with the masks on that these guys weren't pledges. Who wore Wrangler jeans and basketball sneakers? And one of them had a long braid that snuck out from underneath the mask. A silver and turquoise belt. They must be some rez kids Higgins and his crew picked up at the bar. They were totally trying to hustle them.

But everybody was drunk. Maybe they wouldn't notice. Maybe they wouldn't have noticed, except the one kid, the one with the braid, started running the table. Really, running the table. His first time up, he shot six balls in a row before missing a bank shot.

Jenny said she felt the air grow tense in the way it does before boys are about to fight. You can feel it. Like the electric buzzing of the air before a thunderstorm. She said she kept trying to think of a way to end the game, to stop everything before it turned into something bad.

And then it was the other kid's turn, and he made every single shot and was getting ready to sink the eight ball. That's when Fitch started to get suspicious. "Why don't you take your mask off, Igor?"

The kid shook his head.

"Nice belt," Joe said.

And the guy with the Igor mask ignored him.

"I said nice belt. What are you, deaf?" Fitch said, laughing. "Retarded?"

So the guy is about to make the eight ball, and he's obviously pissed and he jumps the cue ball and it flies off the table and hits the cowgirl in the arm.

The next thing Jenny knows, Higgins is ripping the mask off the kid's head and screaming at him. "Jesus Christ, you goddamned featherhead. I told you to play it cool. You hit my fucking girlfriend."

"What the fuck?" Joe said. "You mother-fuckers! You think you're gonna come in here in some stupid costumes and take our goddamn money? This isn't the goddamn Indian casino."

And that's when Jenny said it could have ended. Or, at least, the attention could have turned away from the Indian kids to Higgins and his buddies. They were the ones who were trying to hustle them. But Higgins must have known what was coming and so he grabbed the drunk cowgirl, who was making a big stink about her arm, threw a hundred-dollar bill down on the table, and took off with his buddies trailing behind. "Happy freakin' Halloween, assholes," he said.

Then it was just Joe and Fitch and Jenny and Lissy. And those two boys.

Fitch ripped off the other kid's mask next, the one with the braid, and started in too. "Well, look what we have here—a couple of bush niggers." And then Jenny said he started chanting, "Ki, yi, yi, yi." Putting his hand over his mouth, pantomiming Indian.

She said she wasn't sure who struck the first blow. But the next thing she knew, they were fighting. Fists were flying, Lissy and Jenny were screaming and trying to pull the boys off of each other. And while the first guy, Lucky, fought back, the other one—Ricky—just quietly took it. He didn't strike back. It was the craziest thing she'd ever seen, she said, the way he just accepted the blows. It started to scare her, though, when he finally crumbled to his knees, and the guys stopped punching and started kicking.

While he was down, Lucky must have escaped outside. Because then it was just the brothers, the two girls, and the one kid lying on the floor.

That's when Fitch got the bright idea to grab the bottle of Jäger from the kitchen. "Maybe he needs a drink," he said, bobbing and swaying into the room, where the boy lay prone on the floor. "You know how them Injuns love themselves some moonshine."

Fitch took the bottle and knelt down next to the kid, propping his mouth open and pouring the liquor in. The kid swallowed and spit, but Fitch kept pouring. Finally, the kid struggled to get to his feet and stumbled out the door into the night.

Jenny said she was shaking so hard she thought she might throw up. Lissy ran after her into the bathroom. And then Fitch locked the door behind them, and Joe turned the music up so high she could feel the bass in her heart. And outside, it began to snow.

"He's gone fucking crazy," Jenny said. She was wringing her hands. She and Ben were still alone in the bar, and the bartender was absorbed in a basketball game on TV. "It's like there's a switch that goes off inside his head sometimes. And he does stuff, and it's like the real Fitch is gone. Like he's some sort of animal."

She was crying now, and Ben reached across the table and took her hand. "You have to say something. To the police. And you weren't the only other witness. What about the other girl, Lissy?"

She shook her head. "She's scared. Do you realize who Joe's dad is? I heard about the other boy, that they ran him out of town when he talked to the cops."

Ben nodded. "That doesn't make it okay."

Jenny looked out the window, and Ben followed her gaze. The snow was more serious now, swirling about purposefully, willfully.

"He's *dead,*" Ben said. "He had a life. A family. He had a *sister.*"

Thoughts of Shadi were like the snow. Like cold slivers, melting as soon as they touched his skin. He shivered.

"The police will protect you, if you just tell them the truth. They'll make sure nothing happens to you."

"You don't get it, do you?" Jenny said. "Nobody cares. Nobody gives a damn about what happened to those boys."

"I care," Ben said. "I care. And so do you, or else you wouldn't be here."

Jenny touched the blue-black bruise around her eye. "I really loved Mark," she said, smiling sadly. "We've been together since freshman orientation. He used to sing to me outside my dorm window. He used to bring me chocolate milk shakes while I was in class, sneak into the back of the classroom. He used to be a good guy."

The bartender whooped at something on the TV. "Damn!"

"It was just you and Lissy?" Ben asked softly. "No one else saw what happened?"

She shook her head. "It was just us."

Ben squeezed her hand, pleading. Outside, the storm picked up, snow covering everything in a fresh layer of white. "Do you think you could get her to talk about what happened?"

"I don't know about Lissy. She's Joe's *girl-friend,*" she said. "But I will. Enough is enough."

Ben could barely walk fast enough back to Jack's to say good-bye to Hippo and Ned, to get his truck. The ground was slippery, the new snow quickly turning to ice on the sidewalks. His dress shoes could have been skates. He glided. He wanted to skip, to swing from the lampposts, to howl at the moon. At the intersection as he waited for a car to pass, he closed his eyes, looked at the sky, and stuck his tongue out to catch the snow.

He'd left Jenny his cell phone number. She promised she would talk to Lissy and then call him. He said he would go with them to the police station if they wanted.

Inside Jack's, Ned was standing up on the bar, giving a toast to Hippo and Emily. He had an open bottle of champagne in one fist and a plastic champagne flute in the other. "Bailey!" he yelled as Ben came through the doors. "Get the man some champagne."

Someone handed Ben a glass, and Ned started to speak.

"You guys are the best couple I know. I have never seen such a goddamn happy couple. Makes you kinda sick." He laughed and thrust forward his glass of champagne. "To love!"

Hippo and Emily stood together, Hippo's wiry arm draped across Emily's shoulder. She leaned into him, nestled there like a jigsaw puzzle piece.

"Love you guys," Ned said as he hopped down from the bar. "You wanna say something, Ben?" he asked.

"Sure," Ben said, grinning and climbing up onto the bar.

In all the time he'd worked at Jack's, he had never stood on the bar. Most of the time he was wrestling people down off of it: drunk girls, rowdy cowboys. From up here he could see into the pockets on the pool tables, the grimy veneer tabletops, the dizzying black-and-white linoleum floor.

"If everyone had just an ounce of what you guys have . . ." Ben started. "Then the world would be a better place." He held the champagne glass out and was met by an audience of expectant faces and raised glasses. He felt his gut spin: that wild, wonderful spin from champagne bubbles and everything else. "To love," he said. "To real love."

Outside, his head pounded, and the cold air bit into his exposed skin. The temperature must have dropped twenty degrees since they left the church; he had to fight the wind to get to his truck. He felt like a man on a mission, a man possessed. He felt as though he were on the edge of a steep precipice, just waiting for the gust of wind that would send him over the edge.

He got into his truck and pulled out his phone to check the messages. Sara had called three times. He dialed his voice mail and entered the code. *Hi, it's me, hope you're having a good time. I'm doing okay. Just kind of bored and thought I'd check in. Call when you can.* He deleted the message. *Me again. I was calling because I hadn't heard from you. I'm actually wondering if you had seen my iPod. I can't remember where I put it, and I know I'm not supposed to be walking around. If you've seen it, call me.* By the third message, the lilt in her voice was gone. *Hey, I hope your phone is working. This really isn't cool. What if there were an emergency? Call me.*

He dialed home and she picked up after the first ring.

"Hey, I think I saw your iPod in the drawer of the end table by the couch."

"Something wrong with your phone?"

"No," he said. "I had it on vibrate. I was at a wedding. And it's loud at Jack's. I had to come outside to call you."

He could almost feel her hand clenching her phone.

"The reception's at *Jack's?*" she asked. And there was the slightest hint of something mean-spirited, something nasty in her tone. Just a little something, a twang of disapproval. Then, when he didn't respond, as expected the sarcasm came out. "What's on the menu? Cheeseburger Bourguignonne?"

Ben was silent.

She laughed. "Hamburger Wellington?"

Ben sighed loudly.

"I'm just kidding," she said. "Lighten up. It sounds totally *romantic*."

"Listen, I have to go. It's fucking cold out here."

"Where did you say the iPod was?"

"In the end table drawer," he said. His mood deflated and was left sagging like an airless balloon.

"Thanks," she said. "I love you."

But before she finished, he had clicked the phone shut.

He took a deep breath, and when he exhaled, he willed his shoulders to relax, his fists to unclench.

He clicked his phone back open and dialed Shadi's number. His body trembled as he waited for her to pick up. But it just rang and rang and rang. *Shit,* he thought. He couldn't wait to tell her the news about Jenny.

He turned the key in the ignition and revved the engine. The windshield wipers made wide, sweeping arcs through the new snow. Heat blasted through the vents, and *Exile on Main St.*, which he'd picked up at Gopher Sounds the last time they were in town, blasted through the speakers.

He knew he should go back to Phoenix, drive the hundred and forty bleak miles back to Sara. He could forget all of this, let the girls go to the police alone. *They* were the witnesses. He was just the guy who found the body. There was nothing he could do for Ricky that he hadn't already done. He could go to Sara, hold her tight, pretend that he loved her. Pretend that he loved their palm tree, dry heat, chlorinated life. He could pretend that his whole body wasn't aching for Shadi. That he wasn't in love with her. Or he could stay. He could find Shadi and hold on to *her*. He could go to her and admit finally that *home* was here, in this glittering world of snow and ice.

He rubbed his hand across his jaw; the new hairs there bristled and scraped his palm. He looked in the rearview mirror at his shadowed face and tired eyes, and pulled out of the parking spot onto the street. Then, he stared into the glistening snow, flicked his blinker, and turned down the street that would take him home.

The forest was quiet and cold, but by the time he pulled into the RV park, Ben was sweating. His heart was pounding in his ears and in his chest. He gripped the wheel tightly and drove slowly down the twisty dirt road, savoring the wild anticipation of it all. He couldn't keep from smiling, his jaw and cheeks burning with the effort. He loved every drop of perspiration, every kerplunk of his heart. It was dark in the forest, with only the dim porch lights of the other RVs. His headlights made bright narrow beams on the road, illuminating nothing but trees.

At first he thought he'd turned into the wrong drive. It didn't make sense. The pastel pink RV next to Shadi's was there, pink flamingos knee-deep in the snow, the corrugated tin awning threatening to snap under the weight of so much snow. The giant pine with the address nailed to it was there, but the Airstream was gone. The lot was empty. There was just the empty space where she used to live and the drive-in speaker, a chrome monument half buried in the snow.

He pulled into the driveway and turned off the engine. He pressed his forehead against the steering wheel, feeling the blood rushing to his face in a hot flood. He sat back up, hitting the wheel with his palms until it felt as though the heels of his hands were bruised.

The sky looked like an overripe plum, and the snow swirled about the truck listlessly, indecisive. He rolled down the window and let the cold air rush in. Then he got out of the truck and walked to the place where the trailer used to be.

"You lookin' for that girl?" a voice said.

He turned around, startled, and squinted into the light shining in the doorway of Shadi's neighbor's trailer.

"Hello?" he said.

The old woman hobbled down the steps and walked toward Ben.

"It's just awful what they did," she said. She shook her head, shuffled toward him.

He felt his entire body go numb. "What are you talking about?"

"It's a hate crime, pure and simple. That's what Nancy Grace would call it."

"What happened?" he asked. "Where is she?"

Ben imagined all of the awful things that could have happened to her. He could feel bile rising into his throat, the wedding champagne burning his esophagus.

"Where is she?" Ben said loudly.

"Don't know exactly, but after what they did to her trailer, she had somebody with a big truck come down and tow it away. Sweet girl like that. They had no right. She wasn't hurtin' nobody."

"Please," Ben said, his whole body pulsating with fear and anger. "Do you know where she went? Did she say where she was going? Did she mention Chinle?"

The woman shrugged. "Don't know. But I bet she won't be comin' back here. Damn shame," she said and started walking back to her trailer.

Ben got into his truck and slammed the door shut. If she'd gone to Chinle, he would have to find her. And if she'd gone somewhere else, he'd go there. He knew as he raced out of the forest and into the storm, he'd drive wherever he needed to see her again.

He got gas in town, filling the tank and getting a Styrofoam cup of coffee and a map with a list of Arizona campsites inside the neon food mart. The coffee was so hot it burned his tongue and the roof of his mouth. "Shit," he said, spitting out his first swallow. It steamed on the pavement. He unfolded the map and looked for campsites and RV parks in Chinle. It looked like there were a couple of campsites, both at Canyon de Chelly. Unless she'd taken the Airstream to her grandmother's land, he figured this is where she would be. He got in the truck and it roared to life. Mick Jagger crooned, the guitar twanged its bluesy blues, and Ben set out to find her.

Ben used to love to drive at night. It made him think of the times when he and Dusty were little, and his family would drive down to Florida to visit his grandmother, who lived in West Palm Beach with her three sisters. They always left just before bedtime, he and Dusty putting on their pajamas and then piling into the car, which was already packed.

Dusty usually fell asleep within a few minutes when the general excitement of the impending journey wore off and the engine lulled her to sleep, but Ben stayed wide awake. He loved the feeling of hurtling through the starry darkness, the quiet sound of Dusty sleeping. The sweet smell of his mother's perfume captured inside the car. His father's arm stretched across the back of her seat, absently playing with her hair. He almost always fell asleep to the sound of the radio broadcasting whatever station would come in clearly, and, when reception was bad, the static hum of the spaces in between the channels. And by the time the sun came up, and he and Dusty woke up, they'd be in Florida. They would stop at a roadside stand for oranges for breakfast, and sleepily peel them at the side of the road, the juice running down their hands.

Tonight, despite every impulse to rush forward, he drove slowly. The snow was hypnotic. Ben could feel his eyes growing heavy as he concentrated on the storm in front of him. When his eyes closed for a few seconds, he turned off the heat and rolled down the window. Turned up the stereo and shook his head. There were no other cars on the road.

Finally, the snow began to lessen and the caffeine kicked in. Now he just wanted to get there. To Shadi. Jesus Christ, what had they done to her?

He pulled into the Spider Rock Campground at around nine o'clock, the bright yellow sign at the entrance boasting solar-heated showers and mocha espresso. Ben stopped at the camp office and spoke with the owner of the campground, who offered to arrange for a tour of the canyon in the morning as well as wireless access. Ben said, "Please, I'm just looking for my friend." The man looked suspicious.

"She's from here, from Chinle, but I know her from Flagstaff," he said. "She's got an old Airstream?"

The man smiled. "Only one person staying here tonight. You tell me her name, and I'll show you to her site."

"Shadi Begay," Ben said. The magic words.

The man slapped him on the back, grabbed a pencil from his back pocket, and scratched a map of the campsite on a napkin.

Ben drove along the bumpy path; it was barren land spotted with scrub foliage and a few trees. When he saw the Airstream in the distance, his heart hammered inside his ribs.

It was dark, but as he pulled into the drive, his

headlights illuminated the trailer. Ben caught his breath. In white paint across the side of the Airstream, someone had scrawled *DIRTY SQUAW PUSSY* in giant letters. The door had been dented, one of the windows smashed. There was cardboard and plastic duct-taped over the hole.

Shadi came outside of the trailer, wearing a flannel robe and boots. Her hair spilled over her shoulders like ink. The smoke from her cigarette curled up into the bruised sky.

Ben got out of the truck and walked quickly to her.

"What are you doing here?" Her voice was flat.

"I went to find you, in Flagstaff, but you were gone," Ben said. "I was worried. And then your neighbor told me that something happened. What happened? Are you okay?"

"I'm okay," she said.

He reached his hand out and took hers. Her skin was warm and so soft it felt almost liquid. He squeezed her hand.

"Were you home?" he asked.

"No," she said. "I was at the studio at school."

"Thank God."

"They would have killed me, Ben."

Ben rubbed his temples. The idea that someone had gone to her home, had hoped she'd be there, was almost more than he could fathom.

"You should go," Shadi said, flicking her cigarette ash to the ground. "I don't need any more trouble. Nobody's going to come for me here, unless they're following you."

"Listen," he said, squeezing her hand, smiling. Anxious. "I talked to someone, a girl who was there that night, at the party. She saw what happened. And she's going to go to the police."

Shadi let go of his hand and folded one arm across her chest. She took a long drag on her cigarette and exhaled. "How do you know she'll really go?"

"I just do," he said. It was taking everything he had not to touch her. "I trust her."

She flicked her cigarette to the ground and stomped it out.

"Why are you here, Ben?"

"I just told you," Ben said. "I went to find you, and you were gone. This is what we needed, Shadi, someone to come forward. Someone the police would listen to. She has a friend who was there too. This will happen."

Shadi looked up at the sky; the moon was bright. She closed the screen door of the trailer. "You want to go for a walk?" she asked. "There's an overlook not too far from here. You can see down into the canyon."

He nodded, and she led the way.

They watched the moon set over the canyon, the rocks below them glowing in the waning light. He told her what he knew now, about what happened that night.

"Ricky was so afraid of Spider Woman," she said. "He really believed that if he was bad, his bones would wind up on her tower in the canyon with the rest of the naughty children's. So he never made a fuss. Not even when he was provoked. When Daddy was still around, he'd get drunk and egg Ricky on, try to get him to fight back. But he wouldn't do it. Daddy called him a pussy. Said someday somebody would beat the shit out of him and he'd deserve it."

"Jesus," Ben said.

They stood together until there was nothing but darkness beneath them, until they couldn't even see their own hands anymore.

"Thank you," she said softly.

Ben felt his body fill, expand. He could have floated up above the canyon, a hot air balloon rising over the rocky spires.

Silently they made their way back to the trailer, stumbling awkwardly over the unfamiliar terrain. By the time they got to the Airstream, they were both breathless, their legs and arms scratched from the brush.

"You can come in," Shadi said.

Ben nodded and followed her up the steps into the trailer. She lit a kerosene lamp, and the inside of the trailer was illuminated in soft light.

"You don't listen," Shadi said. "No matter what I say."

Ben shook his head. "I tried," he said. And he

felt tears welling up in his eyes. "I really did."

Ben thought about Sara at home, imagined her asleep in the wide expanse of their bed. He thought about the swell of her belly, the way her eyes fluttered in sleep, her brow furrowed into a scowl. He thought about how he had disappointed her. About how many times he had failed her. His leaving her might actually set her free. Even if she hated him. Even if she never spoke to him again. Even if it meant he would never know his daughter. His *daughter*.

He looked at the corner where her loom usually was. It was empty now.

"What happened to your loom?"

"They built a campfire with it, right outside my trailer."

"No," he said. "Christ."

Shadi blew warm air into her hands. "Brr. It's cold."

"Did you at least finish the blanket you were working on?" he asked. "They didn't destroy that too?"

Shadi shook her head. She stood up and went to a cupboard underneath the built-in sofa. She pulled out the blanket, unfolding it. She laid it across the tabletop, gently traced the patterns with her long fingers.

"May I?" he asked, and she nodded.

He touched the sunset colors, could almost feel their warmth, despite the chill inside the trailer.

She sat down in one of the kitchen chairs. "I started making it for Ricky. For his new apartment."

He touched the woven colors, the descending sun. "What is this?" he asked, touching a lone strand that hung loose from the rest of the blanket.

"It's called the *spirit thread*," she said. "The Diné believe that when you make a rug or a blanket, a part of your spirit or soul becomes trapped inside. The spirit thread allows the soul a way to escape."

He touched the string, thought about escape. About freedom.

"I want you to have it," she said.

He shook his head.

"Please," she said. "It's the least I can do. For all you've done."

How could she not know what she had done for him already? How could she not know that she was the only thing he thought about, the only thing that mattered, the one true thing in his life now that everything else was gone?

And then a hot current ran through his body, and he was moving toward her, touching her face with his hands, running his thumbs across her cheekbones. Tracing the line of her jaw. He could feel that fluid skin, and he just wanted to sink into her like a warm pool of water.

She closed her eyes, nodding, and he turned the

key on the kerosene lamp. It was as though they had been swallowed into the belly of an animal, it was so dark. He reached for her and tore at the flannel robe, at the soft cotton nightgown she wore underneath. He dropped to his knees and yanked at her boots, feeling the scratch of her wool socks on his face. He kissed her foot, her calf, tasting the tendons, tracing the muscles with his tongue. Her body trembled, her hands clawed at his back.

She stood up and they moved together toward the bed at the back of the trailer. She pressed her hand against his chest, pushing him away, but then leaned her ear against it. The feel of her cheek against his bare skin was almost more than he could bear.

He slipped her nightgown over her head, the cotton as soft as her skin but with none of that crazy warmth.

"I need to tell you something," she whispered, her lips grazing his earlobe.

"What?" he asked, touching his tongue to her neck, tasting the bitter musk of the absinthe oil she wore.

She was breathless, her entire body quivering. "I didn't come here because of Ricky, because I was afraid of those boys. Those men. Whoever did this."

He inhaled the smell of her. The oil, her skin. His eyes burned.

"What do you mean?"

She touched his face. "I came here because of you," she said quietly.

"I don't understand." He felt like he'd been running; he couldn't catch his breath.

"I need you to promise me something," she said.

It was so dark he couldn't see her. He reached for her face and felt cool tears on her cheeks.

"Anything," he said, burying his face in her neck again, in her hair. "Anything you want."

"Tomorrow. You need to make a choice. And once you've decided, you can't go back. Not even if it's the wrong choice. Not even if it hurts someone. Not even if it hurts me."

Blood rushed to Ben's temples.

Shadi took both of his hands in hers. She rubbed the back of them with her thumbs. "Don't mistake this for love. We share the same sorrow. And you think if you can fix mine, take it away, then yours will go away too. But it doesn't work like that."

Ben was shaking his head. He squeezed his eyes shut, and in the darkness he saw Dusty's empty rain boots standing by the front door. They were red with black spots, like ladybugs. The mud from the puddles she had splashed in still hadn't dried the day after the accident. And he remembered thinking she couldn't be dead, not when there was fresh mud on her boots. Not when her raincoat was still wet, hanging on the hook in the hallway.

"You need to do what is right," she said. "And what will make you happy."

"*This* is right. *This* makes me happy." He was crying now.

"Promise," she said. "Or go."

Somewhere a coyote howled, and it was the sound of his grief, of their shared loss. The sound of pain, the melancholy moan he'd been carrying in his body since he was eleven years old. He thought of his father's empty drawers after he was gone, the cockeyed hangers in the closet. The empty shelf in the medicine cabinet and the vacant look in his mother's eyes.

The coyote wailed, and their bodies moved together, pressed together until he couldn't tell where he ended and she began. And he knew she was right. It was time.

When the first pale light of dawn glanced across his face, he reached for a blanket. It was cold, and he was naked. The air in the cold trailer was like an icy breath. He opened his eyes slowly and saw that he was tangled up in the blanket Shadi had made, but Shadi was gone. Only the vague smell of absinthe and sweat lingered in the air. She must have known that he wouldn't be able to leave if she were still there.

He wrapped the blanket around his shoulders

and walked out of the trailer. Sunrise and a soft layer of snow glistened, glittering in the light of a new morning. He promised Sara he would be home before she woke up. And he'd made a promise to Shadi. And later, as she slept with her cheek pressed against his naked chest, to himself.

His cell phone didn't get reception until he got to Winslow. He would call Sara, apologize for being late. He would tell her he was sorry. That he was on his way.

Then he would tell her everything else. In person. He owed her that.

He pulled into a gas station for coffee and gas. He stretched and yawned and got back into the truck. He clicked his phone on and saw that there were six messages. Jesus. He felt that old familiar anger welling up inside him. And a new, wonderful and terrifying resolve.

Just calling because I can't sleep. You're probably still at the reception. Love you. Beep.

Delete.

A long sigh and then *click*.

Delete.

It's midnight. Maybe I'll call over to Ned's.

Shit.

He thought about deleting the remaining messages but went ahead and listened.

Ben . . . a whispery static. *Benny, I'm scared. There's something going on outside. There's a car parked across the street and some guys . . . goddamnit it, where are you? Beep.*

Oh God, Ben, I'm calling 9-1-1. Beep.

His hands started to shake and some of the hot coffee spilled on his lap.

Frank's voice. *Ben, it's Frank. Where the hell are you? Beep.*

And that was it. The last message. *Shit, shit.* He scrolled through until he found Frank's number and pressed SEND.

Frank picked up after the first two rings. "I don't know where the fuck you are, but you better get your ass down here."

"Where are you? What happened to Sara? Is the baby okay?"

Frank's voice grew fainter. "Jeanine, talk to him. I can't fucking talk to him." Ben heard the rustle of the phone being passed over to Jeanine.

"Oh, Benny," Jeanine cried. Her voice was raw. He could barely understand her. "Just get to the Mayo Clinic in Scottsdale." She hung up before he could ask any more questions, and as he pulled out onto the highway, the bars disappeared from his cell phone.

He didn't remember the drive back to Phoenix. His eyes were blurred with tears. His hands ached from gripping the steering wheel. By the time he pulled into the hospital parking lot, the memories of everything that had brought him here had faded like a hazy dream, leaving his mind blank and his joints crippled.

He stopped running only to check in and find out where Sara was. By the time he got to her room, he was clutching his chest, wondering if he might be having a heart attack. Frank stopped him at the doorway, held up his hand, and said, "Stop."

"Where is Sara? Is she okay?" Ben craned his neck, trying to see into the room.

Frank pointed his finger into Ben's chest and pushed so hard, it felt like a weapon. "I don't want to know where you were. I don't want to hear any goddamned excuses. I have no idea what you're wrapped up in. I don't fucking care right now. What I want to know is what you were thinking leaving her alone at the house. How could you think it was okay to leave her by herself?"

"What happened, Frank? I just want to know what happened. I just want to see Sara."

"Goddamn you. *Goddamn you,*" Frank hissed, his eyes burning a furious red. He wiped at them as he began to cry.

"Please let me see her," Ben said. "Please let me go to her. I'm sorry."

When Ben entered the room, Jeanine rushed out, holding her hand across her mouth, shaking her head.

Sara lay in the bed, her face colorless, all of that sunshine faded. Ashen. She was staring out the window. She was hooked up to an IV, clear liquid dripping down a meandering tube that crept under her skin, tethered there with a strip of surgical tape.

Ben touched her feet, and her legs jerked reflexively away from him. He moved to the side of the bed and sat down in the chair next to her. He leaned toward her, brushed her hair out of her eyes.

"Sara," he said, but before he asked, he already knew the answer. "Sara, what happened?"

She didn't speak. She didn't move. She just opened her mouth, silently, as though someone had stolen her voice. As if she'd been completely emptied out. The color drained from her face. She was a husk. A shell.

"I wish I were dead," she said.

Later, he would get the story in fragments. The two men who pried the patio doors open, the ones who crept into the living room while Sara cowered in the locked bathroom upstairs. Sara had told Frank that one of them kept saying, *You sure this is the right house? Then where the hell is the bastard?* And then the sound of their footsteps coming up the stairs, the slam of the nursery door, the slam of the bedroom doors. Maude whimpering. *Hey, look at this fucking dog. Some watchdog, huh?*

And while they looked for him, Sara crouched in the bathtub.

Where the fuck is he? He's not here.

He wasn't there. Jesus, they finally came looking for him, and he wasn't there.

Wait. Did you hear that?

Sara had slipped and fallen in the tub, which was still wet from an earlier bath, and they kicked the door down. Came at her, ripped back the shower curtain.

Jesus, who's that? He didn't say nothing about a girl.

Please, she said. *Take whatever you want. I'm pregnant. Just don't hurt me.*

Then: *Let's get the fuck out of here.*

It was Frank who told Ben about the blood. That the paramedics found Sara in the bathtub, sitting in a pool of her own blood. That the fall, the stress, had been too much. It was Jeanine who slapped Ben across the face when he apologized, who pounded her fists against his chest. But it was Dr. Chandra who told him the rest. Sara was lucky to be alive, she said. During the C-section, she had started to hemorrhage. They gave her a transfusion. But it wasn't enough.

It wasn't enough. If Sara had gotten to the hospital sooner, then the baby might have been saved. But there was too much blood lost. It was too late.

It was too late, they said. And to stop the bleeding, they needed to perform an emergency hysterectomy. It was the only way to save her life. They couldn't save the baby, but they could save Sara.

Sara.

Sara stared out the window, untenanted. Every bit of light snuffed out.

Later, as the sun set, the sky like the inside of a blood orange, the nurse brought the baby to them. To say good-bye. They should take photos, she said. It might seem grim now, too difficult, but if they didn't, they might regret it later. There was a company that could touch up the photos, Photoshop out the bruises and discoloration. She would give them a brochure. Sara leaned over and vomited into the plastic bin they offered her. And then she curled onto her side, facing away from Ben.

The nurse said to Ben as Sara trembled silently, "We have a certificate for her, with her footprints."

Ben sat down in the visitor's chair and held out his arms. The nurse gently offered him the bundle. "I'll give you some time. As much time as you need. Just hit the buzzer when you're ready for me to come take her."

Ben held on, despite his body's quaking. Despite the awful aching thud in his head. Despite the sounds finally escaping Sara, even with that terrible keening, Ben held on.

That night, he dreamed again of snow.

He was wearing snow boots, each heavy as night as he walked through the woods. It was spring elsewhere, but not here. Here the ground was cold with six inches of freshly fallen snow. The sky was black but littered with a million stars, pinpricks of light and an enormous moon. The path was illuminated in cold blue light. His boots sank into the snow, each step an effort almost too much to bear. He ground his jaw, concentrated on moving forward. He thought about how many storms they had endured this winter, about how many snowflakes had had to fall to make the crusty layer of snow beneath him. He wondered how far down the earth was.

It was difficult to walk with his arms full. Each step was careful and calculated. Tentative. If he were to sink into the white, he might drop the bundle in his arms. He could disappear with it forever. On each side of him, the giant pines reached up into the sky while still bearing the weight of winter on their arms. This gave him strength.

It was so cold, his back and legs ached with it and his face had gone from stinging to numb. He could taste the cold, a bitter lozenge melting on his tongue. He felt mucous in a warm lump in his tonsils. He sniffed and hacked and spit his steaming insides into the snow. His throat ached.

His legs ached.

Finally, he got to the clearing, to the place protected by the thickness of trees. The foliage was so dense it had kept out the storms and now kept out the moon. It was dark and cold without snow or light. He peered into the shadows at what he carried. He rested the quiet bundle on the ground. And then he dropped to his knees.

The ground was exposed but frozen. He pulled the sharp spade from his back pocket and knew he should have brought a shovel. This could take days instead of hours.

It was still here, the silence like something alive. Not even wind was allowed into this fortress of quiet. It was so dark, he couldn't see his own hands. And so it didn't matter as he closed his eyes.

The two hot tracks on his cheeks felt like a betrayal of the cold, and so he wiped them away. His glove was rough and clumsy. He peeled it off and tossed it to the ground. And with his exposed fingers he began to unwrap the parcel from the blanket made of sunset.

He was a blind man, studying a stranger's face. His fingers touched and hesitated, both discovering and recognizing the angles. The predictable architecture of bones, but in miniature. His clumsy thumb stuttered at the place where the quickening flutter he'd both seen and heard but never got a chance to touch now lay buried. That place between tiny throat and sternum, that place inside the small citadel of bone, once beating, now, under his touch, as still as snow.

I should kill you," Frank said.

Ben, kneeling next to him in the hospital chapel, only nodded his head. He'd been sitting like this, his hands pressed together in prayers that could never be answered, for hours. Sunlight was starting to come through the small stained-glass window over the pulpit. It dappled their hands in fragments of orange and red and gold.

"I want you to start at the beginning, and I don't want any lies. I don't want any candy-coating, no marshmallow fluff. You owe me that goddamn much."

And so Ben began at the beginning: a snowstorm, a Navajo boy beaten to death, his blood like a flower blooming in the snow. He told Frank about the hospital, about Shadi, about the long drive to the funeral. About all the other ghosts. He told him about Dusty, about the sorrow he'd held inside like a precious bug in a jar. As Frank shook his head, fuming, Ben tried to explain how he had come to be so cruel. Then he gave him the blue Mustang, Mark Fitch, and the two girls. He told him about Lucky, about the frat party. What he knew about the fight. And then he told him about Joe Bello.

"*Marty's* kid?" Frank said, rubbing his temples

with two thick thumbs. "Marty Bello?" Frank took a deep breath and clenched his fists.

"Listen, Frank. He had Ricky's friend beaten up. He vandalized Shadi's trailer. And he's the one who hired those guys to get me. That's why they were at the house. They were there for *me*." Ben felt vertiginous, the stained-glass colors turning like a kaleidoscope, making him dizzy. Sick. "I'm sorry," Ben said. "I'm so sorry."

"You fucked up," Frank said.

Ben nodded and wiped fiercely at the tears he hadn't wanted to escape. "I know."

Frank stood up and rubbed his hand across his head. Straightened his shoulders. "We need to make this right," he said. "*You* need to make this right."

Ben nodded again. "But how?"

THE GLITTERING
WORLD

Summer arrived on time in Phoenix with its requisite sun and heat. In the mornings, Ben rose at sunrise, slipped out of bed, out onto the patio, and into the cool green of the swimming pool. He let the cool water fill his ears as he floated on his back and considered the aquamarine sky. Above him, the palm trees genuflected to the dawn.

Sara would wake in an hour after he had already showered and shaved. He shaved every day now, running the razor along his hollow cheeks and sharp jawline. He didn't recognize himself sometimes in the bathroom mirror. The early summer sun had turned his skin a deep gold color. It made his eyes look paler. Like blue ice. When he was finished, he would run the water over the razor, watch the soap and tiny black hairs swirl down the drain.

Sara ironed his dress shirts each night, starched them to a crisp perfection. The smell was strong, clean as he slipped them on and buttoned them to his collar. His suits were swaddled in dry cleaner's plastic bags, which were as thin as whispers. He polished his shoes, knotted his tie.

When Sara woke, he would have her coffee waiting for her. Cream, no sugar. In her favorite coffee mug, the heavy pottery cup the color of a robin's egg. While he read the paper, Sara would make breakfast. Soft-boiled eggs perched in little white egg cups, golden buttered toast, fresh-squeezed juice from the orange tree in their backyard. They would sit across the table from each other and make plans for the evening. For the following weekend. Where to have dinner. Which movie to see. Her parents came on Tuesday nights for dinner, and tried to pretend that things were the same. On Sundays, Sara and Ben went to brunch and then a matinee.

Later, after Sara had showered and changed into fresh scrubs, she would collect her purse and keys and recite the list of things Ben needed to do. Pick up the dry cleaning, deposit a paycheck, buy mayonnaise, toilet paper, soap. Before she walked out the door, he would go to her, kiss her, and say, "Love you. See you tonight." Then he would watch from the window as she backed the car out of the drive and headed to work.

Despite her parents' objections, Sara had transferred from Oncology to the Neonatal Ward, where she held infants smaller than ripe peaches in her hands, fastened tiny tubes to tiny chests, rocked their diminutive bodies to sleep. These were the babies born too soon, the babies born to addicts, the babies ill-prepared for the world outside their mothers' wombs. Every day she kept another baby alive was a good day. And on the other days, Ben held her as she allowed the grief to wash over her like rain.

Every day was an apology.

One morning in early June, as Sara cracks the top of her egg with a spoon and scoops out the soft liquid center onto her toast, Ben reads in the paper that two arrests have been made in the case of a Native American man found dead last November in Flagstaff. *A hate crime,* it says. And one of the young men arrested is the son of a prominent local politician: one who, until now, had been a dark horse with a chance, albeit it a long shot, at taking the GOP gubernatorial primary this week.

Ben skims the article, his heart beating like a hummingbird on cocaine in his chest. But he pretends, he has to pretend, it's just like any other bit of news.

In addition to two female students who have come forward as witnesses, there is a third witness, a young Navajo man from Tuba City, who was brutally beaten earlier this year after initially contacting the police. Surveillance footage that recently surfaced has resulted in the arrest of two additional men, who have been charged with this assault. And based on a tip from an anonymous source, an investigation is now being conducted into Martin Bello's involvement in the attempted murder-for-hire of this witness.

Shaking, Ben runs his hand across his smooth

chin. He sips his coffee, folds the paper, and sets it next to his plate. He imagines Frank reading the same paper at his own kitchen table, just two blocks away. Understands that they have both done what they needed to do to make things right.

When Ben signed the statement, the one Frank prepared, his hands had trembled. He barely recognized his own name, in shivering ink on the snow-white page. Frank had friends in the Coconino County Attorney's Office. Everything would be taken care of, and Ben's name would be left out of it. Justice would be served. For Ricky. For Shadi. And Sara would never know what he had done, only what he had failed to do.

Sara comes to him, her white Crocs squeaking on the kitchen floor. "I have a fitting this afternoon, for my dress. I'll be a little late. And can you just call the caterers and make sure they know we want the ganache instead of the butter cream?"

He nods and then kisses her, breathing in the antiseptic scent of her hair, the Clorox smell of her clothes bleached clean.

She looks at him, her eyes wide and vivid with sorrow still. He aches.

When she has gone, he gathers his own things and says good-bye to Maude, who is lying in a pool of sunlight on the floor. He locks the front door behind him and goes out into the bright blue day.

He knows he should be grateful for the semblance of forgiveness that Sara has offered him. For the effort she's making. And he believes, he *must* believe, it is love, not spite, that keeps her here. Ben should be thankful to Frank, who has also tendered him a certain quiet clemency. Ben should feel lucky for Jeanine's unadulterated mercy. Her anger, her violence, has softened now into a sort of gentle pity. But Ben also knows that the reparations he has tried to make will never be enough, that atonement for some things is futile.

Inside the truck, he rolls the windows up despite the heat. The upholstery burns through the fabric of his slacks, and the steering wheel blisters his palms. The adhesive molding holding the rearview mirror has started to melt, leaving the mirror dangling awkwardly. His eyes sting in the sun. His skin burns with the heat. He imagines his perspiration staining the crisp white shirt beneath his dark suit jacket.

As he drives the familiar route to the dealership, he watches the early morning heat make waves on the pavement, glimmering mirages. And suddenly, the mirrored surface of the hot pavement reflects a different landscape, creates the illusion that he is not in Phoenix at all but traveling on a dusty dirt road, following behind a black truck with a casket bouncing around in its bed. He can feel the chill air, and, as he follows behind it, his heart fills with hope.

He closes his eyes for a moment, capturing a thousand fractured images. Shadi's long brown fingers, the shiny silver rings. Her hair, her spine, her breasts. He smells the bitter green of absinthe and pure bright snow. *Hope.*

But then there is the green, yellow, red of a stoplight, a honking horn, screeching brakes as he awakes from the dream, and his truck slides dangerously into the intersection. An angry face pressed against glass, a man flipping him off, the hot rush of adrenaline as he backs the truck up and out of the way of oncoming traffic. The dirt road, the pickup truck was only a cruel chimera, a daydream. And the slivers of her melt like snow on hot pavement.

He has made his choice. And, from now on, he will keep his promises.

When the light turns green again, Ben pulls out onto the street, listens to the hiss and honk of rush-hour traffic, and rolls the windows back down to the unbearable heat.

Hope. He knows now that hope is a stillborn child, conceived but never realized. It is the dream ended while still asleep. The unanswered prayer. It is simply the fragile thread that a desperate man clings to, even as it unravels and unravels and unravels.

Discussion Questions

1. Discuss Ben's relationship with Sara and how it changes through the course of the novel. Why is he attracted to Shadi? What does she represent to Ben?

2. Ben experienced two significant losses as a young boy (the death of his sister and his father's abandonment). How did these two traumas shape him as a man? How do they play into his relationship with Shadi?

3. How does Ben's relationship with his own father affect his decision to stay with Sara when she discovers that she is pregnant? Do you think he would have made a good father?

4. How do you feel about Sara? Is Ben justified in his treatment of her?

5. Why do you think Ben became so involved with finding out what happened to Ricky? Was it a sense of morality? A sense of responsibility? Or was it really for Shadi? Do you think Ben would have done everything he did if he weren't attracted to Shadi?

6. If you were in a similar situation to Ben's, if you had woken up, gone out to get the newspaper, and found someone near death in the snow, what would you have done? Would you have dropped the whole thing and let the police ignore an obvious case of assault?

7. Contrast Hippo and Emily's relationship with Ben and Sara's.

8. Discuss the use of snow imagery. How does it echo Ben's emotional state throughout the novel? What do you make of the dream that he has after their baby is stillborn?

9. There is a great deal of injustice in this novel: from the original crime committed against Ricky to the police department's initial dismissal of his death as an alcohol-related accident. At one point in the novel, Lucky suggests that there is "no such thing" as justice. Do you agree? If not, is justice served at the end of the novel? And, if so, at what expense?

10. The Navajo art of weaving is a central metaphor in this novel. Discuss the different senses in which the metaphor is manifested. How does the "spirit string" fit into each of these?

11. At one point, Shadi calls Ben selfish. Do you agree with her? What does he do that's selfish, and what does he do that's selfless?

12. The novel is divided into the five "worlds" of the Navajo creation myth. Why do you think the author decided to structure the novel in this way? How are the colors of each part symbolic of what happens in that section?

13. How much do you think Sara really knew about what was going on? Do you think she knew Shadi was related to Ricky when she told Ben she wanted the rug commissioned? Do you think she knew Ben was involved with Shadi? How much do you think Melanie knew?

14. Near the end of the novel, Shadi gives Ben an ultimatum, demanding that he choose between her and Sara. Is this, ultimately, truly his *choice?* Do you believe he will keep his promise and stay with Sara? Was this the right decision? Why or why not?

15. Ben is faced with a lot of choices throughout the novel: whether or not to go to the hospital to check on Ricky, to go to Ricky's funeral, to search for Ricky's attackers, to move to Phoenix and work for Sara's father, to buy

the drive-in theater speaker for Shadi, to marry Sara, and the eventual choice between Sara and Shadi. What do you think of every decision he made? Were there any you disagreed with?

16. The definition of a tragedy is a story in which the hero comes to ruin or experiences tremendous sorrow as the result of both circumstance and a disastrous character flaw. In tragedies, readers should experience both fear and pity for the hero. Would you call Ben a tragic hero and this novel a tragedy? Why or why not? If so, what is Ben's tragic flaw?